TIME & FATE

ALSO BY T. G. AYER

Young Adult Paranormal

THE VALKYRIE SERIES

Dead Radiance

Dead Radiance Audio

Dead Embers

Dead Embers Audio

Dead Chaos

Dead Chaos Audio

Dead Wrath

Dead Silence

Joshua - Dead Radiance

Joshua II - Dead Embers

Joshua III - Dead Chaos

Joshua IV - Dead Wrath

Joshua V - Dead Silence

THE HAND OF KALI SERIES

Fire & Shadow

Blood & Gold

Time & Fate

Fury & Virtue

Spirit & Soul

THE DARKWORLD ORIGINS

Pyros (Logan)
Ailuros (Kailin)

~

THE DARK SIGHT SERIES

Dark Sight
Cursed Sight
Vissarion
Shadow Sight
Dark Prophecy
Cursed Prophecy
Shadow Prophecy

~

THE APSARA CHRONICLES

Immortal Bound
Gods Ascendent
Dominion Falling
Vengeance Born
Last Legion

~

A SEASON OF ASH AND BONE

Heartfyre

~

TIME & FATE

A HAND OF KALI NOVEL #3

ISBN-13: 978-0995112698

TIME & FATE

USA TODAY BESTSELLING AUTHOR

T.G. AYER

AUTHORS NOTE

Hindu Mythology is a living religion.
Like, Christianity, Islam, Judaism & Buddhism, Hinduism has
millions of followers around the world. Fiction featuring Hindu
gods is not merely a matter of choosing a god, and placing them
in a fictional situation, mainly because you risk offending that
deities devout worshippers. Unlike the Greek, Roman, Egyptian
& Norse Pantheon, Hindu & Buddhist gods must be treated with
the utmost respect in any fiction. I hope I have maintained this
ethic within my series.
I have tried to maintain as much respect as possible while still
using fiction to both entertain and educate the reader. The Kali
series is filled with details of the various deities currently
worshipped across the world.
Some rituals and powers are fiction, of course.

There is much in the Kali series that is part of my own journey in
life. I hope my travels in India have lent some level of
authenticity to the Indian scenes.

Demons, Zombies, Undead & other creatures and spirits are as per mythology texts and are available online to research. Much of how to eliminate these creatures is anecdotal & fictional. Sorry guys, if you come across a Vitala, you're on your own.

CHAPTER 1

Outside the window, cotton-candy puffs of bright clouds were shredded into whispers of white fluff by the metallic bulk of the airplane as it knifed through the sky. The surreal view from on top of the world made Maya Rao feel tiny and insignificant in the greater scheme of things, the peace and pure beauty at which she stared, emphasizing just how small a part she truly played in the world.

She hadn't expected the flight home to be so bittersweet. Retrieve Lord Shiva's bow, check. Return Kas to Patala, check.

Mission success.

But they'd left Ria behind at the refuge in the wilds of Mumbai. And, she'd expected to miss her, but her friend's absence had drawn a pall of sadness over Maya's mood, the feeling that none of her own actions would amount to much if she can't protect her own friends.

The aircraft jittered, slamming her into the seat back, taking her from regrets to a tiny frisson of concern. Maya grimaced and gave the clouds outside a wary glance. Given the turbulent ride of the last ten minutes, the serenity of the view was more likely courtesy of her imagination. The bones in Maya's neck clicked with the impact and she grabbed hold of the seat-arms on either side of her, her knuckles a little too pale.

Maya's brows knit together as the dull roar of the engines drowned out the softer exclamations and gasps of shock. Not even an A380 engine could hide the piercing shriek that rent the canned air of Economy. The sound reached out, knives to her eardrums, and Maya rolled her eyes and prayed the woman would shut up quickly. Just the sound of her cries was agitating the kid in the row behind Maya and she gritted her teeth as he began to kick her seat for the millionth time since they'd taken off.

All this bouncing around was inconvenient and more than a little annoying, but really nothing to get worked up about. Take Maya's neighbor for instance; the sole reaction from her so far had been a click of the tongue when her book had bounced off her knee and she'd lost her place.

Seasoned traveler to the core.

A russet-haired flight-attendant sashayed past, all long legs, gleaming chignon, and a touch too much makeup. She hunkered down beside the frantic woman, her face the picture of calm. Maya had to hand it to the girl. She dealt with the highly strung old lady with ease, her soft voice soothing, and within seconds she straightened, giving the woman's bony shoulder a kind pat.

Then, with a cursory glance over her shoulder, the redhead scanned the rows behind her before striding off toward the curtains up ahead. The navy-blue fabric hid a small galley from curious eyes as the crew prepared the evening meal.

Maya wrinkled her nose. The bouncing plane and the pungent odor of pre-packed, super-heated airplane food that wafted through the gap in the curtain weren't exactly a match made in heaven.

Gross.

Their cabin had been intermittently receiving their dinner amidst the constant waiting provided by the persistent turbulence, the smell hung in the air, thick and nauseating. Maya swallowed hard as her stomach rebelled. She'd stick with the butter and bread and the fruit, rather than try food that stank like stale cabbage. It was a wonder more people in the cabin weren't reaching for their barf bags.

Up ahead, the flight attendant almost made it to the doorway when the aircraft shuddered again, this time dropping so sharply that Maya envisioned a nosedive from the sky, a fiery death as the plane plunged into the earth, and whole villages decimated on impact.

A one way trip to Patala, and not all that exciting since she'd been to the underworld a time or too already.

But, the experience was eerily reminiscent of the Discovery Channel docos about air crashes that people seemed to watch with bizarre fascination just before they were about to take a plane trip. Maya tried to ignore the drama. Not easy as books and magazines hit the carpeted floor, plastic cups and food-wrappings tumbled from laps, headphones yanked from ears, people exclaiming in varying degrees of shock.

Maya sighed, releasing the arms and feeling the stiffness in her fingers from her death-grip on the handles.

Okay, so maybe she didn't like imminent death any more than the next guy.

This was a perfect argument for god-assisted teleportation.

But seriously, people liked getting worked up about nothing, unlike her blond neighbor with her nose in her book who hadn't twitched since the first rocking and rolling began. Maya grinned and scanned the skies again. At least the oxygen masks hadn't fallen from the ceiling. The sudden drop of bright yellow masks would send the entire cabin into a sure state of panic.

But even as the passengers awaited the worst, the plane righted itself and all was well with the world again.

She glanced over at Joss who was still reading, oblivious to the near-death experience they'd just had.

She gave a soft sigh and left Joss to her book, tilting her head left and right to ease the soreness in her neck before leaning back against the seat. Somewhere, within the pit of her stomach, an ache had been building slowly. And her thoughts meandered back to thoughts better avoided.

A rush of hot shame snaked its way through Maya's veins as her thoughts drifted back to Ria. How many times had she criticized Ria for behaving the only way she'd known how; by maintaining the status quo in order to protect herself?

Now, she blinked hard at the memory of Ria's injuries, the bruises, the black eye. Her fingers curled into a fist, the flesh of her palm growing warm. The anger inside her swelled, frustrated, as if it wanted out.

And Maya exhaled.

"Easy there, Blaze," said Joss, leaning close to Maya's ear, a note of warning in her teasing.

Startled, Maya glanced at Joss's strained face. But she wasn't looking at Maya. Her friend's eyes were trained on the air in front of Maya's face.

Maya shifted her gaze and the blood within her veins went from volcanic to frigid in zero point five seconds flat. She stifled a gasp at the handful of dancing flames sprouting from her lips. Fire that had seeped into her throat, that had coated her mouth, now escaped her lips in the form of super-heated flame.

She coughed and spluttered, tasting heat and shock and a touch of anger. She pulled the power from the flame as fast as she could, and sucked it deep inside her core. The flames fell away into nothing, wisps of hazy smoke curling in front of Maya's face, twisting as it rose to the ceiling of the cabin.

"Crap. You think it'll set of the fire alarms?" Maya asked, her words a soft croak as she tried to keep her voice down. Then she frowned. "Do planes have fire alarms?"

Joss just stared at Maya's face, shaking her head as if she dealt with a three-year-old, steady patience mixed with a dollop of pity and a hint of amusement.

Maya waved a hand in front of her face, a desperate attempt to dissipate the pale cloud of stubborn smoke. Was it shock that made the flailing tendrils take the shape of a smoky dragon whose expression, though amused, bordered on the maniacal? She batted it away again and sighed, still feeling remnants of heat bathing her cheeks.

"Talk about being full of hot air." Joss snorted, still staring at Maya, her deep blue eyes oddly dark, shadowed by thick black lashes as she studied Maya's face.

Maya knew that look; Joss was worried but was battling a powerful need to show concern by discussing Maya's sudden fire-breathing talent in a cabin filled with potential eavesdroppers. Bets on, she'd force it out of Maya, before long, regardless of the consequences.

And she did.

"What the hell was that, Maya? When did you start belching freaking flames?" Joss's voice was a loud hiss, which thankfully remained deadened by the roar of the plane.

Reluctantly, Maya shifted her gaze to meet Joss's narrowed eyes. She lifted her chin a little and shrugged, holding tightly onto her calm because all she needed was a tiny little push in the right direction and she'd go all padded-room on Economy.

"Just now," she said with a nonchalant bob of her shoulder, grateful her parents were up ahead in Business.

Joss rolled her eyes. She sat back, spine stiff.

Not good.

Finally, she sighed and stabbed a finger into Joss's shoulder. "Okay, fine. I'll keep a lid on it. And as soon as we get home, I'll start practicing. Who knows how this will come in handy?" Maya was making light of the new ability, but she had to admit the whole fire-surging-from-her-mouth-thing scared her witless.

Was the dragon-flame a manifestation of the fire ability, or was this something totally new?

Joss lifted her hand and began to raise one slim, neon-blue digit at a time. "Self-generated saunas. Instant smores. Ooh, hot tub. We could sure use you if the power ever goes out." Joss bobbed her head, eyes gleaming with pride at her suggestions.

With her lips tightly pursed, Maya rolled her own eyes. "Whatever." She wasn't sure she liked the idea of being the serviceable equal of a gas-lamp.

Joss huffed softly and opened the books lying on her lap. Leaning in, Maya snuck a peek at the titles. Expecting a contemporary romance, or shock-horror, maybe even a paranormal one, she was surprised to see they were along the lines of meditation and chakras.

She stuck her elbow into Joss's arm. "You're going to look strange when you start floating cross-legged through Economy."

Joss raised her middle finger, flipped her off calmly then settled in to read her scintillating textbook.

Maya took that as her cue to return to her musings, this time concentrating on keeping a tighter rein on her fire, keeping all thoughts on Ria at bay.

The last thing she needed was to crash the plane by spontaneously combusting.

CHAPTER 2

*H*ome sweet home.

The girls sighed in unison as they walked straight into Maya's darkened room, dropped their bags on the floor and fell face-down onto the bed, echoing each other's groans.

They lay on the soft mattress for a few minutes before turning over and scooting up onto the pillows. Kicking their shoes off onto the carpet, they remained in the semi-darkness, neither one moving to open the drapes and let in a little of the fading afternoon light.

Maya found herself listening for the sound of clicking toenails on the floorboards. She gave a tiny shake of her head, amused to discover she actually missed Sabala. For a black-as-night, four-eyed hell-hound he sure had a way of growing on a girl. Chayya had sent Sabala back to Patala while Maya had been busy with Lord Shiva's mission, but that didn't mean the four-eyed canine had a supernatural ability to sense Maya's presence. She'd have to ask Nik to send him home.

A few moments of pleasant silence passed, a strange dearth of sound after the constant hum of the aircraft engines.

Then Joss cleared her throat. "You think she's okay?"

Blood thrummed in Maya's ears and she took a moment to inhale sharply. Then she nodded, taking a certain comfort in knowing Joss was as worried about Ria as she was. "I'm sure she is. Mom said they'll take good care of her." Despite that assurance, Maya's concerns about Ria still persisted, strong and nagging.

A pregnant pause ensued, which Joss ended with a low chuckle. "A new identity, huh? Not sure how our Ria will handle that." Then she let out a sigh. "You think we'll be allowed to see her?"

Maya laughed softly, a sound already indicating the impossibility of such a thing. You didn't keep in touch with people in what was pretty much witness protection.

"You'll see her again, but only if you can both keep your mouths shut," came an amused voice.

Or maybe you do?

Both girls shifted onto their elbows to stare at Maya's mom as she stood leaning against the door jamb, a fluffy towel in her hand. Leela's almost-black hair, so like Maya's, framed her oval face and hung way past her shoulders in luxurious waves. She looked like an older version of Maya, and though her looks were awesome, Maya often hoped she'd inherit her wisdom too. Her mom knew stuff.

"When?" asked Joss and Maya in unison before glancing at each other in anticipation and relief.

A corner of Leela's mouth turned up, a smile that did nothing to hide her fatigue. She tilted her head to look at the girls, revealing that she understood their need to see Ria only too well. Maya felt a frisson of sadness for her mom's past grief.

At least Ria would have contact with her friends, unlike Leela's experience. Maya still reeled from learning of her mom's previous marriage, the abuse, and of how she'd had to run from everyone she cared for. Even today, her family had no idea where she'd gone.

Maya blinked back the film of moisture that suddenly covered her eyes and forced herself to concentrate on her mom's voice.

"A few weeks," Leela was saying, giving them a reassuringly calm nod. "She just needs to do some training and learn to live with her new self." As she spoke she ran her fingertips back and forth over the soft towel, a soothing gesture that probably had more to do with her own heart than with comforting the girls.

"New self?" asked Joss, her forehead scrunched.

Leela nodded, her dark eyes a little sad for what Ria had to do to ensure a better life for herself. "They'll get a few things fixed for her. Shape of her eyes maybe. Nose too. Just enough that she'll still be comfortable with what she sees in the mirror, but enough, too, so her family won't recognize her the moment they set eyes on her."

"But if it's only her nose and eyes, surely the people close to her won't be fooled." Maya couldn't fathom being unable to identify her parents even if they had a nose-job or other work done. Surely cosmetic surgery couldn't make someone look that different.

Leela's eyes narrowed at the possibility. "There is a chance, but she can still manipulate her eye and hair color. All that combined will make her a totally different person."

Leela's jaw tightened, affected by Ria's situation. She'd never spoken to Maya about her past, not even a hint of the horrors of her life before she'd met Maya's dad. And then, when Ria's own horror had been revealed she'd finally told them all the truth.

Maya nodded, sticking a cheeky grin on her face and hoping to banish the sadness on her mom's face. "Yeah. She could even get away with blond hair." Maya could imagine the color working well on Ria, but she wasn't entirely sure her timid friend would attempt such a drastic change. Ria had always been a bit of a prude when it came to makeup and clothes.

Joss snorted and shook her head. "Totally. That chick's whiter than I am."

They all burst out laughing and Leela pushed off the door jamb before saying. "You two shower and come down. Dad's getting takeout."

"Ooh. What are we having?" asked Maya, her stomach suddenly pinching with hunger.

Talk about the power of suggestion.

"Thai Fire noodles." Leela winked. She knew it was one of Maya's favorite meals.

Joss gave a strangled laugh. "Bet Maya can give them noodles a run for their money."

A pillow sailed through the air, hitting Joss square in the face. She didn't even see it coming.

Leela disappeared, quietly leaving the two girls to argue about violence, and the importance of being nice to the people closest to you.

CHAPTER 3

Maya turned on the shower and slipped her fingers into the strong stream to test the temperature. She'd always loved her showers hot, even in the middle of summer.

Showers, a thing unheard of in the middle of the Indian jungle, as she'd found out not too long ago.

Thank goodness for waterfalls.

Maya smiled, remembering the rush of icy cold water slamming into the top of her head when she'd stood beneath the falling rivulet. She could still taste the cool fresh water on her tongue, and smell the wet sand on the banks of the pond.

Now, beneath her fingers, the water seemed lukewarm, just not hot enough to satisfy Maya. As she stepped beneath the spray she adjusted the heat and waited tapping her finger against the tiles of the shower wall.

But even though the water grew hotter, with steam billowing around her, Maya remained dissatisfied. Not hot enough. Not even close.

She adjusted the heat again, and raised her eyebrows as she stared at the faucet wondering why the temperature hadn't changed. The water crashed onto her body, lukewarm and unsatisfying. Must be something wrong with the hot water heater.

After vigorously scrubbing down, Maya leaned her head against the shower tiles and stared at nothing, frustrated and annoyed. Lord Shiva's mission was still bugging her. When Lord Shiva had zoomed in at the last moment to take the Bow to safety, he'd left Maya behind. To fend for herself.

Was she being presumptuous to expect him to have save her?

But did she really have the right to feel betrayed? He was a god; the creator, the preserver, the destroyer. He would certainly know what's best in the greater scheme of things.

Wouldn't he?

Maya sighed. Who was she anyway to question Lord Shiva's actions?

Why should she expect help from a god she hadn't even believed in five minutes ago?

With a groan, Maya shrugged the negativity away, finding she'd fisted her fingers again, her palms now filled with burgeoning heat. She forced her hands to unclench, forced herself to inhale and then let the breath out slowly.

Control, Maya. Keep it together.

Maya blinked, the unusual silence within the shower cubicle penetrating her deep concentration. Her gaze snapped up at the shower head and her eyes widened. The water no longer flowed. Had she turned the shower of without realizing it?

Glancing at the faucet, Maya's eyebrows hit her hairline. The faucet was turned all the way to the hottest setting but the shower head was now dry.

Hot. And dry.

Maya froze as heat enveloped her, emanating so strongly from the breath she exhaled. She blinked, her eyeballs tight and dry as she stared around her, at the bathroom filled with steam. Maya sucked in her breath, lifting her hand to her mouth to test the heat she generated.

Her breath simmered at boiling point. Her body, too, radiated so hot the air around her shimmered like heat rising from the blacktop on a scorching hot day. Her power was turning the water into steam within seconds of it leaving the shower head.

As she dried off, she snorted.

Another power manifesting, and this one wasn't even all that cool if all it did was evaporate much-needed water, and spoiled her enjoyment of her shower.

With the towel tightly wrapped around her, Maya exited the bathroom, passing Joss on the way.

"Wow, you really steamed this place up," grumbled Joss, waving her hand in front of her face.

"Yeah," said Maya dryly. "You have no idea." She hoped Joss hadn't picked up on the edge of nerves in her voice.

She closed the bathroom door to leave Joss in peace, and heard the shower running while Joss began to hum the notes of a pop song.

A shrill shriek ripped through the closed door, the pain in the scream sending Maya slamming the door open and racing back to the shower cubicle.

Her heart thudded painfully against her ribs as she stumbled to a halt before Joss who stood beside the open shower door, holding a shaking reddened palm to her face and inspecting it, her face pink and wet as pain and tears mingled on her cheeks.

"What happened?" asked Maya, even as she suspected it had been all her fault. A glance at the faucet confirmed it was still on this hottest setting. Maya had left it that way and Joss hadn't checked it.

And she'd been burned.

Thank goodness she'd tested the water with her hand, the way Maya always did. Maya suppressed a shudder at the thought of what would have happened had she stood under the super-hot spray instead.

She closed in, taking Joss's hand into her palm as carefully as she could. The burn looked angry and painful. Joss never shed a tear about anything. Joss moaned and sucked in a sob. Her hand shivered as Maya bent to inspect it, the jerking movements worsening when Maya gasped softly.

"Is it bad?" sobbed Joss softly. She was breathing hard and Maya wasn't sure if she needed to worry about shock. Why hadn't she done a proper first aid course yet?

She glanced up at Joss, unsure what to say. All she knew was, if she could feel the heat emanating from the burn, the injury must be a very bad one. There were degrees that described the severity of a burn, but Maya was unable to recall which one was the worst, or which one best described Joss's ugly red palm.

For now, Maya figured honesty was the way to go. She nodded. "I think it is bad. We need to get you to the hospital."

"Good thing I hadn't gotten naked yet," Joss looked Maya up and down, giving a short laugh that ended in a pained sob. Even her funny wasn't helping to ease her pain.

Still clad in her bath-towel, Maya gave her injured friend a narrow glare and was about to say something rude when a memory flickered in her mind.

While climbing the side of the palace of Swargaloka, Nik had told her that they both, having the power to control fire, also possess the power to heal. She'd promptly forgotten his words, partly because it had seemed so far-fetched. But now, even far-fetched was a chance she couldn't ignore.

She met Joss's eyes and gave her a firm nod before reaching for her hand. Joss pulled it away, her expression filled with pain as she curled the injured hand toward her body.

"Give it back. I want to try something," Maya said firmly.

Joss glowered, her eyes narrowing on Maya. "You want to experiment on me while I'm in agony?" The skin on Joss's face had bloomed a deep pink as she struggled with the pain, and even her eyes had darkened to sapphire with the effort.

"No," said Maya shaking her head, wanting to reassure Joss

that she wasn't about to do anything that would hurt her. Then she paused. "Well, yes. I guess." She kept her features relaxed, disliking that she could either fail, or cause her friend more pain.

"Yes, you guess?" repeated Joss, her eyebrows and her tone rising dangerously, the color of her cheeks slowly matching the angry red of the burn.

"Stop being such a wuss," said Maya. Reaching over, she gripped Joss's wrist before pulling her hand back. She gently placed Joss's hand onto her own palm and inhaled slow and deep, hoping Joss wouldn't pick up on her scrambled nerves. At least her hands weren't shaking and giving her away.

Yet.

She cleared her throat and spoke, iron coated in soft silk. "I'm going to try something, but it's not guaranteed."

"What is guaranteed is that my palm is totally effed up. Once I get to the hospital they'll confirm it. I've seen burns like this before. It's not pretty and the scars aren't fabulous either." Joss watched Maya as she stuck her hand out in front of her, a lamb offered into the flames. "Do your worst. I don't think you could damage it more even if you tried."

Relief, in the form of cool sweat, slid down Maya's back, and she said nothing. She just bent over her friend's ruined palm and threw a mental net around her fluctuating concentration.

She drew on that energy from the deepest part of her soul, and a sense of overwhelming peace enveloped her. Somewhere, too, like the distant cry of a wounded animal, was the primal fear that whatever she tried wouldn't work.

But Maya couldn't afford to listen to fear right now, couldn't afford to surrender control to what would inevitably cause failure.

She took a deep breath, then slowly allowed her eyelids to flutter closed as she exhaled. Reaching out, she hovered her palm over Joss's red skin, guided solely by the steady stream of heat emanating from within the soft flesh of her friend's palm.

Maya stiffened her muscles, urged the heat to enter her own flesh, fervently wishing Joss free from the pain.

Nothing happened.

And Maya suspected she knew why. Fervent prayer wasn't going to be of any help in this situation. Maya needed action, not wishes.

She glanced up at Joss and a spike of relief skittered through her veins. Thankfully, Joss's attention was focused on her burnt palm and not on the doubt in Maya's eyes.

She gathered her wits again and forced her mind to clear of all her doubts. She could do this. She'd done much bigger, more powerful things with her fire. Drawing heat from a person's body isn't something that should pose a problem. And Maya didn't have the time to wonder what the source of her current misgivings were. She needed to succeed.

For Joss.

Again she focused, drawing a veil of peace and tranquility around her mind, filling her consciousness with the fluidity of nothingness. Once she gained the purity of utter calm, Maya focused on the fire within her Atma, her soul. There, she ignored the whispers of doubt that swam around her and teased the surface of her mind, and filled her thoughts with her fire.

Then she pushed the flame down. So far within herself that soon the deepest yearning for the heat began to surge through her, as if she'd become so accustomed to Kali's fire that it had become an intrinsic part of her.

Maya shuddered, the need for the fire making her stomach twist as if even her body hungered for it like it did food. She swallowed and breathed through the need, knowing her craving for fire was what she'd wanted, what she'd aimed to create in order to succeed.

Now, she focused that need on Joss's hand, feeling her mind drawn to her friend's blistered palm, like a bee to the exquisite simmering heat that broiled beneath the surface of her skin.

And Maya exhaled slowly, until her lungs emptied of every atom of oxygen. Then she drew the fire from Joss's palm into her lungs, inhaling the very energy of the burn. A small part of her wondered how she was able to do this, to wing it, trying whatever methods she could to get things done. But she wasn't about to question her ability now. Not when it might actually work.

With her hand still hovering over Joss's palm, Maya could still feel the heat from the injury, and she could also sense the decreasing warmth as she drew the fire of the burn deep inside her.

Slowly, Maya's core began to fill with the fire of the burn, while Joss's skin went from blistering ruby to a pale baby pink, from superheated to body temp.

Joss let out a whispered gasp. "Maya?" The awe-filled question hung in the air between them, a bright and fiery blaze of tempered relief, blatant shock and burgeoning happiness. Maya had managed to shock her friend.

Again.

Maya didn't respond. With her neck bent, she didn't stop until she'd stripped all the simmering energy of the burn from Joss's hand. Only when she shivered, lightheaded, only when her head tipped forward, did Maya yank her mind from the hold on Joss's injury.

She slid down the side of the glass shower door, and sank to the cool tile of the bathroom floor. A strange weakness in her knees had taken hold of her limbs.

Joss's free arm curled around her shoulders. "Hey, are you okay?"

The words echoed in the distance, disembodied and ethereal. Taking a shuddering breath, Maya blinked away the encroaching darkness.

"Yeah. I'm good." She reached for Joss's hand and was pleasantly surprised. "Wow. It's healed."

"Er . . . Yeah. That's what I was just saying." Joss snorted. "You did it. Whatever mojo you have, you managed to save my hand."

Maya nodded absently as she stared at Joss's palm. The skin was still blistered and wrinkled, though all the redness had disappeared.

"But your hand is still injured," she said, feeling the hollow of failure.

"What were you expecting to do? Magic?" Joss shook her head. "Maya. Whatever this power is, it's certainly not magic. You were able to take the heat away, but the damage had already been done. It wouldn't have gone away just because you took the heat. And I wouldn't have expected it either."

Maya turned her gaze back to Joss's, where the expression on her face was tender and understanding. And grateful. But, despite Joss's attempt at comforting her, Maya couldn't help feeling the ache of disappointment, a frigid fist in her gut.

Joss lifted her palm to Maya's face, her skin streaked with dried tears. "So, I'm good. And you can leave."

Maya raised her eyebrows at the curt demand then snorted when Joss said, "You need to put some clothes on."

With a glance down at her towel-wrapped body, Maya laughed and got to her feet. She made a show of dusting her hands, then left Joss to it and headed into her room, her stomach growling loudly.

And for a little while, the mundane made her forget the truly amazing.

CHAPTER 4

*D*ressed in a pair of bright blue pajamas patterned with little yellow-beaked ducks, Maya headed down to the kitchen, glad for once that jet-lag put paid to any sort of ceremony regarding mealtime. As she passed the family's temple room, an odd sound caught her attention and she stopped in her tracks.

She listened for a moment, then turned on her heel and headed to the little prayer room that her dad had built when they'd first bought the house; a commonplace room found in many a devout Hindu's home. A place to perform daily prayers as well as larger ones where the lighting of a havan, or blessed fire, is required to perform cleansing rituals.

The door to the room always stood open and Maya paused on the threshold, a gasp perishing within her throat.

A woman stood beside the carved marble statue of the God Shiva, staring silently at his dark unmoving features. Her figure curved at the waist, her hair flowing in dark generous waves down to her waist. The light falling on her profile reflected blue.

The Goddess Kali had dropped in for a visit.

Not for the first time, Maya recalled the many artists renditions of this goddess, depicting her in an almost demonic form, unruly black hair, protruding blood-stained tongue, large staring eyes, a scary image even before you take into account the necklace of bloody demon-heads or the girdle fashioned of blood-drenched demon limbs.

All symbolic of the destruction of evil in thought, word and deed, of course. But some artists took that symbolism a little too far. Maya suppressed a shudder, supremely glad that the goddess in reality was a damn sight more pleasant to behold.

Now, the Mother goddess smiled as she met Maya's gaze, her kohl-lined eyes dark and mysterious. "Namaste, Maya."

For a moment, Maya hesitated, unsure of how she was meant to greet the goddess. At the last second, she placed her palms together and bent in a short bow, the universal Namaste. When she straightened, she was relieved to see the tilt of a satisfied smile on Kali's lips. The wordless greeting had been deemed acceptable.

Maya took a deep breath. "You know what I did?" she asked softly, suspecting there was one very specific reason she'd received a personal visit from Kali.

Kali nodded slowly, the gemstone in her nose-ring glistening in the light from the lamp Leela had lit earlier. The single amber flame rose from the cotton wick, drawing fuel from a small well of oil, a source of light that went back thousands of years, and one revered on a daily basis by followers of the Hindu faith.

"I know all that happens when it concerns you. And more . especially when it is related to my power." Kali's smile gave Maya a little relief as she didn't detect either annoyance or anger in the goddess's expression.

"Did I do something wrong?" Maya asked tentatively.

But, Kali shook her head and smiled. The action rounded her cheeks and she looked positively radiant, if one can look radiant being blue and all. "On the contrary, you have progressed naturally, developing your skills so well that I believe you are ready for the next level."

"The next level?" asked Maya, feeling a little stupid as she parroted the goddess.

"Yes, Maya." Kali tipped her head to one side, studying Maya for a long moment, her dark eyes almost glowing with latent power. "The abilities granted to you are manifold. Your power to control flame; given to you to enable you to eliminate demons and any other dangers at will, and of course for protection. And your blood power, to detect and find evil, in essence to track down anything bad. So far you have honed it to track demons, but there is more to that power, and with time you will learn to use it for far more than mere demon tracking."

Maya nodded, a little unsure. Kali's revelation that her powers were even more than she'd expected hadn't been such a revelation, especially coming within minutes of healing Joss's burned hand.

Kali's soft voice broke the hollow silence of the tiled room. "There is one more power that you have not yet received." The goddess straightened her head, focusing squarely on Maya's face. A frisson of discomfort slid down her spine. Would Kali judge her on her reaction? The last thing she wanted was to come off as an airhead.

She fidgeted, her fingers tugging the bottom hem of her pajama top. "Another power?" Maya asked. Her conversation skills were more than lacking and didn't bode well for Kali's impression of her as an intelligent human specimen.

Too late, though. She certainly couldn't turn back time and take it back.

A grin spread on Kali's face and Maya stiffened. Had she heard her thoughts?

Damn.

Kali laughed softly, gentle and almost loving, the sound of a mother's amusement when her child did something cute. She glided towards a slim waist-high brass stand that usually held oil and a multitude of burning cotton wicks. Now, they were unlit, but the goddess swept her hand across the tops of the oiled cotton and all six sprang alight, flickering and casting a gentle glow onto Kali's face.

"Don't worry, Maya. We only read minds when we want to know something that you are not willing to tell. Fortunately, you are . . . how do you modern souls say . . . an open book?"

Maya nodded, a little embarrassed. Open book, indeed.

Kali laughed again. "Other humans will find it a little harder to read you, my dear. Gods, though, are a different story." Then she leaned forward, her expression eager. "Now. Pay attention. You must learn how to call me when you need me. I believe Chayya has provided you with a method to easily call her to you?"

Maya nodded. "She gave me a brass pot," she said, still amused with Chayya's version of an emergency text.

"And I will also give you a vessel. One which is significantly different." Kali extended her right hand and bared her palm. A breath later a bowl appeared, dull and yellowed marked with a million cracks and imperfections. Unimpressive to say the least.

Kali bobbed her hand, and Maya reached for the bowl, taking it into her own palm and turning it over. When it finally sunk in as to what the bowl really was, Maya almost dropped it on the tiled floor.

She had to force herself to maintain her grip on the bowl. Or more accurately, the skull.

Maya glanced up at the goddess, a little afraid of what she would be expected to do with this particular receptacle. Appearing on a multitude of images of Mother Kali, it often collected the blood that dripped from a severed head the goddess held with another one of her eight hands. Of course, the head was another symbol, this time of human ego, the mother being depicted as the destroyer of ego. A garish image, but apt.

Kali tapped the ragged edge of the skull. "You can call me to you with this kapala." She smiled at Maya's fearful frown. "Do not worry, child. I will not require a human sacrifice."

Maya's eyebrows rose, and then she grinned at the mirth in the goddess's eyes. Kali was teasing her.

Then Kali glided closer. "Well, it is, in a way, a human sacrifice."

Okay.

Maya held her breath.

"You will be the sacrifice. Or at least, a part of you."

Maya's eyes shifted from Kali to the kapala, her heart beginning to thud harder against her ribs. She wasn't too sure of where this was going and she mentally crossed her fingers.

Kali chuckled. "Enough teasing. You will prick you finger and place a drop of blood inside the kapala. Then you must light a piece of sambrani. The blood and the incense will do the rest."

Maya hesitated again, the sight of the skull giving her the creeps.

"You do not need to be afraid of it," said Kali, softly. "Tell me, what do you see?"

Maya's forehead creased. "It's a human skull."

"And if you look closer?"

Maya lifted the kapala to her face, turning the bowl over to study every inch of it. To her surprise she found the cracks seemed to be hand-drawn, the surface too smooth, the shape too perfect. "It's man-made," she said, relieved.

"And what does it tell you?"

"That it's a representation or a symbol?"

Kali nodded, satisfied with her response. Then she dusted her hands, as if that resolved Maya's curiosity regarding the human skull, and moved toward the raised platform set against the back wall of the room. The little dais held a pair of black stone carvings, one of Lord Shiva, the other of Kali herself. Maya's parents had always put both deities on an even footing, and even the inclusion of Kali at Shiva's right hand was unusual when Parvathi was his consort.

Technically.

Maya forced herself to concentrate as Kali knelt before her likeness and waved her hand. The air shimmered and a brass tray appeared. Upon it sat a small pile of camphor shards and a little rock of frankincense.

Kali shifted, the deep red fabric of her sari rustling as she glanced over her shoulder and beckoned Maya closer. Maya obeyed, stopping beside Kali and sinking to her knees, feeling more than ridiculous in her bright blue pajamas next to the silk-and-gold clad goddess.

"Place the kapala here," she pointed beside the tray. Maya obeyed and sat back on her heels. "Now, for the blood."

Maya looked around the temple, wondering what she was meant to use to puncture her skin to draw the blood. With the wave of her hand, Kali produced a small silver pin. "This will suffice. No need to get fancy."

Maya took the pin without a word, pierced her forefinger and pressed the tip to encourage a bead of red to form. Then she rubbed the blood onto the bottom of the kapala. Strange, and a little creepy but who was she to judge?

Kali motioned at the camphor and Maya sprinkled a dusting of grains onto the blood smear.

"Light it."

Maya obeyed, reaching automatically for the box of matches that sat beside the main brass lamp.

Kali clicked her tongue and the sound danced off the tiled walls. "Not with that. What is the use of having fire power if you do not use it?"

Maya nodded, trying to hide her smile at the goddess's obvious irritation. Kali certainly didn't have qualms about using mystical power to perform everyday tasks, so why should she?

Maya proceeded to pull a flame from within her core before setting the camphor alight with a soft sputter.

She reached for the frankincense, what she'd known all her life as sambrani or loban, and dropped a small rock into the burning flame. Almost immediately the outer surface of the grey-and-white speckled resin began to melt and a smooth white smoke rose into the air, filling the room with the unique fragrance.

It had always been strange knowing this particular incense was so commonly used among all of the other major religions. Sometimes the simplest of things show how very little difference exists between people.

"Now, once the sambrani is burning, you call to me."

"What do I say?"

Kali frowned, genuinely puzzled. "What do you mean?"

"Is there a chant or something?" asked Maya. She probably had to recite a few Sanskrit verses or something.

"Do not be silly, child. Just use your words and speak to me. I will hear you and come as soon as I can."

That's it?

It was Maya's turn to frown. "So why do the priests chant those verses and mantras if that doesn't call the gods to the temple?"

Kali smiled. "The chanting is a form of purification, a means to center the minds of the worshipers. Most people's minds are filled with too much thought and emotion, too little peace and serenity. They are unable to focus long enough to allow their plea to leave their souls and make its way to us."

"So anyone can summon you?" Maya glanced nervously at Kali. She'd used the word summon as if the gods were at her beck and call. "I'm sorry. I didn't mean . . . "

"Do not worry, Maya. That is what we are as gods. We exist merely to serve you. Sometimes we cannot come the moment we are called, but we will come." Her expression was serene, unaffected, pure.

Maya nodded and swallowed. The goddess's assurances had failed to console her. "So I perform the ritual, and ask to see you. Then I wait?"

Kali nodded. "You would not need to wait too long. A few minutes, perhaps a little longer. If you call me I will find you wherever you go afterwords. I will, of course be discreet so only you will see me." Kali smiled in such a way that Maya could have sworn she'd winked at her.

Maya cleared her throat."How come you don't reveal yourself to others?"

"Because they may not be the one who needs me. I go where my people need me. Appearing to all and sundry would be a waste of my energy and would probably cause too much of a commotion."

Maya grinned. "You would qualify as a celebrity."

The goddess laughed softly. "That is the last thing any of us would aspire to."

Then Kali got to her feet in one smooth move. "I must be going, but I will return soon to begin your training for your final power."

"What is this power?" asked Maya, curious now that the word training had been mentioned, making the mysterious new ability all the more real.

Kali gave a half smile, her lids lowered. "You will have to wait and see, my dear."

Maya pouted but didn't dare demand an explanation.

"See you soon, Maya Rao," said Kali as she walked across the tiled floor and then disappeared into thin air.

Maya let out a breath, feeling the tension escape from her body along with the air from her lungs. She should have been used to visits with gods and goddesses, but Kali was different.

Kali had bestowed Maya with her powers. Fire, and then blood.

Now, she had one more to look forward to.

Maya's stomach turned over and she swallowed against the queasy roll in her gut.

Who knew? Maybe the new power would come in handy.

CHAPTER 5

Joss stood at the little stereo beside the coffee machine, swiping the finger of her now-healed hand across the screen of her iPod as Maya walked into the kitchen. Her dad was busy unpacking paper bags of Thai food and the delicious smell of spiced noodles and fragrant rice drifted toward Maya, eliciting a symphony of grumbles from her stomach.

Dev smiled as the air filled with the soft jazz sounds of Melody Gardot and Maya suspected they were in for Joss's special play-list that included Norah Jones and Joss Stone. If Maya didn't know for sure, she'd have bet money that her friend was named for the famous Joss. With the music set, the girls helped to lay out plates and cutlery.

Anything to get stuck into the meal faster.

Maya sighed and as she sank gratefully into her seat, she pulled the Styrofoam box filled with noodles closer to her plate. "Come to mama," she cooed at the box before letting out a soft grunt. "Airplane food sucks."

"I'll second that," said her mom as she walked in bearing a

large bottle of orange juice. She grabbed a pitcher from the cupboard and filled it before setting it onto the table.

As Leela took her place beside her husband and began dishing, Maya gave the jug a glare, remembering the glass of OJ she'd melted not too long ago. Her gaze slid to the burn that still adorned the aged wood of the kitchen table, and a pulse of guilt rippled through her. Neither one of her parents seemed to be in any kind of hurry to be rid of the constant reminder of her tantrum.

The silence in the room was broken solely by the clink of Maya's fork, she being the only one utterly incapable of eating with chopsticks. Deep within a strange meld of satiation and peace, it was only when Joss poked her in the arm that Maya looked up from her plate.

"What?" she asked, sending a grumpy glare at her friend, slightly annoyed at the intrusion as she'd finally managed to sneak a few minutes without worrying about strange fire abilities and how she was going to manage them without incinerating herself and the rest of the country.

"So, you breathe any fire yet?" Joss asked, grinning as she spoon rice into her mouth.

Crap.

Maya had forgotten to tell Joss to keep her lips zipped until she got the fire-breathing under control. Like with most siblings, she blabbed unless she was sworn to secrecy. She wasn't ready for the twenty questions they were sure to fire at her.

Maya went still, hoping her parents had missed Joss's indiscretion.

"Breathe fire?" asked Leela as she leaned forward, curiosity brightening her eyes.

Double crap.

"Yeah. Maya was full of hot air on the plane." Joss smirked. Maya suspected she was hoping for a big reaction.

As if performing on call, both her parents looked from Joss to

Maya, and the silence that filled the following moments held a hint of a threat with which she was quite familiar.

She dared to give a tiny sigh but it ended up just a hiss of breath discernible exclusively to her own ears. Lifting her chin the tiniest bit, she said, "It's nothing. I just breathed a little fire. That's all." She gave a shrug and hoped they would drop the interrogation.

But her dad's forkful of noodles hovered mid-air a few inches from his mouth and her mom still remained motionless.

"It's fine. Really. I'm going to speak to Nik about training so it doesn't happen again." She spoke all in a rush and then came to an abrupt stop, deafening silence now crowding the room.

Dev cleared his throat and set his fork, still laden with noodles, back on his plate. "What happened before you . . . did your dragon impression?" he asked, his lips turning up slightly at one corner.

Leela gave him a withering glare but he barely blinked an eyelid, just waited for Maya to answer.

"I was thinking about Ria. I'm assuming I lost control because of it. I'm still so pissed off about that." Maya sighed and leaned her elbows on the table, completely unaware that she'd used a word on the *bad* list. "My anger made me lose control and I know that. I'm going to be responsible about it and speak to Nik as soon as possible."

"And in the meantime?" asked Leela, her almond-shaped eyes still dark, fatigue and worry now deepening the shadows etched beneath them.

"In the meantime?" asked Maya, straightening in order to tackle her food. She planned to tackle Joss later.

"How do you plan to control it in the interim? You don't exactly have the boy on speed-dial."

Mom, you have no idea.

Maya merely gave a short nod and tried to keep her facial muscles under control. She had enough on her mind that was related to the conspicuous absence of *the boy* without letting her mom know that she was bugged about it.

"What do you suggest, Mom?" she asked, genuinely interested. Her mom would have something in mind already, or she wouldn't have asked the question at all.

"You should try some Yoga." The expression on her face claimed she was actually being serious.

Maya groaned. "Mom! The last thing I need is to be wasting time on some flaky, hippy stretching."

Dev snorted, the rough sound drawing the studied attention of all three women at the table. "What?" he asked, his face the picture of innocence. "Not too long ago she was denouncing gods as just myths and folktales, and see where that got her."

Leela and Joss turned to look at Maya, neither able to hide the width of their grins. Seems they'd forgotten all about their food.

Thanks, Dad.

Then Joss cleared her throat. "Your dad has a good point there, Maya," she said between bites. "Don't knock it 'til you try it."

"Of course, *you'd* say that," Maya said with a stony glare, her emphasis on the word *you* sounding as all-encompassing as she'd meant it to be.

"What do you mean?" asked Joss, her eyes flickering with amusement. She knew exactly what Maya meant.

"Do your research. There weren't many *brown* hippies," Maya snapped before shoving a forkful of noodles into her mouth. Despite the ribbing, she was still enjoying her noodles.

Joss burst out laughing. "Sure. Blame me for the mistakes of my entire race."

Maya jumped at the opening. "So you're admitting the whole hippie movement was a mistake?"

Joss chortled. "Not a freaking chance. Where would humanity be without Kaftans, boho chic and weed?"

Maya couldn't maintain a straight face any longer. The whole conversation had devolved into a bunch of nonsense.

Despite the mention of illegal substances, Dev and Leela were also chuckling and Maya knew they were laughing at her. And strangely enough she was actually fine with it.

A little teasing never hurt a girl, fire-breathing or otherwise.

CHAPTER 6

$\mathcal{E}$arly next morning, far too early courtesy of jet-lag, Maya trudged into the kitchen to find they had a visitor.

"Claude! What are you doing here?" asked Maya with a bleary-eyed grin.

She'd barely stopped speaking before Claudia Romero, her mom's closest friend and her adopted aunt, enveloped her in a hug that almost squashed her flat.

"Air," croaked Maya, pointing to her throat and pretending to choke. Both her parents ignored her from their seats at the table, eyes trained on their devices, neither moving a muscle to save her. Their amused expressions reassured Maya that they had no intention of helping her out. At last, Claudia laughed and let her go, and immediately Maya felt bereft.

Funny how that goes.

"Good trip?" she asked, giving Maya a sober head-to-toe examination.

Maya made a face and sank onto the nearest stool. "Successful mission, yes. Good trip, no." She placed her elbow on the table and rested her head into her cupped palm, then closed her eyes, feeling a wave of bone-searing fatigue begin to swallow her whole.

Claudia patted her arm, pushing it out of the way and Maya's head dropped so sharply she had to straighten hard to ensure her face didn't smack into the table.

"What was that for?" she grumbled, giving her aunt a dark look.

"Because you need to get moving." Claudia was already behind her, grasping her upper arms and helping her to get back onto her feet.

"Moving? Where?" asked Maya, a little disoriented and almost heartbroken as she watched her seat being pulled away.

"Prague."

"What?" asked Maya, finding herself wide awake all of a sudden, her gritty eyes widening. "Prague? As in Prague, Czecho-slovakia Prague?"

Claudia rolled her eyes and put her hands on her hips, her dark hair cascading in rich waves down to her waist.

"Could have sworn I spoke in English," said Claude, an impatient gust of air exiting her throat. Her body language implied she was already half way out the door. Dressed in her fighting clothes, jeans, dark boots and a leather jacket over her signature silky shirts, Claudia made a bad-ass picture.

But, Maya ignored her and said, "You mean another international flight?" Her tone was dry and impatient. She was too tired for games. And as much as another hunt would be interesting, she still felt like she was walking under water. Surely nobody could be ever-ready to function under these conditions.

But Claudia was nodding vigorously, clearly oblivious of Maya's fragile condition. "Yup. Sorry, chica. In this business you need a go-bag. Ready at a moment's notice."

Maya groaned. "My go-bag went and only just got back."

Claudia chuckled and patted Maya's back with deceptive

gentleness. "Get moving, honey. Missing girls, possible rakshasa demon. Our flight leaves in two hours so we need to head out to the airport like . . . now."

"Are you serious? Am I being punked?" Maya asked, half hoping Claude would admit it was all a joke.

Her dad dragged his gaze from his laptop. Looking at her over the tops of his glasses, he said, "It's no joke Maya. They've requested you for this particular case. No turning it down."

"Why me?" she asked, successfully holding in the whine in her voice. Something told her she didn't really want to know.

"They need a bloodhound," was all he said before looking back at the screen, his expression indecipherable. Maya had the distinct feeling that he was laughing at her despite his stern composure.

"Move your butt, Maya. We don't have time to waste." Claudia's tone rang a little sharper than Maya expected and her eyes widened.

She threw her hands up in front of her, making a show of defending herself against Claudia's cantankerous tone. "Okay, Miss Grumpy Pants. I'm going." As she moved away from the table, she grumbled, "I just wish Nik was around to help get us to Prague without having to take another flight."

"Well, why don't you dial your driver and tell him to pick us up?" Claudia folded her arms and then raised an eyebrow. She too was well aware that when Nik was gone, nobody could contact him unless Maya had Sabala to send a message.

And, of course, Maya had no Sabala.

Filled with annoyance, disappointment and fatigue Maya turned on her heel to head back upstairs and ran face first into a chest. A firm, well-muscled one at that.

Firm, and familiar.

Nik.

Maya took a step back from him, for propriety's sake of

course, and lifted her annoyed gaze to meet the demigod's pleasantly unaffected one. Yes, she had a right to be annoyed with Nik, though she did manage to rake him from head-to-toe with a gaze that bordered on hungry. Good thing she was facing Nik and her parents couldn't see her expression.

Damn he was good to look at. Those dark, smiling eyes, wavy hair that cried out for Maya to run her fingers through them . . .

Cut it out, Maya.

A glance to Nik's left, did confirm that Claudia had witnessed Maya's face in all it's besotted glory, but right now, her aunt knowing her lascivious Nik-related musings was the least of her concerns.

She closed her throat on a sigh. It made a kind of cosmic sense that Nik would appear when he was truly needed, not just because Maya had missed him, or because she'd needed to talk to him. And now that she'd gotten over her initial feelings when first seeing him, she accepted, to a certain extent, that she had no right to be annoyed with him.

It's not as if they were married, or even in a formal relationship. What they had had developed as she'd learned to control her powers. What they had was a little strange too, considering Nik was a 62-year-old demigod.

But she could handle it if he could. Her parents didn't seem to have a problem wrapping their heads around their daughter *dating* the half-god son of Yama, Lord of Death.

Maya swallowed hard, her suddenly parched throat protesting the action and making her muscles constrict.

Could it even be called dating?

"So how can I help?" Nik gave her a soft smile. His dark hair hung ever-so-casually over his forehead, high cheekbones shadowing a firm jaw. His patrician nose and bearing were a dead giveaway of his regal upbringing.

Maybe she should have clarified the actual status of their relationship, but she'd never broached the subject with Nik. Probably because she was afraid of what he'd say. And right now, she couldn't handle the rejection.

Dev cleared his throat, the sound almost making Maya jump. "We need to get Maya and Claudia to Prague. Is there a way you could give them a lift?" he asked.

Beside Nik, Claudia had a nervous smile on her face, and Maya suspected she really didn't want to be zapped from the kitchen to another country half way across the world. Claudia thrived on control.

Nik grinned. "I'm happy to take you. But I may have to leave you there and return later to fetch you."

Maya's ears buzzed and she blinked away a wave of dizziness.

The room around her fell into heavy shadow, the lines of strangely placed furniture and the sense of a low roof and close walls made Maya feel all the more disoriented.

The odor of dust and rain filled her nostrils, an oddly pleasant smell.

Thunder rumbled and a door to the left let in murky light that in a blink was blindingly bright as lightning crackled somewhere overhead.

The tiny shack, with its dirty white walls and roof of almost rotted wood, smelled of warm metal and burning wood, scented heavily with fried food.

A low grunt bounced against the walls and Maya shifted her gaze to the woman standing beside a rough-hewn wooden table, a cellphone in her hand, a look of disgust smeared across her face like an eerie shadow.

"Where is he?" asked Claudia, fingers fisted, forehead crumpled in frustration.

In some strange way, Maya knew she meant Nik. Like in a dream, she sensed more about the scene than was obvious, like the gut feeling that Nik's absence meant a whole lot of trouble.

In the vision, Maya shook her head and she heard herself

speak. "I don't know." Her hollow tone held a deep sense of hopelessness, and fear.

Maya's throat tightened. What was this strange vision?

A premonition?

One of being stranded in Budapest, unable to return home because Nik had disappeared.

Maya's stomach clenched painfully, and she let out a strangled cough as the dilapidated room disappeared and her mom's kitchen returned to surround her with comforting warmth. A coziness that felt a little empty after her vision.

She cleared her throat. "Er . . . I think we should have an alternate plan. Just in case."

The silence around her seemed deafening, filled with shock and criticism as her parents stared at her as if she'd been unforgivably rude to a revered guest.

Nik's gaze snapped to Maya, his eyebrows curved with curiosity. Despite Maya's concern, she couldn't see even a hint of annoyance or judgment.

"In case of what?" He genuinely wanted to know.

Maya shrugged. "You never know. Something could come up for you." She hoped she'd kept her tone neutral, but from the tiny frown now creasing the demigod's brow, she knew he was suspicious. "All I mean is, we should be prepared. If we enter the country without stamping our passports what happens if we have a problem when we try to leave?"

"Oh, don't worry about that. I can easily get you into the airport and past the security checkpoints." Nik grinned, his white teeth flashing cheerily.

"You can?" asked Maya.

Really Maya? Way to ask a dumb question.

Heat bloomed on her cheeks as her parents chuckled, while Claudia snorted and said, "Duh."

She gave Claude a quick glare. "Of course, you can," she said, giving Nik a sweet smile, unable to keep the dry note from her tone.

Nik smiled, unaffected by her strange mood. "You are right, though. You do need a contingency plan. I'll get you to the airport and grab a couple of disembarkation forms for you so it looks to the customs officers as if you have arrived from a recent flight. They wouldn't suspect otherwise. And when you're done, I will come to fetch you. But I do understand. Peace of mind is important."

The strange edge to Nik's tone pulled at Maya's heart. Had she hurt his feelings? Or was he just preoccupied?

With a deep breath she gave her parents a look that said she was sorry, then grabbed Nik by the arm and guided him out of the kitchen and into the living room across the hall.

For a moment, they stood just inside the door, enveloped in uncomfortable silence.

Get to the point, Maya.

"I'm sorry. I didn't mean to hurt your feelings." She folded her arms over her waist and waited, keeping her eyes on Nik's face.

He shook his head, his expression neutral but now the hint of tightness at the corner of his eyes said her words had affected him, even if it had been in a small way. Raising his hands up before him he said. "You didn't-"

"I know I did. But I have to explain."

Maya's tone must have had a no-nonsense edge to it because Nik remained silent.

She took that as her cue and said, "Something strange happened. I kind of saw us, like a memory, or déjà vu or some-thing. We were stuck in an old house in the country, waiting for you, but you never came."

"And you saw this like a vision?" Now she had his attention. The tight lines around his eyes were all gone, which made Maya inordinately happy.

She nodded. "Yeah, it was weird."

"Okay. Best not to ignore it. Could be a sign."

"You believe in signs?"

"Of course. There is more about the universe that humans could learn in five lifetimes."

Maya gave a weak smile.

Humans.

Nice reminder that they didn't even belong to the same race.

Technically.

$\mathcal{M}$aya kicked her closet door shut before dropping a couple of changes of clothes onto the bed. Joss was folding them, strangely silent as she packed Maya's bag while Maya scurried around getting dressed.

She was dropping Kali's kapala and Chayya's pot into a side pocket of the rucksack when a knock on her room door had both girls glancing up.

Dev stood on the threshold, a comforting smile on his face. "You don't have to rush, you know. Now that Nik is taking you two, you are ahead of schedule."

Maya shrugged. "Better to get it over and done with."

"Just so you know, you aren't needed only as a bloodhound." Maya raised her eyebrows finding that unlikely.

"Like I have any other skill KALIMA would want." She snorted.

Dev laughed. "Well, maybe you're right. So a quick rundown?" Maya nodded. "The Eastern Europe sector became aware of this case yesterday. What the police think is a serial-killer could possibly be a demon. A string of girls have gone missing over the last few months, all late teens, all of a similar look; dark hair, on the shorter side, all independent. Many of them were back-packers and students."

"What makes KALIMA think it's a demon?"

"He's not the most efficient of killers. Along with personal items, the abduction scenes contained traces of non-human DNA."

Maya raised her eyebrows. "And *we* have the technology?"

He nodded. "Yes. Our bio-engineering department have a lot of fun studying demon genetics. The cops passed us some of the DNA found at the scenes and our tests indicated a presence of Rakshasa. That's where you come in."

Maya said nothing.

Joss grunted.

"What's wrong?" asked Dev, his smile amused.

Joss pointed a thumb at Maya. "*She* gets to have all the fun." She pouted.

Dev chuckled and stepped into the room to take a seat at the window. "I have a mission for you. If that makes you feel any better?"

Joss's face lit up. "Really?" She crawled to the edge of the bed, packing forgotten.

"We have a report of suspicious activity out in the San Fernando Valley. Someone complained about Eastern cult prac-tices out in the desert and Leela is going to have a look." He smiled, his expression truly fatherly as he spoke to Joss. She'd become one hundred percent part of the family. "You girls don't have to worry about school either."

The *girls* both shared a surprised glance.

"Do tell," urged Joss, leaning forward.

"Together with Joss's parents, we've prepared the paperwork to remove you two from the schooling system."

"What?" Maya raised her eyebrows.

Joss managed a soft, "Wow."

Dev nodded. "With all the running around that we have to do, sometimes formal schooling can prove to be a problem. So your mom and I will oversee your studies. You both only have less than a year left before college so we thought it best you have some flexibility."

"Um . . . Thanks?" said Maya, a little uncertain how she felt about this change of schooling method.

School had never been a comfortable place to be, but being removed entirely from it was a little bit of a shock to her system.

Joss's shell-shocked expression said she felt the same.

"Hey, you two. Don't stress. It's not finalized so if you still want to go to school then we just do nothing."

"More hunting? Less timetables and teachers? What's not to love?" asked Maya.

Joss was nodding vigorously and Maya's dad smiled. "Okay. Joss, you go get ready. Leela is leaving in half an hour."

Joss jumped to her feet, gave Maya a wink and waved as she hurried out the room. Maya shook her head and smiled. To her dad she said, "That was nice of you, giving Joss something to do."

He nodded. "She's been keen to go on more cases. She's been training hard and studying up. I think she deserves a shot at being an agent."

Maya grinned. That explained the meditation books on the plane.

"Well, you just made one girl very happy."

She threw her toiletries bag into her rucksack and zipped it up. When she faced her dad, she frowned.

"What?" she asked, unable to keep the defensive note out of her voice.

Damn. That was sure to get Dad on her case now.

"Nothing," he said with a shrug, hopelessly failing to hide a smile. Then he cleared his throat. "You really should cut that guy some slack, Maya."

Her gaze narrowed. "What is that supposed to mean?" Good thing she sounded less defensive.

"Cell-phones don't work in the underworld. Nik has to learn to adapt to a relationship and I'm assuming it's going to take time."

"Time for what?" Maya said, her voice a little too harsh as the advice hit home. She managed to soften her words with a self-deprecating smile.

Dev tilted his head and studied her face. "Time for him to adjust to being in a relationship where he is expected to reciprocate according to modern norms."

"Oh." That put Maya in a state of confusion.

Thankfully, he left that topic alone. "We are both very proud of you, Maya." Dev's eyes darkened. "Your Mom and I have been very impressed with the way you've handle your responsibility. We just think you need to ease up on the pressure you put on your shoulders."

Maya shook her head, the movement sharp and frustrated. "You don't understand. Responsibility is the last thing on my mind." Suddenly she fell silent. Did she really want to talk about this with her dad right now?

He must have sensed her rejection because he rose and came to sit on the bed beside her. His arm tightened around Maya's shoulders.

Giving her a little shake, he sighed. "You can tell me anything. You always have been able to, so you know my ear is here whenever you need it. No judgment zone." The silence hung heavy as Maya's brain went a mile a second. "All you need to do is let yourself trust me," he said close to Maya's ear.

Maya frowned. Why shouldn't she talk to someone about what worried her the most? Her parents had taken care of her from the beginning, protected her all those years, knowing the day would come when Maya would come into her power. A power that they'd kept a secret ever since they'd found out the truth.

Maya let out a soft sigh.

"You are not alone in this, honey. You must remember that." Her dad's soothing voice brought back countless memories of bowls of butter-drenched popcorn and late-night movies, sneaking out for ice-cream with him when her mom was asleep, and brushing the crumbs from stolen cookies under the rug so her Mom wouldn't find out they'd taken them.

She cleared her throat, shoving her tumultuous emotions aside. "Okay. Maybe you can help. Even if it's just to listen to my first-world problems." Maya made a face.

Dev nodded, approval gleaming in his eyes. "That's my girl."

Maya quickly gave him a rundown of the fire-breathing incident on the plane and didn't leave out the fact that her emotions had gotten the better of her. But when she described healing Joss, his body stiffened beside her.

"Maya," he whispered, and Maya could feel the concern in his voice.

"What's wrong?"

Maya shifted her gaze to meet his eyes. And then she shook her head, feeling a tightness grow in her chest.

"See? I knew I shouldn't have told you anything. I didn't want you to worry, and now you're worried."

Dev chuckled. "Worrying is part of the deal."

"What deal?" Maya asked, a little distracted.

"Parenthood."

Maya made a face.

"We've always looked out for you. So whatever you have on your plate will affect us too."

Maya studied the lines on his face. "So you're really okay with this?" she asked, suddenly absurdly terrified that he would say she needed to stop with the crazy fire stuff.

He gave Maya's arm one last squeeze before saying, "Of course, we're okay with this. We're all in this together, Maya. Your powers are not solely your responsibility. We've been in this business long enough to know that normal is not what any of us were destined to be. Actually, we kinda like not being normal."

Maya gave a short brittle laugh. "Normal? All this started with me just wanting to be normal."

He frowned. "What do you mean?"

Maya shrugged. "I was tired of being different."

"You were never different, Maya," he responded, sounding annoyed that Maya would even think so.

Maya shook her head. "See? You don't know what I mean. I was never normal. Indian, not American. Hindu, cultural, strict upbringing. Everything that wasn't considered normal. All I wanted was to fit in and little did I know normal wasn't even an option for me."

Maya's lips turned up in a wry smile. "Normal was all I'd ever wanted to be. Until flames burst forth from my fingertips and roasted a guy to smithereens."

Dev sighed, his eyes darkening a smidge with sadness for Maya's dead dreams. "I'm so sorry, Maya. I wish I could have given you the normal that you wanted so much."

Maya bobbed a shoulder. "Hindsight and all that."

"Really?" he asked, his eyebrows rising, two little quarter moons dividing his forehead. "After wanting normal for so long, *now* you're happy being different?" His voice held a trace of disbelief that made Maya smile.

Giving a short laugh, Maya poked a finger into his arm. "I know what you're doing and you don't need to. I stopped wanting to be normal a long time ago."

Maya opened her palm and a ball of fire appeared. It hovered two inches above her palm and she nodded at the fiery sphere.

"That's the reason. The moment I felt that course through my veins, the moment I was able to see the fire that I could create, everything changed. After that . . . there was no going back."

Saying words out loud held a satisfying finality.

"Are you sure that's the only reason?" Her dad waggled his eyebrows and gave her a teasing look.

Maya rolled her eyes. "Thanks for the chat, Dad." She got to her feet and hefted her rucksack over her shoulder. "The demons await," she said giving him one last grin before heading out the door.

She heard him chuckle, but her own words echoed in her head.

The demons await.

CHAPTER 8

Maya's stomach did an uncomfortable somersault as Nik transported her and Claudia to the Prague airport. No one was more surprised than Maya when they materialized inside of a dark closet, barely large enough to hold four people. A single light shone from a tiny fluorescent that threw a dull flickering glow onto the gigantic metal sink below it.

She blinked and glanced around to ask Nik where the hell he'd taken them, when a disembodied, tinny female voice rang out around them. The announcement came over a PA system, the accent thick, the vowels rounded, but Maya managed to make out a few words which in turn allowed her to guess at the rest.

Last call for a flight from Prague to Paris, and apparently passengers Hermann and Muir were about to miss plane.

"Nice idea," she said, with an approving glance at Nik.

"Very nice idea, " murmured Claudia even as she scanned the tiny room with a moue of distaste. "I'm assuming we're just inside international arrivals?"

"You assume correctly," said Nik, giving her a rakish bow. The self-satisfied curving of his mouth made Maya smile. "You just have to give me a few minutes to locate the correct arrival declaration forms. I'll be back."

Maya was still nodding when Nik disappeared.

Light from the fussy fluorescent shivered, on, then off again, and the closet was drenched in deep shadow for the second time.

With an annoyed sigh, she lifted her hand, palm facing up and spread out her clenched fingers. In a breath, a ball of fire burst into eye-watering brightness, and hovered an inch above Maya's skin.

Claudia shaded her eyes and squinted as Maya glanced at her apologetically. "Sorry. Sometimes I forget to tone down the power." Maya lowered the energy output of the fire and the light dulled a fraction, becoming more bearable, and less painful to their eyes.

Claudia chuckled and winked. "Happens more often when you allow your feelings to take over, eh?"

Letting out a short laugh, Maya shook her head. "No, Claude. It's just when I forget the amount of energy I feed into the fireball. Maybe I need more practice." Maya smiled, and hid the burst of anger she felt. She hated having witnesses when she lost control.

Thankfully, Nik materialized, bearing three blank arrival forms.

Maya let the fireball loose to float above them. She and Claudia each took a form and pulled their passports from their pockets when Maya choked on a bubble of shocked laughter.

She gave the dark blue book in Nik's hand a look of amusement.

He shrugged, barely raising a dark eyebrow as he stared back at her from beneath the ebony strands of hair that hung low over his forehead. Even in the almost dark he still managed to look so good.

"What?" he said, challenging her. "I even have a social security card and a driver's license. And they are all legit. Just so you know."

"All legit? You're kidding." Maya laughed softly, looking at him out of the corner of her eye as she filled in her form.

He shook his head, his expression dead serious. "Nope. Not kidding. It's part of creating a believable identity in the human world. If I'm stopped by the police or anyone in authority, it helps to have a legitimate identity. And besides, I *am* a real, honest-to-goodness US citizen." He grinned, clearly enjoying himself.

Maya snorted. "It's not as if you can use *that* passport anyway," she said dryly. "Technically, you're supposed to be dead, or very nearly dead."

"Hey! Sexagenarians are not considered nearly dead. I have at least twenty years to go before I reach *old*." Nik shook his head. He pulled a pen from his jacket pocket and proceeded with the mundane business of form-filling.

Like a human.

Once done, they filed out of the closet, past the toilets and joined a cluster of passengers hurrying towards a sign that proclaimed 'Customs' in three languages. They joined the line and passed through without a hitch.

Nik accompanied them through to arrivals where they strode past the baggage carousels. The airport looked more like a gigantic warehouse, with its super-high iron rafters and wide open space, and Maya found herself unimpressed as they headed outside to catch a cab.

As they waited, Maya watched Nik from beneath her lashes. Finally, unable to control her tongue, she asked, "How come you're staying?"

"I thought I'd tag along for as long as I'm able."

Maya nodded. "How long do you have?"

"Probably not long."

There, he'd said it. Again, she only had him for a brief time and waiting to grab a cab was not the best place to have a reunion.

Claudia drew out her phone and swiped through her messages. Then she flipped it around so Nik could read it.

"Here's the address. You can zip us over there, can't you?" she asked, smiling at Nik. Claudia was not immune to Nik's charms.

"I definitely can. Let's go somewhere a little more private. Can't be disappearing in full view."

They both nodded and followed Nik as he headed towards the toilets. The passage that led to doors to both male and female facilities contained a glut of passengers heading to and from the toilets. Maya pulled out her phone and Claudia followed suit as they loitered.

Nik didn't waste any time. The moment the corridor was empty he grabbed hold of Maya's waist and Claudia's arm, and flitted them away.

Despite the roiling of her stomach, Maya quite enjoyed the feeling of Nik's arm curling around her body.

Pity it didn't last.

They arrived inside a darkened room, the drapes drawn and shadows owning the large space.

Maya was about to thank Nik when he held up a hand, his expression almost cross-eyed as he appeared to be listening to something.

When his shoulders dropped, Maya knew immediately what was wrong. "You have to go?"

"I'm sorry. But yes, and it was a strange call. Something is very wrong so I can't afford to waste any time."

"That's okay. You go and do what you have to." While Maya's smile remained unaffected, disappointment stabbed deep within her heart.

"I'll leave Sabala with you."

Nik waved a hand and the four-eyed dark-as-night hellhound materialized beside her. Maya reached out and scratched

Sabala's head, her happiness to see her old friend tempered by her disappointment.

Then, before she registered what was happening, Nik curled his fingers around Maya's arm and said, "Claudia, I'll bring her right back, okay?"

Claudia nodded and Nik and Maya disappeared.

The sound of waves rushing to the shore filled Maya's ears as they materialized on soft sand. A look around her made her smile. Her favorite beach. Her favorite spot.

They'd come here a few weeks ago. Here was where Nik had revealed his true identity as the son of Yama.

Now, he smiled as a gust of wind played with his hair. He leaned close and tipped her chin up with one long finger. "I'm sorry. This happens to us way too often. I'll make it up to you, okay?" he said.

He looked so upset that Maya's heart melted and she found herself nodding and giving him a bright smile.

Nik bent close. Cupping the back of her head, her pressed his lips softly on hers. She sank into him, lifting herself onto her toes as he wrapped his arm around her waist, bringing her closer.

Heat sizzled through her body, but this time it wasn't her flames that filled her veins with fire. This particular fire was all Nik. And now, within his embrace she could barely breath. The waves crashed to the beat of her heart as Nik kissed her over and over again.

He'd missed her too.

But the moment was bittersweet, filled with longing and frustration. When he pulled away his apologetic smile was enough for Maya to forgive him anything.

The rush of the breeze did nothing to cool her heated flesh and she blushed as she looked up at him.

"I will go and check this out and I promise I will come right back." Maya nodded. "And I have something for you."

She raised her eyebrows but waited in silence as his hands

went around to the back of his neck and he unhooked his gold chain.

He handed her the glinting pendant and said, "This is mine. Given to me by my father. If you hold it in you hand and think of me I will hear you. It will connect me with you."

"Like Chayya's shadow pot?" Maya asked with a frown. The Goddess of Shadows, Chayya had been so kind and helpful she'd even left Maya with a method of summoning her, what she called her version of an emergency text.

Nik shook his head. "Not really. This is more of a mental or emotional connection because it's mine. I can feel you through it. And I will feel you, more in an emotional way than hearing you. All you have to do is hold it and think *to* me."

And then he grasped her waist and returned her to the room, now no longer dark. Claudia turned from the window, where she was busy opening the drapes, but she didn't get to say anything. With a wave, Nik disappeared.

The pendant warmed her palm, providing her with much needed comfort.

CHAPTER 9

The alley stank, the spiky fumes of urine, the rotting stench of three-day-old knedliky and svickova, even the murky puddles of water that dotted the surface of the cobbled street, all combined to envelop Maya in a blanket of gag-worthy aromas.

She picked her way deeper into the shadow-laden alley, treading carefully along the narrow cobbled ledge that masqueraded as a sidewalk. Here, the smooth round stones were dark, the edge of the street heavily draped with shadows.

Hunting an elusive demon possibly on a gory killing spree was turning out to be more complicated than they'd expected. They'd been so busy since they arrived that Maya had barely given Nik's absence a second thought.

Barely.

"Damn it." Claudia groaned as she hunched over something, her eyes focused on a greasy looking puddle soaked in darkness.

Maya suppressed the urge to grit her teeth as she maneuvered her way through the broken remains of the streetlight and closed in on her aunt. A dull click sounded and Maya peered over Claudia's shoulder as yellow light from her flashlight flooded the cobbles making them glisten.

If they hadn't been looking for it, they would never have found it. Not everyone heads out for a stroll through the streets of romantic Prague with the intention of looking for pieces of ripped skin, bloodstains and broken jewelry.

"Bag," said Claudia holding a palm up.

Maya scrambled to tug a plastic packet from her pocket, then handed it over to Claudia before she asked a second time. In her brief time spent on the job with Claudia, Maya soon learned that her aunt had a few pet peeves, one of which was having to repeat herself.

She'd always known the woman was a perfectionist but this bordered on being a pain in the patootie.

Claudia took the bag, then pointed a pair of tweezers at the glinting remains of a silver bracelet, the kind that usually held a jumble of charms. She used the instrument to retrieve the chain and slip it into the safety of the bag. She handed it to Maya before giving a pointed look at the rest of the dark and silent alley.

With a short nod, Maya rose and dug into her pocket for her own pair of tweezers with fingers a little sweaty inside her latex gloves. Claudia had insisted she use them, but now that they'd found the bracelet, Maya admitted it had been sound advice.

At least they wouldn't be contaminating the evidence with their presence. With the discovery of the bracelet, things were beginning to look up.

No longer a dead end.

Maya's heels made soft thudding sounds as she walked, but the sharp click-click that accompanied her were nothing but soft. Sabala's claws always managed to echo loudly around. It was very likely a good thing he was almost always glamored, making him invisible to human eyes.

Now, as Maya walked on, he trailed her, his eyes focused first on the street up ahead, then behind them. He did his job as guard-dog pretty well, so she wasn't about to banish him back to the underworld yet. Maya had to admit that she'd missed the mutt.

She cast her eyes back and forth along the street, looking for the tiniest glint or sparkle that would indicate the presence of charms that matched the bare bracelet.

Anna Polaski had been missing for a week. Maya had studied the photograph from Anna's blog; brown eyes, black hair to her waist, a penchant for brightly patterned head scarves which tempered the severity of her high cheekbones. For a backpacking eighteen-year-old that wasn't a long time, but the dark haired, adventure-seeking student was also close to her parents. She sent them daily text messages, giving a quick rundown of her day, and she posted a more detailed version on her travel blog. No messages and no blog activity for six days was entirely too unusual for the normally fastidious Anna.

She'd come to Prague to trace her ancestry and then disappeared.

That was the *what*. The *why* was proving much more complicated.

Missing people were one thing. Serial kidnapping's a whole other ballgame. No bodies had surfaced, so it hadn't escalated to serial murder.

Yet.

But Maya had a hard time believing they'd soon discover all the missing tourists alive in a house in the woods singing Kumbaya. Some things were often too good to be true.

A gleam to the right beside the wall caught Maya's eye and as she sank to a crouch to inspect it, Sabala let out a soft warning growl, the sound rumbling in his throat.

Here too, the light-bulb was busted and the shiny object turned out to be glass shards. Disgusted, Maya was about to stand up when something else caught her eye.

A dull glint, a hint of silver catching the shine of the meager light from along the curve of the alley. Maya hunched down again, reaching out with her tweezer to tease the object from the narrow space between a cobblestone and the roughly hewn wall.

A diamanté encrusted ball.

She lifted the bauble to get a closer look as to why the charm hadn't shone to its full brightness.

Blood.

Slick, glistening blood.

Blood that held the strong odor of rancid meat and spices.

"I'll be damned," muttered Maya as Sabala walked a circle in place, click-clicking before he finally stopped to sit back on his haunches.

The soft tap of Claudia's heels drew closer as Maya fished a plastic bag from her pocket and dropped the bauble into it. She held it up for her aunt to get a good look. Claudia took the packet and studied the charm as Maya got to her feet and pocketed her tweezer.

"Is this what I think it is?" asked Claudia, her voice husky as she aimed for a whisper.

Maya nodded, "One hundred percent pure Rakshasa." She wrinkled her nose. "And from the way that single drop assaulted my olfactory organs, I'd hazard a guess we are looking at a high-level female."

Claudia's eyes narrowed as she looked from the jewel to Maya. Then she waved the packet close to Maya's nose and said, "You know you want to." The look on her face said she was enjoying the offer far too much.

Maya shook her head and held up her hands, waving them in front of her, the pale light glancing off her short fingernails. "Nuh-uh. Let's keep the taste-testing for when we get back to the room." She made a face, then shuddered.

Of all the powers in the world to have been gifted to her by a real-life goddess, Maya's blood-tasting was the least glamorous.

Making it all the more unappealing was the specificity of her talent; Demon blood tasting.

Maya shifted her gaze and scanned the curve of the alley, toward the shallow decline that would have encouraged more than a few charms to tumble their way down to the bottom of the street.

She glanced at Claudia who was busy taking pictures of the scene. "We may find more bling at the bottom of the alley."

Claudia raised her eyebrows and gave a sober, unaffected half-nod, but Maya knew she'd like that suggestion. Especially since she hadn't come up with it herself. Maybe Maya was showing more talent than what her nose possessed.

She and Claudia headed off down the alley, heads moving back and forth, scanning grid by grid as they searched the cobbles. Neither one of them would want to miss even one square inch in case the police ended up finding something significant.

Maya had suggested the continued search as a means of escaping Claudia's amused gaze, but she soon found herself wondering what else they'd discover. Her stomach did a little nauseated jump as she considered the killer and the trail of evidence he'd left behind.

Well, the 'he' in question may now be a 'she', considering the demon blood, but that fact still needed confirmation. And Maya's tongue would manage to do the job instantly.

Just gross.

She gave a delicate shudder before taking another step, ensuring she moved with care so as not to slip on the wet cobbles. Another glinting object caught her eye, a shine that was oddly different from the charm. When she hunched down to get a closer look, it became clear why.

The smooth, unpolished surface leaned slightly in the direc-tion of the next streetlamp, reflecting a meager amount of the vapid yellow light. The raw edge, ragged and red, sent a shiver down Maya's spine.

A fingernail.

The remnant of the missing girl lay half-hidden on the cobbles, and mere chance and circumstance had allowed Maya to find it.

She reached into her pocket for the tweezer again, with a hand that held a slight tremor. The sight of the fingernail had affected Maya more than she'd expected. She bent closer and gripped the nail, lifting it to what little light she could catch.

Its bloody, ragged end indicated a struggle violent enough to brutally rip the entire nail from its bed. Maya turned the nail over to inspect it for residue in case the victim had scraped onto anything or anyone. She stiffened.

The girl had grabbed onto something alright.

Grabbed on hard enough to get skin and blood under the nail before it had been yanked off. Sabala let out another growl, the sound reminiscent of an underground train, rumbling beneath Maya's feet, the vibrations making more of an impact on her than the threat of sound. And she understood the hell-hound's agitation.

The scent was strong enough to announce its ownership.

Maya gritted her teeth as she slipped the nail into another clean plastic bag.

She looked up as Claudia returned from her inspection empty-handed. Her aunt shook her head, dejection hanging over her like a dark cloud.

"Nothing," she said with a sigh. Then her eyes fell on Maya's discovery and she leaned closer to inspect the bag. "Well done, Sherlock."

Maya snorted but was still happy to accept the compliment. "Thanks, but the sooner we get back to put these into sealed containers the better. The aroma is about to fry my nasal passages to a crisp."

Claudia nodded and headed up the alley with Maya hurrying after her. Her stomach grumbled and she wanted to laugh. Neither the scent of rotten flesh, nor that of rotten Czech food had affected her need for sustenance.

As they walked, a light rain began to fall, and Maya closed in on her aunt. She slipped her hand into the crook of her elbow and said, "Let's move. I'm hungry."

Claudia laughed as they entered the narrow street, still bustling this late at night. The route would take them back to their hotel. She grinned at Maya, her mouth half-open to say something smart or insulting.

A man walked straight into them.

Aiming for their locked arms, he bumped into their shoulders with such force that he sent both stumbling to either side while he simply hurried off down the sidewalk.

Maya nose twitched as the stink of rotting meat seared itself into her nostrils.

She watched, frozen in place, as Claudia fell, tilting slowly toward the busy street, unable to regain her balance.

A horn blared, the sound jarring against Maya's eardrums. Around her, pedestrians began to slow down, taking notice that something was wrong. Maya paid them no attention, just lunged forward, desperate to grab onto Claudia, a hand, her clothing, anything to stop her from falling into the road.

But her grasping fingers clutched dead air.

Brakes screeched and Claudia hit the cab with an ominous thud, clipping her hip. The impact tossed her over the hood where she landed with a harsh crunch, her weight and momentum denting the metal. While the horn still blared and the brakes still squealed, Claudia slid down the hood of the vehicle. She dropped in front of the car in a tumble of sprawling arms and legs and disheveled hair.

Skidding off the sidewalk onto the street, Maya stumbled towards Claudia, watching helplessly as her aunt hit the ground, her outstretched hand falling to the street just as the wheel of the car halted inches from her fingers.

Maya sank to her knees beside Claudia's unmoving form, her shaking fingers shoving aside the collar of her silk shirt, searching for a pulse. Then she sighed and almost sank to the ground herself, barely hearing the horns blaring around her, barely noticing the gathered crowd of onlookers, eager to get a glimpse of blood and death.

Claudia's heartbeat pulsed steadily against her fingers, confirming she still lived. More than Maya had expected.

With her body stiff, her limbs wooden, Maya's heart fluttered. She'd come so close to losing Claudia. And all the powers bestowed upon her by the goddess Kali had counted for nothing.

She'd been utterly powerless to stop Claudia from getting hurt.

And that was an irony she did not appreciate.

CHAPTER 10

At just after midnight, Maya strode in circles across the carpet outside Claudia's bedroom, flicking her thumb back and forth across the top of a spare plastic bag. She couldn't even recall picking the packet up. Her mind had remained so focused on Claudia and her condition, that sleep had evaded her.

She barely paid attention to the apartment itself, a small part of her acknowledging the designed ceiling, the old cornices and the patterned wallpaper. A beautiful example of old Prague interior design that went mostly unappreciated by Maya.

How the hell had that happened? Was it deliberate? If she were honest with herself she'd admit her instinct was telling her the man, or demon, considering his particular aroma, had slammed into them deliberately. Had he followed them? Watched them at the scene collecting evidence?

That opened up a can of rot Maya wasn't ready to contemplate.

Right now she was in bed, recovering from the accident. She'd refused to go to the hospital and assured Maya she was still in one piece. She'd also mumbled something about being tougher than the last batch of Seals the Navy had produced.

Maya had left her to rest just a couple hours ago, but now, a tortured sound brought her worried pacing to a halt. She tilted her head and listened intently. A groan emanated from inside the room, the sound not dissimilar to someone being choked to death. Was that the sound of pain? Or something worse?

"Claude?" asked Maya, placing an ear to the door. "Are you okay?"

"I'm fine." She sounded annoyed and not in the least bit sore. "Can you do me a favor?" she asked, her voice hopeful and a little too bright for Maya's liking.

"Sure," Maya said, eager to help in any way she could. "What do you need?"

"You can stop your damned pacing and have a rest."

Maya snorted, then gripped the handle of the door. "Hope you're decent."

She shoved the door open and entered the room to see Claudia standing in the middle of the room, in her underwear, lifting a pair of neon pink weights.

"What in God's name are you doing?" Maya found she was almost yelling, her voice so high it broke on a screech.

Claudia went very still, both dumbbells held above her head, blue and purpled bruises standing out starkly on her bare skin. She stared at Maya, lifting her chin a little in the face of the heat from Maya's furious glare.

"I need to ensure I stay strong?" Her tone was meek and she didn't meet Maya's eyes.

Maya folded her arms and nodded, her expression serious as she said, "So, flying through the air and landing on a car, then on the ground, are not reasons enough for you to take it easy?" Maya deliberately stared first at Claudia's colorful ribs, then her bruised shoulder.

But Claudia shook her head, her hair bouncing in the high ponytail she'd used to keep it away from her glistening face. "I have a responsibility. To your parents, to you."

"Responsibility?" Maya asked, her ears catching the sound of clicking on the wooden floors coming closer and closer.

"Yes. While you're with me, you're my responsibility. There's no time to waste lying in bed. We need to get a move on this case and part of that means I need to be strong enough to protect you if the shit hits the fan."

Movement behind Maya told her that Sabala had come to a standstill in the doorway and when he let out what sounded like a choked sneeze, Maya had a hard time trying not to laugh.

"What the hell was that?" asked Claudia, eyes going wide as she stared intently at the open doorway.

"Sabala," said Maya, unable to suppress her grin.

"What's wrong with him?" Claudia asked, looking blindly at the empty threshold.

"I'm assuming it's not often that he gets to see a sweaty, bandaged chick in hot pink lace underwear lifting a pair of hot pink dumbbells."

Claudia started to laugh but she quickly choked it off with a wince that twisted her face into something fit solely for a horror movie. She took a step back and sank onto the bed, letting the weights fall onto the carpet.

It was Maya's turn to wince as the heavy metal hit the wood floor, and wonder if the downstairs guests would complain about all the noise they'd made since they'd returned from their foray in and on the streets of Prague.

"Where the hell did you get those dumbbells anyway?"

"The apartment is well-stocked," was all she said.

Maya sighed. "Claude," said Maya, speaking slow and with gentle care, as if she was trying to persuade a child to part with a dangerous toy. "You have to rest."

Claudia grunted and threw her a glare.

Shaking her head, Maya threw both hands in the air. "Okay, fine. At least get back under the covers."

"Why?" Claudia asked, her dark eyes flashing.

"I don't think Sabala's sensibilities can handle that much naked flesh for too long."

Claudia snorted, then dived under the blankets muttering something about respect and kids these days. She pulled the sheet up to her neck and sat with her back to the carved wooden head-board, glaring at Maya.

"Happy?" Her tone wasn't much different to an Arctic ice-shelf "Very."

"Now what?" Claudia asked, almost meek, but Maya didn't buy it.

"Now, I tell you what I found after partaking of my little demonic delicacy."

Claudia's eyebrows shot to her hairline. "You found something?" she asked leaning forward. "Well, don't make me wait, kid. I'm still the adult in this outfit."

Maya smirked and considered taking advantage of the situation and making Claude wait in suspense for a while longer, but she couldn't control the urge to reveal what she'd discovered.

She hurried over and sank onto the foot of the bed.

"Watch it," Claudia snapped as the spongy mattress shuddered, sending her bouncing up and down.

"*Now* you're worried about your injuries?" asked Maya, shaking her head. The woman was impossible to figure out.

Claudia waved a hand, dismissing the question, then gave Maya a pointed glare. "Out with it."

Maya leaned forward. "I tested it twice, and both times it came up the same." She paused while Claudia tried unsuccessfully to dissolve the expression of disgust on her face. "It's Rakshasi. High-level female. But we knew that. The nail though, that I wouldn't have guessed. It doesn't belong to the victim."

"It's not human?"

Maya shook her head as her heart thudded. She wasn't liking the way this case was going. "Nope. The victim gave her a pretty hard time. The nail belonged to the demon perp."

"Wow." Claude shook her head and leaned back again. "Not a smart move leaving a piece of oneself behind at the scene."

"She may not have realized it. We know demons use their human hosts to get around, but sometimes they aren't fully in tune with it. And, the older the host the more likely it is that vigorous activity, like murder, could loosen a body part or too." Strange, talking about demonic body possession as if she was discussing nail-polish shades or the latest blockbuster movies. She suppressed a sigh.

"If we took the nail to a full-scale forensics lab, maybe they could tell us something about the health of the possessed person, and maybe their age too." Maya got to her feet and went to the window. "I'm thinking the nail tissue could tell us something. Don't hair and nails continue to grow after you die?"

She shifted her gaze to Claudia who was nodding.

"We can courier it to the Amsterdam office. We have a good facility there. Enough to perform the testing." Claudia was nodding, her mind already moving a mile a minute.

"We have a facility in Amsterdam?" Maya wanted to bite her tongue the second the question slipped out. Of course, they did. They had properties all around the world, and employees in offices worldwide.

"Still trying to get your head around the whole thing, eh?" asked Claudia. Her face, showed the effects of the accident, a purple bruise coloring the left side of her face from cheekbone to temple, another marring her right along her chin.

Maya shrugged, threading her fingers together. Nails clicked on the floor and a soft whine emanated from her side. Sabala didn't like being so close to the demon's remnants, and she understood his discomfort.

Then she laughed. "I guess a secret organization having little pockets in cities all around the world, isn't so bad. Not when you compare it to inheriting the ability to throw fireballs and sniff out demons. And certainly not when you compare it to the fact that the freaking gods are real."

"It'll get easier," said Claudia, clearly saying what she hoped would make Maya feel better, but knowing it probably wouldn't.

With a soft smile, Maya said. "I'm getting the hang of things."

Claudia blinked then snuggled down under the blankets and suppressed a yawn. "So . . . when do you start your next training?" The words were slurred a little as fatigue took its toll.

"How do you know about that?" Maya asked, shaking her head. "Are there no secrets left in my life?"

"Nope." Claudia struggled to keep her eyes open. "Families don't have secrets," she whispered. A low hiss of breath left her lips and Maya smiled.

She'd finally fallen asleep. With what the woman had been through you'd think she'd have passed out hours ago, but not Claudia. She'd go down fighting every time.

Maya slid off the mattress slowly and left the room with Sabala in tow. She shut the door as softly as she could, before heading to the couch where she'd piled pillows and blankets. Autumn in Prague wasn't exactly the Riviera.

Sabala followed close on her heels, choosing a spot beside the large brocade sofa where he sat back on his haunches to watch over her.

Maya shivered, huddling close to the fire, moving the glowing logs with the iron poker from a metal stand beside the fireplace. The apartment was heated, but the fire warmed Maya to her bones, in a way that central-heating simply couldn't.

Not unlike the way her own fire warmed her. From the inside, from deep down within the core of her being.

Maya sank onto the couch and rested her head on the soft pillow, and stared at the dancing flames. The wood spat, and embers burst sending sparks flying into the air where they turned to nothing within seconds.

Fire.

Beautiful. Infinitely powerful.

At times like this, while watching the beauty of the element of power, it was easy to feel blessed, easy to see the ability to control fire as the ultimate power. Easy, but burdensome too.

Only when the heat began to fade and only after the flames had died down, did Maya fall asleep, her last wakeful moments spent touching on the unspoken question.

Did she really get to own this kind of power?

Or did the power own *her*?

CHAPTER 11

The next morning Maya found herself gritty-eyed and bone-tired, as if *she* had been the one hit by a car. As she walked to the bedroom, she scraped her knuckles across her sore eyes and yawned twice, so hard her jaw clicked loud enough for Sabala to sit up and take notice.

The muscles of her back and neck were coiled tightly, and throbbed, probably protesting her night on the unforgiving sofa. But she had to admit, having the fire keeping her toasty was a good enough trade-off for any of her aches and pains.

She was in the middle of a satisfying stretch when she stopped cold at the threshold of the bedroom.

Claudia was already up and dressed in jeans, boots and a silk shirt, her hair curling in the steam escaping the attached bathroom. If it hadn't been for the incredibly colorful bruising on her face, Maya would never have been able to tell what she'd been through.

As Maya raised an eyebrow, Claudia leaned closer to the mirror above the dresser and expertly applied concealer to hide the multitude of bruises. Seconds later she stood back, examined her reflection, then gave a satisfied nod.

Reaching for her backpack, which sat already packed and waiting on the bed, she threw her cosmetic bag inside and closed the zipper. She looked up, giving Maya a faded smile before pointing at the open bathroom door. "You jump in the shower. I have to email Amsterdam to give them a heads up about the test we need on the nail, and I'm hoping the police have come up with some of their own leads. Then we head out for a second look at the alley. Daylight might give us a bit more info."

From the expression on Claudia's face, she wasn't going to take any rest advice from Maya. The set of her jaw, and that hard glint in her eye suggested Maya nod and obey. Claudia was already half way out the room when Maya sighed and turned on her heel.

She soaked in the steam of the bathroom as it bathed her cheeks, eager to drown her fatigue in the warmth of a hot shower. When she finally emerged from the bathroom, she was dressed in much the same way as her aunt, although she preferred her sneakers, teeshirts to those silky creations Claudia loved.

As she headed for her sofa to fold her sheets Claudia sighed and put her tablet onto the table. "So you know how we were supposed to be heading out for a second recon? Well, I just got an email from the Budapest police."

Maya raised her eyebrows, but Claudia's attention remained on her tablet. "A strange discovery at a cemetery that the priests and the police want to deal with quick-fast."

"Our demon?" asked Maya as she zipped up her backpack, and heaved it over her shoulder, annoyed that the right strap had chosen this morning to start fraying, silently cursing about unhelpful pooches who don't have luggage to worry about.

Claudia nodded, her expression dark. "Now, let's hope we find more than just a little piece of this demon." The she proceeded to juggle her tablet, keys, cellphone and backpack, her expression serene as if managing a dozen things at the same time was totally no sweat.

Maya prayed the next case could be solved, no sweat.

CHAPTER 12

The 7.20 am flight from Prague to Budapest had lasted just under one and a half hours so Maya had barely gotten the chance to relax before they had to prepare to disembark again. Add to the fact that she'd spent the majority of her time worrying about Sabala who'd remained glamored and hidden at the back of the plane. She'd left him to do his thing. Given he was a few hundred years old with a lot more experience in blending into modern society, Maya trusted that he knew what he was doing.

She just didn't like not being able to see him during the flight.

Thankfully, he rejoined her as she descended the stairs from the plane onto the tarmac, his nails clacking on the steel risers of the stairs as her cellphone vibrated in her jeans pocket.

Thanks to KALIMA, she'd had international roaming switched on, a perk she'd been very pleased with when Claudia had told her. When Nik had disappeared so soon after dropping them off, Maya's mood had certainly needed lightening and Claudia had found just the thing. At least Maya had been able to keep in touch with Joss who was bound to be incredible nosy about the investigation.

She scanned the screen to read the message, a grin curving at her mouth.

Where the hell are you? What's happening? Have you found the demon yet?

Maya laughed softly and stuck the phone back into her pocket. Now was not the time to be answering that particular message. She followed Claudia into the airport building and through customs, holding doors open that bit longer so the hellhound didn't get squished. The airport was busy for its small size, and with its curving split-leveled design and floor-to-ceiling windows, it was a marked change from the more staid Prague building.

Thankfully, they were processed smoothly and were soon hailed by a dour-looking driver, eyes dark and eyebrows even darker.

Claudia gave the man a curt, familiar nod, then followed him to the car, where he stowed their luggage in the trunk. He'd appeared unassuming at first, but on closer inspection, Maya noted the muscles bulging beneath his old and frayed gray suit-jacket, the way he scanned the area around them, as if on high alert. He had to be a KALIMA man.

Once inside the vehicle, with Sabala occupying the space between Maya and her aunt, the serious driver gunned the engine and they moved smoothly into the curving road heading toward the city.

Claudia made a strange sound; surprised and a little confused. Maya leaned past Sabala to check up on her and hid a grin. Claudia was holding her tablet in the air, pressing it lightly against Sabala's shoulder.

She couldn't see the hell-hound, but he was solid enough.

With a hand at the back of Sabala's neck she guided him off the seat to take up a more cramped position at her feet. He gave her a dark look but she ignored him.

"Sorry," she said to Claudia who still looked a little off balance. "I forget sometimes that you can't see him."

Claudia raised a piqued eyebrow, then handed her the tablet. Maya raised her eyebrows at the language, probably Czech. "We can't read that," she muttered, wondering what the point was of having documents you can't read.

Claudia reached across, swiped and opened the next page. "Full English translation here, with copies of the original police reports as a backup. Now read."

Pays not to speak too soon.

Impressed, Maya nodded and began to scan the documents. She read through the police reports with Claudia, and missed most of the journey, barely catching sight of the tree-lined expressway bordered by train tracks. She hid her disappointment, reminding herself that she hadn't come to Budapest as a tourist. That, in fact, beneath the romance of the sprawling silvery waters of the Danube and the domed spires and beautiful buildings of the city, a killer was on the loose. One that the police preferred to keep out of the press.

She glanced up to see they were making their way onto the famous Chain Bridge, with its ferocious lion statues and beautiful archway that led them straight into the heart of the city.

"I'm amazed the press hasn't caught wind of this yet," said Maya as she laid the tablet on the seat between them. She was feeling decidedly empty, as if just reading the documents had sucked the very blood from her veins.

Claudia nodded then gazed out of the window at the sidewalks, filled with people going about their daily business, tourists, backpackers, workers. "Things are a little different around here. Back home, freedom of speech and the public's right to know takes precedence. Here, nobody wants to be accused of scaremongering. And I think the people actually care what the cops have to say."

Maya sighed as her cellphone beeped again and she withdrew

the device from her pocket. Joss again. "I'd better respond or she's going to nag me until I do." Sabala peered at the phone but Claudia was already back to studying the reports when Maya tapped her message out on the screen, telling Joss they had little to go on, and that she'd message her back when they got into their hotel.

The driver pulled up outside a small cafe, and Maya scanned the street. They'd left the busy city centre and the area looked more residential with colored roofs peeking at her from around the corner.

"We need to grab something to eat. The drive is a couple of hours." Claudia rolled down the window as the driver alighted and headed inside. Maya raised her eyebrows. She certainly hadn't expected first class service.

The early afternoon sunshine shone through the open window and provided little warmth. Maya pulled her leather jacket closer, wishing she'd worn an extra layer. Claudia seemed oblivious to the weather as she swiped and scanned images of the mausoleum outside of Budapest in a small town called Debrecen.

She glanced up at Maya. "It's a hundred-and-forty-year-old mausoleum, give or take a few years."

Maya nodded, giving the screen a glance. "Yup. Discovery made outside the crypt by the grounds-keeper." Maya repeated what she'd read feeling Claudia needed to be satisfied she'd paid attention.

Only two things indicated someone had been to the crypt recently. A pair of black HiDunk sneakers and the crumpled stub of a plane ticket. The KALIMA team had tracked down the identity of the ticket-holder; a Deb McGowan from New Mexico. Whether the shoe belonged to her would take a little longer to identify, but the team was working on it.

No sign of the girls body was found.

She suppressed a shudder. "The report said the place was well-fenced, so how did she take the victim there?"

Claudia paused as the driver brought their order, coffee and burgers, not a surprise since she knew what Maya's favorite food was. Soon he pulled into the traffic and headed out of the city.

"Hopefully we can find some kind of evidence that will point at the answer."

"Are the cops going to join us?" Maya asked, before starting in on her meal, finding she was hungrier than she'd expected.

"Nope. This little visit is on the DL."

Maya nodded. "Ah, I see. Covert like."

"Yes. And that's why we'll be heading there on our own," said Claudia. "We need to find whatever there is to find before the police decide to deepen their investigation. They think it's a bunch of unrelated kidnappings, and we'd like to leave it that way. No sense in endangering any more humans than necessary. They say ignorance is bliss."

Maya nodded mostly to herself. She knew that the cops were allowing KALIMA access only because they had a higher security clearance. Seems KALIMA was as respected as Interpol. Impressive.

She was also impressed by the breadth of investigation where the KALIMA hunters were concerned. They certainly considered every possibility, no matter how insignificant. Right now, they would be analyzing the piece of nail and skin in some fancy lab, and Maya crossed her fingers, hoping they would get something concrete from their tests.

True to Claudia's words, the journey took a little more than two hours, and Maya had to repeatedly suppress the urge to wriggle.

But, she didn't suppress the sigh of relief when the driver finally drew to a stop outside the gates of a small cemetery.

An ancient, rusted chain held two metal gates closed, but swung far enough to allow both Maya and Claudia to shimmy through. Sabala walked through without a hassle, giving the driver one last glance before coming to Maya's side.

"So much for security." Maya lifted an eyebrow.

"The priests don't care too much as long as the church is left alone." Claudia was already leading the way up the bank and across a grassy area. A bridge rose on the left, the bare modern concrete a stark contrast to the almost classical style stone mausoleum standing above them on a small grassy knoll, the entrance half hidden by the trunk of a huge tree.

They drew closer, taking in the graffiti and the burglar bars that had been installed to prevent entry. The pungent odor emanating from the inside of the crypt proclaimed those measures had failed.

Maya wrinkled her nose as Sabala let out a soft whine, his ears popping to attention. "Good thing we don't have to go look in there," she said as they both headed to the side of the crypt, the area hidden from the overpass, so steeped in shadow that an observer would have to be within five yards to see anything that happened there, even in broad daylight.

As they grew closer, Maya slowed her steps, taking deep breaths to calm the wave of nausea that threatened to engulf her. Rotten meat and that spicy chili powder smell again.

Crap.

"Got something?" asked Claudia as she watched Maya over her shoulder, her eyes hooded, spine tense.

Maya nodded, and kept swallowing. Someday she was going to beat this urge to throw up. But she had to remind herself that high-level demon's blood would very likely cause this strong a reaction.

And it wasn't every day she came across a first-class Rakshasi.

CHAPTER 13

"Something stinks. Maya took a tentative step toward the odor, despite her brain yelling at her to turn around. She was really trying hard to deny the presence of the demon's odor.

Her heels sank into the soft soil, as if even the ground wanted her to stop her investigation. From the potent strength of the blood she wasn't sure what she was going to find.

"This is so strange. Why is the smell so strong?" Her voice was low, almost a whisper as she talked mostly to herself, and Claudia seemed to understand. She walked with Maya in silence.

They reached the sheltered side of the crypt, moving carefully into the steeping shadows as Maya followed her nose. The section toward the back end of the wall matched the pictures in the file. Overgrown grass grew beside the wall, so high it had begun to bend and curl back onto the ground. A small patch of blades had been smashed down by some kind of weight, while streaks of reddish-brown tainted the edges of the blades, marring the rich green.

Maya wondered about the whole DNA and gene research KALIMA was doing. From her first-hand experience she knew that most of the DNA they find would be that of the human host, but in such minute quantities that even then it would be assumed someone had come into contact with the body rather than it inherently belonging to those chromosomes. Considering these demons were mostly parasites, it was understandable.

Maya hunched down beside the flattened grass and did a bit of analyzing of her own. She drew in a slow breath, concentrating on the nuances of the substance, subtle or not.

Yup. Definitely Rakshasi.

But she needed more to figure out what the demon had done. Had she killed the girl, or just abducted her, spiriting her away to a secluded hideaway in order to partake of her victim in private?

Or had she needed Deb McGowan for something else entirely?

Maya shifted her attention to the splatter of blood on the crypt wall, clearly visible, even in the shadowed gloom. This too had been part of the police report, which had led the cops to believe the girl was dead. Which had also led them to happily hand over the case to KALIMA.

Maya wrinkled her nose.

Now, wouldn't that open up a new field of modern forensics? Demonic genetics included in the human population. What would the world be then?

Maya put her nose closer to the stain, inhaled slowly then nodded.

"Is it hers?" asked Claudia, stepping closer to inspect the streak.

Maya looked at her aunt, unsure which 'her' she was referring to. "It's the demon's blood. Looks like there may have been a bit of a struggle." Maya scoffed. "For a Rakshasi she's allowing herself to be hurt one too many times." Maya wondered if it was possible that the demon was weakened for some reason. Maybe she was old? Or she could be badly injured.

She had to force herself to pay attention as Claudia said, "The kid's been doing MMA since she was thirteen. Mum said that was the sole reason she allowed her to travel on her own."

"Yeah. Looks like she defended herself. Or at least she tried. Caused enough damage to injure and draw blood." In this girl's case, her mixed martial arts background had helped, but it still hadn't been enough to save her.

"Mortal wound?"

Maya shrugged. "Could be. And I'm still smelling demon blood. Strong, so I'm guessing we keep looking. We'll find more blood. Or more demon."

"Or both." Claudia began to search, skirting the crypt and making a circuit of the building before returning with a resigned shake of her head. "Nada."

Maya took a step back and set her hands on her hips. "It's strong." She squinted at the crypt and made a face. "Looks like we have to go inside. So much for assumptions."

Claudia chuckled before swinging a bag around from her shoulder. "Where did you get that?" asked Maya, puzzled. She knew for a fact the bag wasn't Claudia's.

"The driver," she said, her raised eyebrows saying Maya should have known that.

"Ah."

Claudia extracted a bolt-cutter. "These would have been hard to get through customs."

"Yeah. I'm positive you'd need a license for that." Maya grinned as Claudia snapped the chain holding the steel gate shut.

It squealed, nails scraping on Maya's eardrums as Claudia pulled it open. Maya winced, looking around her in case they'd drawn attention. But the place remained deserted.

Claudia pulled a small black box from the bag, flipping the lid open to reveal a blob of gooey-looking gloop that glowed with a sickly green fluorescence. She ripped off a small piece, then stuffed it into the rusted keyhole.

Turning to Maya, she said, "Fire away."

Maya raised her eyebrows at the KALIMA version of C4. "The priests being cooperative, I see," she said dryly.

Claude grunted. "They want the whole thing over and done with, but they aren't being helpful. They even gave the police a hard time when they wanted the crypt opened."

Maya didn't answer. Most likely the priests knew, or had a sense that the killing wasn't of the usual human to human variety. She gave Claudia a short nod, Sabala a warning frown, then lifted her palm and threw a burst of fire into the lock, making sure it connected to the piece of gloop sticking out of the keyhole.

As soon as the flame hit the substance it exploded with a dull pop, letting off a burst of green-gray smoke that stank of copper and sulfur. The door shifted slightly, confirming the lock no longer held it shut.

Mission accomplished.

Maya groaned as she pushed open the metal door a couple of inches, wincing again as it grated on the stone floor. Another unnaturally loud sound in the still afternoon.

Claudia gave the door a shove. She'd been expecting it to move, but ended up being pushed away by the momentum when it refused to budge. She swore softly before glancing at Maya. "It must be stuck."

"Thank you, Captain Obvious." Maya rolled her eyes. Claudia just narrowed her gaze and said nothing."Is that the only way in? No skylight or back door? No secret underground tunnel?" Maya glared at the unhelpful door, already suspecting that the grate was the way in.

She didn't like it.

She liked it even less when Claudia moved away from the door and went around to the grate. "*This* is the only way in." She glanced at Maya.

"No way," Maya responded, shaking her head a little too hard. Sabala moved toward the door, putting his nose into the gap and sniffing the interior of the mausoleum. The dog whined, then backed away from the crypt, his liquid gaze moving to Maya's face. It looked like he was telling her that this was a very bad idea.

She couldn't agree more.

Maya looked at Claudia and nodded at the grate. "Maybe *you* should go. I'm sure you'd fit."

Claudia laughed and pointed at her generous hips and then at her equally rounded butt. "Have you seen these? No way I'm getting inside there. Sorry, kiddo. This one's all yours." Maya growled, the sound receiving a snort from her aunt. "Now, now. No reason to go all rabid on me. Job's a job, kid."

This time Maya snorted. "I can see you're enjoying this far too much."

"Not at all. What kind of aunt will I be if I took enjoyment from your discomfort?" She sounded so innocent. Not.

"You're you. That is all," Maya said dryly, giving Claudia a dark glare before sinking to her knees. She grabbed the grate and gave it a light tug. May as well get it over with.

The movement proved sufficient to shift the grate, and Maya lifted it away easily. Proof the small space had been used as an access point on a regular basis.

Maya dropped her rucksack on the grass and took a deep breath before poking her head into the opening.

"Ugh," she groaned, snatching her head out of the hole in the wall and gasping for air.

"What is it?" Claudia asked, hunkering down beside her and attempting to peer inside by tilting her head at an unnatural angle. Then she winced and straightened, her injuries curtailing her gymnastics.

Maya groaned. "Why didn't we bring gas masks? It stinks in there."

"Stinks like what?"

"What do you think? These days human stink is by far the more acceptable odor of preference," Maya grumbled as she sucked in a breath and maneuvered her way into the crypt.

Usually she hated being so small, but this topped all previous experiences. Even Sabala gave a whoof, as if his nostrils couldn't bear the stench either.

And he was still outside.

"How the hell did the cops not get a whiff of this and break the crypt open?" asked Claudia, her voice pitched not a scale of high annoyance.

Maya tilted her head to the side and studied the crypt. She'd been wondering the same thing. "Do you believe in magic?"

"Quoting lyrics now?"

Maya huffed. "The building, its walls, feels strange. Like it's resonating a power. I'm wondering if the demon could have glamored the place. I know they use glamor to hide themselves from humans, so why can't they hide buildings, especially ones as small as this?"

"A-plus for observation kid. I think we'll keep you."

Maya snorted. Then she crouched and shimmied through the square opening, then got to her knees and peered around the small dark space. She lifted her palm and called up her fire. With a spurt of flickering light, a flame appeared in her palm, brightening the furthest corners of the small crypt.

Maya grunted.

Claudia poked her face into the space, trying to see what had happened. "What's wrong? You okay?"

"Yeah. I'm fine. Demon BO is usually rotten, but this takes it to a whole other level," said Maya, staring at the putrid remains of a body.

She turned her attention to the small room. Whatever remains this mausoleum had been built to store, were now long gone. Not a coffin or a jar of ashes remained. The rotting body currently occupied the space all on its own.

Unless you counted the stacks of paper, the ripped filthy sleeping bag, an ancient lantern, a pile of unopened tinned food, and a stack of yellowed novels. Whoever had lived here had kept the place clean. Probably to ensure they didn't end up sleeping with rats or snakes.

Did Hungary have snakes?

Maya glanced at the entrance and said, "I see why you couldn't open the door."

"Locked from the inside?"

"Yeah. It's got an old drop bar lock thing. It's a bit too wide which explains why the door opened a little. Whoever built this thing had a reason to want to lock themselves up inside it." Maya shoved the metal bar up and out of the brackets, then leaned it against the wall before pulling the iron door open. "Man, I don't know if I've ever been this happy to see the light of day."

Claudia chuckled as she peered into the shadowy interior of the crypt. "Says the girl who has spent time in the Underworld."

"That was different. There weren't any rotting corpses that I could see." Maya moved aside to allow Claudia to get a better look at the remains. The hell-hound drew closer, probably so he'd look like he was doing his job. He was clearly not into rotting remains that smelled like demon barbecue either.

"The Underworld without rotting corpses? That's a new one," Claudia muttered as she tugged a camera from her rucksack. After taking a few photographs she stowed the camera, then tugged out a piece of black plastic.

As she dusted it, Maya grumbled. "You have got to be kidding me." She glared as Claudia lay the body bag on the concrete floor and unzipped it.

"What?" Claudia glanced up, her eyebrows raised in innocent question. "It's just a pile of skin and bones, Maya. The lab will want to examine it."

Maya just made a face and watched as Claudia snapped on a pair of gloves, then threw a second pair straight at her. She caught the flying latex and slipped them on before silently helping her aunt to pack up the remains. It didn't take long before Claudia was zipping up the bag then rolling it into a bundle.

"Watch the evidence," said Maya as her aunt stuffed the package in her rucksack.

Claudia just shrugged. "Makes little difference. The demon's obviously found herself another host. This isn't going to give us much to go on except for confirmation of identity."

"It does give me something to go on," said Maya softly, feeling a strange sensation curl in the pit of her stomach. Claudia zipped up the rucksack and glanced at Maya, her brows scrunched. "The more I use this power, the more I can identify smells. I think I'm beginning to differentiate the blood from different people when I smell this demon's blood. Could even be blood types."

Claude pursed her lips and gave a short nod. "That's good, right? Means we can track the different people this demon has taken so far." She headed out of the crypt and Maya followed closely, not keen on being left behind in the cold room.

She raised an eyebrow. "If you say so."

Sabala kept close to her side, his great black eyes scanning the lengthening shadows around them as they headed back to the car.

Claudia glanced over her shoulder. "What's bugging you, kid?"

Maya shrugged. "I dunno. I'm not sure I like being able to track demons using their blood and the blood of their victims. I'm not much more than a hound-dog right now."

Sabala sneezed, clearly understanding the insult.

"And where would we be without that nose of yours?" Maya glanced at her aunt, a question in her eyes. Claudia shook her head, impatiently. "We'd be back where we were last year, solving only thirty percent of our cases. That damned schnoz of yours is bound to help a lot of people, either to achieve closure or to find a killer. Or to kill the demons responsible for death and mayhem. Pretty important stuff, even if it isn't super glam. Besides, that fire power of yours is freaking awesome."

Maya remained silent as they slipped through the gates and headed for the car. The trunk rose and Claudia dropped the rucksack inside before slamming the lid closed.

Her fire was awesome, but with its recent unexpected fluctuations she had to be careful. Awesome could turn into deadly very quickly.

Soon they were heading back to Budapest, while Maya remained deeply ensconced in her thoughts. Claudia had made a few good points. So why was she still feeling dissatisfied? Was it really her power that was bugging her? What Claude said was true. As nasty as her demon-seeking ability was, it had helped them, especially over the last few days.

Seems she had a nose for the job.

CHAPTER 14

*D*uring the two hour drive, with Sabala's head in her lap, she stared out of the window at the blur of green and brown that sped past.

Maya's phone buzzed and she grinned as she scanned the screen to see a text from Joss.

She tapped off a text. *Did you find a cult?*

A few seconds later, Joss's reply came through.

Waste of time. Turned out to be a group of kids who thought Satan worship was boring and decided that sacrificing to Kali would bring them blessings, or some shit like that.

Bet Kali would love that.

Maya responded with a grin as she wondered what the goddess would think.

Yeah. They've all been arrested. Runaways, and a couple foster kids and juvies. Great way to prey on the weak. Cult leaders suck.

You back home? Maya asked.

Yup. Just walked in the door. I'm crashing in your bed. How you doing with your demon hunting?

On the trail. Just checked out a body outside Budapest. On our way back. Have to catch this bitch soon before she kills more innocent kids.

Wow, Maya. Language much.

Maya laughed silently. *Shocker right? Losing patience here. High-level Rakshasi going Hannibal on Eastern Europe.*

You'll figure it out. Use that nose of yours.

Maya sent her a little emoticon flipping her off.

You in a good mood.

Just a little tired. And grossed out. Dead bodies aren't my idea of a good time.

You be careful, okay?

Joss was being her usual bossy protective self.

I will. Claude will make sure of that.

Maya said her goodbyes and settled into filling her mind with something other than dead bodies.

Darkness began to claim the horizon as they headed back into the city and the tightness in Maya's gut told her it was far from over.

Over or not, this demon was going down.

CHAPTER 15

The car pulled up in front of a two-storied terra cotta building, Opera Garden Hotel from the looks of the gleaming silver plaque on the right hand wall beside the entrance.

Claudia scooted out of the car. "We have a long-term rental here. Let's get our luggage upstairs. I have a feeling this may be more than an overnighter."

Sabala scurried out, landing on all fours just as Maya alighted. They hurried inside, Claudia leading the way with the sure confidence of having been there before. The rooms were beautiful and totally not what Maya had expected. Light wood floors, feature walls in pale colors speckled with gold patterned leaves and flower prints.

It was very modern and thoroughly lovely, yet she wasn't able to enjoy it much more than to drop her rucksack onto her bed and stare longingly at the gorgeous pale blue and brown throw before Claudia's phone began to ring.

Maya left her room and hurried into the living area as Claudia held a stilted conversation with someone, probably from

KALIMA considering the sobriety of her tone, mostly made up of 'Crap', 'this is not good' and 'we are on our way'.

As soon as she hung up, Maya asked, "What was that about?"

Claudia made a face and tucked her phone into her pocket as she got to her feet. She grabbed her backpack and was halfway to the door as she spoke. "Another possible abduction. Get your butt moving, kid."

Maya hurried after her, with Sabala's claws scrabbling on the wood floor as he sprang up to follow them.

Leaving the warm hotel room, and entering the brisk after-noon weather would have been a shock to Maya's system had she been paying attention, but her mind was focused on what could possibly be another victim, while her stomach rebelled by vigor-ously churning her long-eaten burger and threatening to expel it.

Their KALIMA issue car waited downstairs, this time with a different driver, hair, eyebrows and cheeks all a similar shade of red. And he appeared to be not much older than Maya herself, which she found strange. Younger people tended to be life-focused, as opposed to concentrating on the saving of lives. Unless he comes from a family of hunters.

They climbed into the vehicle and as the driver navigated the streets, Maya found him glancing back at her in the rear view mirror every so often. Technically he wasn't staring, just looking. A lot. And every time she caught his eye, he blushed and glanced away.

She wasn't sure about the almost-casual observation. Curious or pervy, she couldn't decide.

They flitted through the busy afternoon traffic, speeding along the city streets, just slow enough so as not to kill anyone on the way, but fast enough that they got to their destination in under fifteen minutes. Soon enough that the trail wouldn't go cold for Maya. The fresher the scent, the stronger her ability to identify it.

At last, they screeched to a whiplash-inducing stop outside a building that looked like it had jumped straight out of the pages of a fairytale. All white, with thin spire-topped towers, it shone in the sunlight, so glaring Maya wished she'd brought her shades.

"What is this place?" she asked as she got out of the car and left the door open for Sabala for a few discreet seconds.

The hell-hound jumped out of the back seat, his four eyes scanning the street and the building they were about to enter. With a bob of his head he rounded the vehicle before her, as if checking the place out before she entered.

Maya shaded her eyes with her hand as she craned her neck to stare up at the highest points of the building. "Pretty."

"It's called the Fisherman's Bastion," said the driver, a nervous ripple in his voice as he looked at her, then up at the building, then back at her face, his cheeks ripe with a blush. "It was built in the 19th century, originally a lookout tower."

"Thanks, Stefan. If you could wait here for us?" Claudia gave him a curt look and Maya had to suppress a laugh at the stern reprimand in her voice. Seemed she hadn't missed Stefan's scrutiny throughout the ride, either.

Stefan now blushed all the way to his red roots and jerked his head up and down so violently that Maya could almost imagine it popping off his shoulders and rolling away down the street. When she glanced over at him again, he'd leaned against the hood of the car, folded his arms and appeared to settle in to wait.

Although the sun was warm, a chill on the air managed to steal its way down Maya's collar and up her sleeves. Seemed she was beginning to dislike feeling cold these days.

As she followed Claudia up the incline she pulled her jacket closer, then let out a soft laugh. How silly of her.

She had the perfect way to keep herself warm that didn't entail additional clothing. She drew her fire up from her solar plexus and directed the heat to the surface of her skin where she left it to pulse, warm and comforting.

As Maya reached Claudia's side, she said, "You were a little hard on him." A glance behind them revealed that Stefan was still watching them intently as they walked across the large court-yard, past a statue; a man on a horse from the brief glance Maya gave it.

Claude turned and looked at her. "That boy has a hard time keeping his head in the game. One day it's going to get him killed." Claudia made a face. "At least he's gotten over his curios-ity. Hopefully now he'll concentrate better."

"Curiosity?" Maya asked as they entered the building and headed for the stairs, Sabala's nails clattering on the floor just behind them.

Maya didn't need anyone to direct her to the scene. The spicy rotten scent of demon blood did well enough to lead Maya toward the scene all on its own

She had to concentrate on Claudia's words as she answered Maya's question. "Yeah. You're somewhat of a celebrity over on this side of the ocean."

Maya stopped in her tracks. "Celebrity?" She didn't like the sound of it one bit.

Claudia nodded. "KALIMA has been waiting for you to come into your power for a while now. Of course, your identity was always on a need to know level but most of the hunters knew the Hand of Kali was going to come soon. So laying eyes on her is a special privilege. Stefan will be a popular guy for a while once he tells his story."

Maya turned on her heel and ducked under a ribbon of police tape that blocked the next stairwell. She headed up the stairs, gritting her teeth. "Too bad he didn't ask for an autograph," she mumbled as she took the risers two at a time, inexplicably angry all of a sudden.

Claudia snorted as she hurried behind Maya. "Hey, don't go thinking you can carve your name in fire on his naked chest or anything."

Maya merely gave a cold laugh, unable to find a good enough response to that.

She didn't have much time to give it any thought either as they rounded the corner and the scent of demon blood filled the air, like the fumes of putrid garbage, or the ripe odor of fresh manure.

Maya tried not to gag.

 aya slowed to a stop, trying to figure out where the odor was the strongest. It didn't help that Sabala was growling, hackles high, teeth bared. Ironic that the demon dog didn't have a soft spot for demons.

They were near a ledge that looked out over the city. Blood pooled on the floor and stained the wall in irregular streaks that suggested an accidental smear as opposed to blood-spatter caused by stabbing or shooting.

Maya hunched down over the crimson puddle, finding what the police had considered a clue to another disappeared tourist. A key-chain with a picture of a little boy holding a Cookie Monster toy. The picture had survived the mess courtesy of its cheap plastic frame. The ring held a single key, which Maya assumed would be nearly impossible to identify. It could be a small luggage lock, or a train station locker or even a key to an apartment door.

Too many possibilities. The key was a dead end.

But the blood was not.

Maya inhaled slowly, trying not to give a full impression of a sniffer dog. The real dog, or as real as a demonic pooch could be, stood stiffly at the sidelines, his ears on end, his lips pulled back. Seems he couldn't stand the smell.

At the end of the hall stood a stiff-spined policeman whose severe expression simply darkened as he watched Maya study the scene. When he took a step toward them, looking like he was about to come over, Claudia hurried around Maya and strode over toward him, her bearing a little more officious than a kid like Maya.

Good thinking, Claude. Keep him busy while I do my thing.

Maya left Claudia to pacify the policeman and concentrated on the scene. She leaned closer and studied the blood, observing all its characteristics including its particular odor. She soon stiffened, her own blood cooling beneath her fire-generated warmth. Claudia wasn't gone long, but Maya was distracted by the tapping of her heels on the floor. She glanced up, her face now as severe as the cop's. Claude's expression went from annoyed to curious in a fraction of a second.

"What? It's another girl, isn't it?"

She looked like she wanted Maya to say no.

"No," said Maya, giving the blood a second glance. "The blood is a combination of both Deb McGowan's and the Rakshasi's." Maya made a face as the odor churned her stomach to boiling point.

"This is getting creepy," said Claudia as she too stared at the ruby liquid as if was about to come alive. She'd come to stand right beside Sabala, who now raised his eyes to give her an appraising look. Claudia remained oblivious that she was standing half an inch from him, and Maya was all the happier for it.

"And it hasn't been creepy until now?" Maya snorted. "Woman, you are getting jaded in your old age."

Claudia clicked her tongue softly. "You don't know the half of it, chica." She gave the scene a nod. "So, break it down slowly for this old woman, okay?"

Shaking her head Maya said, "The blood is fresh, not yet congealed. Same blood as the alley in Prague. They were here not very long ago. Probably left minutes before the scene was discovered." Maya circled the soiled floor and went to stand against the balcony. "It's strange, though," she said, staring out at the horizon but seeing not a thing.

"What's strange?" Claudia prompted her. Maya pulled her gaze from the view and met Claudia's concerned eyes. She'd stopped speaking, sidetracked by her discovery.

She inhaled, the sound harsh even to her own ears. "Sorry. But it's totally weird. The blood was not dripped onto the floor from each of them individually, not like a wound of any sort. Even if they both opened a vein and bled onto the floor, the patterns would alternate as each drop fell into the pool. One drop, then the next, each one displacing the one that follows. I can only guess that it's been mixed together well before being dropped onto the floor."

"Ritual?" asked Claudia, her voice and expression fatigued. Her injuries must be taking their toll on her and Maya reminded herself that she should keep an eye on Claudia.

Now, she nodded. "Yeah. Definitely some kind of ritual. The blood looks like it was dropped from a container. See on the right, that configuration of drops." Maya pointed as the scattered collection of irregular sized blood droplets. "It looks like the contents was tipped onto the ground but at a slight angle so there is a small amount of splatter on the one edge. And there are traces of holy basil leaves and graveyard ash, and I also smell camphor."

Claudia frowned. "Pray tell, how the hell you know all this without forensic training?"

Giving a shrug, Maya said, "It's got nothing to do with training. It's more like I can see and sense how it happened. Almost like a vision of it pops into my head and I can see it happening, the bowl tipping, the blood falling, hitting the ground, splashing on the edges." Maya paused as she put into words what her process of tracking had evolved into over the last few weeks.

"Don't forget the whole sniffer dog routine."

"Hilarious," said Maya as she faced the view again, still distracted. "She's alive," she murmured half to herself.

"What?"

Maya glanced at Claudia over her shoulder. "Deb McGowan. She's still alive."

"How do you know that?" Claudia's tone sharpened as she stepped closer to Maya. Sabala got to his feet, watching her intently before deciding she wasn't a danger.

Maya shrugged, then gave a pointed glance at the mess on the floor. The blood was beginning to cool and congeal, looking a little gluggy around the edges. "There isn't enough blood there to indicate she'd been bled dry. And the demon must want her to perform this ritual again, because it sure looks to me like it failed big-time."

Maya sucked in a breath sharply as her sight began to fade, darkening at the edges as if she was about to pass out.

Not again.

She grabbed tightly onto the balcony and blinked vigorously. But even as her sight slowly returned she knew she was seeing something other than the expansive view of the city.

Her eyes focused and she found herself watching a girl sleep, watching the vein beat at her temple, her low hairline almost hiding the pumping vein with a shock of jet-black hair. The girl's eye's were shut, but somehow Maya knew they were a dark, brown like her own.

Maya sucked in a shocked breath as her stomach pinched and she a deep hunger pierced her belly. She stifled a gasp at the pinch in her throat, the insatiable thirst which confirmed *she* was the one who craved the taste of blood, who wanted to consume every last drop the girl could offer.

A part of her mind reminded her that this was a vision, not

real, just images in her head, but the taste on her tongue making her mouth water, and the hunger in her gut pushing her deep need to insane levels, made her wonder.

She found herself turning her gaze slowly to face a man whose features were hidden by shadows. The room was familiar too. The smells, the walls and roof.

She'd seen this place before.

The shack from her vision

CHAPTER 17

And with a start Maya recognized the shack. The same shack from her first vision when she'd known that Nik would not come back for them. Was this how it connected? Would he have abandoned them in the demon's hovel if they hadn't taken other precautions?

But Maya didn't have to ponder what would have been. She forced herself to concentrate on the subject of her scrutiny; the man who also seemed so familiar.

He shifted, a step closer and the shadows changed, revealing his long, gaunt features, his unusual height. The man who'd shoved Claudia into the road. The demon, who answered to the killer Rakshasi.

Now, Maya paid full attention.

"Find me another one." The words left her own mouth, but she wasn't the one speaking. "This one is soon going to be of no use to me." The woman's voice was soft, and husky. And familiar.

What the hell is going on?

"Will you perform the ritual again?" The man's voice grated on Maya's bones and she found that she somehow knew that she despised him. That she wished he was dead, but accepted that he had his uses.

"We will perform the magic again and this time it will be a success." A new voice made her turn to the speaker, a younger woman, the muscles of her face tight against her bones. She was dressed in a long simple garment, a large hood covering her dark hair, her face so familiar. She couldn't put her finger on it yet.

Any second now.

Behind her stood a group of girls, all with the same strained expression, all with cheekbones that seemed to stand out garishly from faces framed by dark waist-length hair. All bearing the same expressions of fealty, devotion.

Maya's head nodded, and she sensed approval of this girl.

And then she was pulled back to her own consciousness. But the last image in the vision made her blood run cold.

Claudia was standing beside her, holding onto her waist tightly. "Maya, what the bloody hell just happened?" she whispered harshly into Maya's ear.

Maya gasped, taking a sharp breath of the cold late-afternoon air. "I don't know. It happened again. When Nik offered to help us get to Prague I 'saw' us stranded in this old house. In that vision, he didn't come back for us and we were in danger." Maya looked at Claudia, feeling her stomach tighten into a knot. "The same thing just happened. I had this vision of the same house. It was so real, I could have sworn it actually happened."

The seconds ticked by as both of them remained silent, absorbing Maya's words.

Eventually, Claudia asked, "Tell me exactly what you saw."

"Demon eyes. They had demon eyes," Maya whispered.

"Maya, what are you talking about." Claudia gave her shoulders a shake and it seemed to do the trick, bringing Maya back to reality.

She blinked and glanced up at Claudia as her aunt stepped

away to give her some space. "She's not alone, the Rakshasi. She has a colony, for want of a better word."

"Shit, Maya. You sure know how to push things up a notch."

"What can I say, I do try," said Maya wryly, still feeling the craving for blood in her veins. She gritted her teeth and pulled her fire forth, sending it surging through her veins in the hope that it would obliterate that awful desire. Then she cleared her throat softly. "Oh, and the Rakshasi is a bit of a psycho female."

"The vision told you that?"

Maya nodded. "It's almost like I felt what she was feeling. She's filled with rage. And she's killing young girls because she wants their blood."

Claudia scowled. "The blood? For the ritual?"

Another nod. "And for her nourishment. It feels like she needs the blood to survive." Maya paused. "There is something else, too. It's like she has this terrible hatred for the girls too. As if they'd done something to her and she needs to punish them for it."

"That doesn't make sense. All the girls had nothing in common except for being alone at the time they disappeared, and that they seemed to be of similar coloring."

"Dark haired?" asked Maya remembering the sleeping girl and all the other acolytes. She recalled the one demon girl who'd seemed so familiar. Why couldn't she remember?

Claudia nodded. "It is a factor, but it isn't a deal-breaker."

"What if they came across the demon on the street and they dissed her or something? That could explain her deep anger towards them."

"Could be. Or maybe it's something more sinister. We can only go on what you saw." Claudia was looking at her, her frown skeptical.

Maya opened her mouth, about to assure her she wasn't playing games when Sabala growled loudly and someone crashed hard into her side.

What the hell?

She scanned the area and caught a glimpse of a man, running for the stairs. He glanced over his shoulder and Maya's eyes widened as she recognized him only too well. Instinctively, she shifted to give chase and it took a split second to realize that she couldn't because she was in the process of falling.

Falling over the edge of the balcony.

Maya flung her arms out, trying to regain her balance, knowing in the pit of her stomach that there was no way to save herself.

She was going to die.

Claudia grabbed a hold of the front of her clothes, jacket and all. Fingernails dug into the skin of her chest as they gripped and pulled hard. Maya's body swayed from falling over the edge, to being pulled back to safety in the fraction of a blink.

She fell to the ground inches from the congealed blood, sucking in a deep grateful breath. Sabala sidled close to her, giving a soft whine as he nuzzled her ear.

"What the hell just happened?" she asked, more indignant than inquiring. She gasped for air as she surged to her feet.

"Someone pushed you."

"I know." Maya spun on her heel and took off down the passage. "It's the same creep who shoved us last night," she yelled over her shoulder as Claudia caught up with her. There wasn't time to apprise Claudia of the man's demonic ancestry.

Maya skidded down the stairs, racing for the entrance and the front steps. From her vantage point she could see the gangly demon racing across the open courtyard heading for the street. The sun was low on the horizon as dusk fell and Maya knew they didn't have much time if they expected to catch the creep.

She ran, taking the steps two, three at a time, barely paying Sabala any attention as the hell-hound click-clacked beside her, keeping pace. In a flash of black, he dashed forward, giving a woof as he sped after the demon.

Maya yelled, "Stop him Sabala," before realizing that he wasn't visible and she was going to look nuts yelling instructions to the air around her.

As she passed their car, a stunned Stefan watched her speed by. He pushed off the car and Claudia yelled something at him. Behind her, Stefan slammed the car door and gunned the engine. She ran, keeping the demon in her sights and upwind. She hated to admit it but she could smell him very well, and had found the best way to track him now was to follow his stink.

She sensed movement behind her and a car squealed to a stop so harshly that Maya smelled burned rubber. Claudia flung open the back door and scooted inside so Maya could jump in back with her. She'd barely gotten into the car before Stefan took off again, with Claudia yelling directions at him.

Maya rolled down the window, barely registering the fact that the car actually had roll-down windows. She stuck her head out of the open window, accepting the irony that she was behaving exactly like the sniffer dog she didn't want to be as she took a breath and scented the air to ensure they were on the demon's tail.

"Keep going, he's heading toward the river."

Stefan glanced back at her, taking his eyes off the road for a little too long.

Horns blared and Claudia screeched, "Look out," before he turned back just in time to wrench the wheel and miss a small truck by inches. "Keep your eyes on the bloody road, you fool. We can't afford an accident right now."

Stefan glanced over his shoulder at Claudia and she smacked him on the shoulder. "Watched the freaking road, Stefan."

That seemed to do the trick as he began to pay closer attention to speed and driving accuracy.

Maya continued to test the air, pointing left and right as the demon sped through the city. Once or twice she caught sight of Sabala on the creature's tail and wondered what would happen if the hell-hound caught up with him before Maya got there.

She crossed her fingers and prayed that wouldn't happen. She'd much prefer to get the demon alive so that she could be the one to make him breathe his last.

They passed out of the city into an area that seemed poorer, darker and much more derelict. The demon led them beyond, to the outskirts of a countryside area, sparsely populated and almost deserted save for the odd house that looked abandoned. Her skin tingled, and a corresponding hum vibrated in her bones.

"Here, take that road," said Maya, pointing at a dirt road heading off the blacktop, leading deeper into the valley.

"There's no road there, Maya," said Stefan, peering in the direction she pointed.

And her eyebrows rose a few inches. "You can't see it?" she asked, looking from Stefan to Claudia. Both shook their heads.

She glanced back at the dirt track, again feeling that strange tension in the pit of her stomach. "They must have warded it with some kind of magic. Makes sense why this area looks abandoned," she said, looking back at Claudia who nodded, her face pale with tension.

"You okay?" Maya asked softly.

Claudia narrowed her eyes, giving Maya a dark look. "I'm fine. You just do your job," she snapped.

So it's going to be like that.

CHAPTER 18

Maya had to hide a grin when Claudia rounded on Stefan and poked him in the shoulder. "Follow instructions. Use the radar."

"Radar? What radar," asked Maya, her attention focused on the road ahead.

"One of our hunters discovered that radar bypassed most wards. So even if you can't see it with your eyes, the radar still picks it up. We've been using it ever since."

Although Maya was profoundly impressed, she had no time to respond as Stefan took the car off the road and they bumped up and down for a while.

It didn't take long before she got fed up with the jumpy ride and yelled, "Stop." She was out the car before he even came to a halt.

"Where are you going?" yelled Claudia as she too exited the vehicle. Her usually well-coiffed hair stood out in numerous directions giving her a decidedly harpy-like look.

"I'm going on foot. I don't think it's too far away. It's getting darker but I can already sense more demons, and the scent of our creep is much stronger."

Claudia nodded, for once unable to come up with an alternate plan on the fly. "Fine, let's go." She turned to Stefan. "You stay with the car. No heroics. We need to be able to get out of here fast once we rescue the girl."

The boy nodded, though he didn't look too happy to be missing the fireworks. Maya understood, but as she watched him stare at them, her stomach did a sickening turn.

Then she and Claude were hurrying through a field and down into a small valley. A tiny building sat at the bottom of the hill and Maya's heart tightened. They'd found the demon's lair.

She slowed and drew Claudia behind an old tree stump. "This is the place, but maybe I should go in alone." She glanced at Claudia. "Either he was stupid to lead us here, or this is a trap."

"No way." Maya opened her mouth to state her case when Claudia raised a firm hand. "Don't waste your breath. I'm coming."

Maya stepped away and took a deep breath. Then she jumped almost a foot off the ground when a wet nose nuzzled her palm.

"Sheesh. Sabala. You really shouldn't be sneaking up on a girl like that." She turned to face the hell-hound. "You're here, so I'm assuming they are all inside the hut?"

Sabala's expression seemed to indicate a 'yes' and Maya shifted to face the house again. A thin stretch of smoke curled from a hole in the metal roof and Maya could picture the inside of the building, knowing exactly what it looked like.

The power of prophetic visions.

"So what's the plan?" she asked Claudia, understanding that whatever her own, god-given talent, it was still Claudia's show.

"We watch for a while."

Maya couldn't help but roll her eyes, glad the growing darkness hid her expression. "While they drain her blood until she's almost dead?"

"No, Maya. Just to see what's going on." Claudia turned to face her, her expression determined. "How confident are you that you can fight them?"

Maya nodded. "I can do it, no problem." In fact, Maya had never been this ready for a fight. Something about a demon trying to kill both her and Claudia that got her hankering for his fiery death.

"How many did you say there were?" Claudia asked, keeping her voice low.

"Ten in all. Not counting the girl. Queen b-word, our demon attacker, and eight minions."

"Really, Maya? You want to fight all ten of them?"

Maya gave a curt nod. "You get the girl out, leave the demons to me and Sabala."

Claudia fell silent for a moment. "I'll get the girl out, but I will come back to help you." At least Claudia had the sense to see Maya's point.

Maya nodded. "Fine. We wait until it gets darker. Should help you ward the place without being made." She nodded at Claudia's bag. "You have stuff to create the ward?"

Claudia nodded. "Whatever we know how to use. I'll get to work on it as long as you cover me."

They both slid down out of sight, watching the building through a stand of shoulder-high grass beside the rotten stump, while Sabala chose a small outcropping to keep a closer eye on the place.

Nothing stirred down in the valley, but Maya could smell them.

While they waited, Claudia pulled out her cellphone and found, to no one's surprise, that they had no reception. When she pulled a sat phone out of the backpack Maya shook her head. KALIMA had every possible situation covered.

She kept an eye on the house while Claudia called their position in and requested backup STAT.

It didn't take long for all light to disappear entirely and soon night took over with a vengeance. Away from the glare of the city lights, the sky positively overflowed with stars, an endless canvas sprinkled with an overly generous dose of twinkling diamonds.

But she had no time to appreciate it, what with keeping a solid eye and nose on the lone house.

Maya had to admit the reprieve had been good. She was now rested, and calmer. Finding it easier to call her fire.

As darkness threw its black cloak around them, Claudia sank to the grass and placed a small clay-lamp on the dusty ground. She dropped a shard of frankincense into the bowl and lit it with a small lighter; all part of her on-the-go magic bag.

A regular Mary Poppins demon-hunter she was.

As the smoke rose, she bent over it, allowing the tendrils to drift into her hair and soak into her clothing. Before long, she smelled like a living piece of frankincense.

The stuff was almost magical when it came to demonic life-forms. The fragrant resin had the ability to chase away any species of demon, and also enabled the user to render themselves invisible to a demon if they wished. Maya was glad she'd paid attention to Claudia's intermittent ramblings aimed at giving her a more rounded education in hunting. As if Maya's schnoz-on-steroids wasn't enough.

All done, Claudia crept toward the house, with Maya keeping a few meters away. Sabala picked his way closer to the building and came to a standstill in front of the door. Maya watched her aunt go from one corner of the shack to the next, pausing for a few moments to bury something in the ground before moving on. She made quick work of circling the house and soon came to hide with Maya behind an old rusted tractor a few meters from the house.

Shadows moved eerily against the windows which were covered with gray sackcloth. Maya glanced at Claudia and they nodded in unison.

"We should move while you still have the frankincense working," said Maya.

Claudia didn't wait for a second invitation.

CHAPTER 19

Claudia was off at breakneck speed, a foot behind Maya as she passed Sabala and rushed at the door. Putting the full force of her body behind her shoulder, Maya slammed into it, thinking as she hit the flimsy wood that perhaps she should have studied the material of the door first before racing at it with such brute force. Too late, she struggled to control her momentum as the door cracked in two, like a gigantic stale biscuit, and the broken half fell awkwardly to the ground.

Maya, unable to stop herself, ended up somewhere in the middle of the single-roomed hovel, and unfortunately right in front of the gathered demons.

The stunned occupants, mistress and followers alike, turned to Maya in shock. All except two. The girl lay pale and unmoving on a stained pile of blankets in the corner on the left side of the shack, but thankfully Maya could sense her blood, fresh and flowing within her veins. She was still alive.

Maya celebrated her survival with a split-second glance at Claudia, who'd kept running even as Maya had come to a slightly unbalanced halt. Claudia was already at work untying the girl so Maya turned her attention to her audience.

Nobody moved.

On Maya's right, the second figure who'd taken Maya's sudden intrusion without even a twitch of the eyebrow, stood very still, face hidden by the folds of a black cowl. The Rakshasi stared at Maya, and though she couldn't see the demon's eyes, Maya could feel the hair rise on the back of her neck.

And then, as if her minions possessed a hive mind, the group moved toward Maya, eyes glowing amber, fingers lengthening and growing deadly sharp claws that shone even in the meager light within the hut.

Just my luck. I'm stuck in one of those really bad zombie movies, with the fake blood, the terrible hair and even worse special effects.

Still invisible, Sabala ran at one of the demon girls, the one from Maya's vision who'd seemed so familiar. The hell-hound's teeth clamped on her skinny arm. His eyes had begun to glow amber, the only part of him now visible, a sight that put the demon-girl into a full panic. As she struggled, trying to pull her arm free from her invisible attacker, Maya caught a glimpse of bright color around her arm. A gaily-patterned headscarf tugged at Maya's memory and she stiffened.

Anna Polaski.

The Rakshasi was turning these girls into demons. Stunned, Maya watched as the hell hound gripped hard onto the demon's arm, the girl's skin beginning to burn away. Hell-hounds were often tasked with finding demons who'd gone AWOL, and their ability to terminate a Rakshasa at will usually subdued the creatures long enough for the dog to take them back to Patala.

But this demon seemed like she planned on dying before he would have her. And Maya refused to add to the girl's torment. Something deep within Maya told her that there was no hope for these girls. That whatever had been done to them was a one-way street.

She called her fire and threw three super-charged fireballs in quick succession. Anna and two more demon-girls fell burning to the ground, clutching at their bodies, fingers entering gaping holes in ribs and legs and faces.

The hell-hound stood over Anna's remnants, giving Maya an accusing look that implied she'd spoiled his fun.

She wasn't for you, pooch.

A glance to her right and Maya was relieved to see Claudia throwing a ragged blanket over Deb's head and half-carrying half-dragging her out of the shack.

The Rakshasi wasn't paying her once-human victim any attention. Her eyes seemed to be soley for Maya, penetrating all the way to Maya's bones. With three of her mini-army incinerated, mere pieces of soot floating to the ground, it left Maya to face six more including the male. He stood at the Rakshasi's shoulder, watching with a smirk on his gaunt face, as if he was dead certain that Maya would lose this little battle against his mistress.

Mind games.

Something moved at the corner of Maya's eye. Sabala flitted past, an ebony shadow, and launched himself at the demon-girl closest to the door. The hell-hound grabbed the creature by her ankle and held on, tugging left and right. The demon shrieked, staring around, unable to see what was attacking her as Sabala had dispensed with the glory eyes.

While the room's attention remained focused on the hysterical demon, Maya sent a streak of fire at the Rakshasa closest to her. It was strange that they didn't seem to be fighting her. Had she come in and surprised them so much that they couldn't defend themselves?

Or was Kali's fire so destructive to them it made them unable to defend themselves. The first time she'd killed a demon he'd had no chance to save himself. And just like him, these Rakshasas were falling beneath the power of Maya's fire.

Ball after ball of flame she sent into their midst and within seconds they disappeared in explosions of sparks and black soot.

But when pain ripped into her side, she knew she'd underestimated at least one of them. She turned to face the single demon remaining, shocked as she placed her hand over her wound, her fingers sinking into warm, sodden fabric of her tee.

A deep sadness welled within Maya.

She could do nothing for this girl now. She was too far gone, whoever she was. And she was a danger to Maya, and Claudia.

Maya drew her fire, coaxing it from her core and up through to her chest. The pressure built in her lungs and Maya had no choice but to set it free. Fire burst from her mouth, a wide stream of superheated flame that, in seconds, encased the demon who'd attacked her, incinerating her almost instantaneously. Ash and flakes of soot were all that was left of her as Maya turned back to face the Rakshasi, tamping down her sadness.

Her fire followed swiftly, a sphere of flame more potent than the heat of the sun, raised by fury, powered by pain.

In the end, all that remained were the demon male and his Mistress.

Maya tried to ignore the burn of her injury and turned her head just as the Rakshasi glanced up at her henchman. Maybe she meant to give him the instruction to attack, but when Maya caught sight of her face, her gasp of shock stilled his movements.

"Priya?" Maya asked, stunned at the identity of this rogue demoness whose killing spree had left Eastern Europe paralyzed by fear of a serial-killer in their midst.

The Rakshasi reached up with a pale, blue-veined hand, and pushed back the hood that had hidden her face. She raised her chin and gave Maya a defiant glare.

Priya, the Rakshasi who had been Nik's right hand, part of his personal guard in Patala. Priya, who was supposed to be dead.

"So the rumors are true," was all she said, her dark glare turning amber for a few seconds before fading back to black.

Maya didn't bother to ask her what rumors she referred to.

She could guess. But there was one question she did want to ask her.

"I thought you were dead?" Maya bit the words out angrily, recalling Priya's betrayal and how she'd endangered Ria's life not too long ago. More especially, how she hadn't cared in the least that she'd almost killed Maya's best friend.

Priya sighed and tugged at the gleaming clasp at her neck. "Things are not always as they seem."

Maya's gaze narrowed on the demon's face. "But I saw you die. Are you sure you aren't some sort of undead demon or something?" asked Maya, still finding it difficult to believe that the Rakshasi had survived after Kas had made a proper show of roasting her alive because she had a problem with loyalty.

But the look on Priya's face stopped Maya in her tracks. Her skin paled and her fingers tightened on the cloak so hard that her knuckles went white. Had Maya hit on some sort of truth without even expecting to?

Demon undead? Could it be?

CHAPTER 20

*M*aya laughed harshly. "I can't believe it. I'm right, aren't I?" Maya took a step closer, watching both Priya and her side-kick closely. "You did something, didn't you? I'd bet you sold your soul." Maya frowned. "Do demons even have souls?"

Priya snorted. Ever since she'd first met the demon in Patala, Maya had admired her striking beauty. And Maya had never trusted her. Not that looks had anything to do with trust. It had just been a gut thing.

Now, the demon laughed, her hazel eyes glinting in the light of the weak fire. "Of course, we have souls." There was an odd tension in the way she said the word 'souls'.

And Maya sprang on it. "But you don't have one anymore, do you?" asked Maya, her gut telling her she was onto the truth. "You actually sold your soul? I can't believe you did that." Maya shook her head, somewhat disappointed in the Rakshasi.

Selling her soul, and not being dead, two things for which Maya was unable to forgive Priya.

The Rakshasi scoffed, waving a hand at her demon-goon.

With a slight inclination of his head, he moved a step back, but his dark orange eyes never left Maya's.

"For a puny little human you have a very big mouth." Priya's tone was hard, and filled with anger, and more. A simmering hatred burned in her tone, her eyes, her stance, as if given the chance she'd spring on Maya and rip her to shreds.

Maya had to frown. Was she still angry that Nik had chosen Maya over her?

"Is this about Nik?"

Priya laughed, the sound echoing against the iron roof, but a vein throbbed in her throat. And as Maya watched it beat she registered the condition of Priya's desiccated skin, the gaunt hollows of her sunken cheeks.

"You human females. Not everything is about a boy, you know. Did you really think I was pining for him, making all these plans in order to gain some sort of sway over him?"

Maya raised her eyebrows, her expression telling Priya that's exactly what she'd thought.

"Well, I'm sorry to disappoint. Nikhil's heart is beyond my reach. But, let me tell you something, little human. His heart is also beyond *your* reach."

Something about the demon's words penetrated Maya's emotions, deeper than she'd expected, but she didn't let it show in her eyes.

Instead she laughed. "Whatever floats your boat, Priya."

But the demon just continued to smile at her, her grin looking somewhat maniacal on her.

Definitely psycho.

"Let me ask you a question." The demon glided over to the fire. She stood so still, beside the open hearth that Maya could see the flames reflect in her eyes. "Do you know where Nikhil is right now?" she turned her gaze on Maya, her smile triumphant , and touched with evil.

Then, just when Maya was beginning to wonder why she was

being so persistent, she did an about face, waving a hand and saying, "Never mind. I think we both know you have no idea where he is. But, you see, *I* do. And you will never see him again."

Priya had hit a raw nerve, and her words hit Maya harder than any weapon could. And though she wondered why she gave credence to Priya's words, the pain still ripped through her like a hot lance.

Maya's hands tightened into fists and Priya's spine stiffened as if she sensed the wave of fury she'd brought on. She gave a short nod, a go-ahead to her thug, no doubt.

He flew straight at Maya, hands outstretched, blades growing from his fingers.

She had her fire ready, and would have sent the demon right back to the hell he'd crawled out from, but a gunshot rang out and he was flung back against the far wall.

Stefan ran around Maya, shoving her back, his elbow connecting hard with her ribs.

He held a shotgun up and aimed it first at Priya and then at the demon who was sliding slowly to the ground, looking a little cross-eyed, his hands revealing a slight tremor. The creature grunted while his mistress just smiled and watched in silence.

Stefan's eyes widened as he watched the demon crouch, then straighten. He coughed once, twice. Bullets hit the floor, falling from somewhere within his body and the boy took a hesitant step back.

Big mistake.

The demon flew at Stefan. Instinctively, Maya sent a fireball straight at his head, drawing the energy without a moment's hesitation. But the fiery sphere merely hit the demon's perforated chest and exploded into a million tiny flames.

Dig deeper, Maya.

This demon was far more powerful than the female followers Priya had gathered to her.

Now, Maya sent a barrage of fire at him, each one hotter and more powerful than the next.

He pressed against the onslaught of flames, struggling to reach Maya with his razor-tipped fingers, but at last he sagged, seeming to want to flee, but unable to under the gaze of his mistress.

He gave her one last impassioned glance before he exploded into a starburst of brilliant red sparks.

An odd gurgling sound drew Maya's attention to Stefan, who'd been standing beside her, attempting to guard her. Priya now stood in front of the boy who'd fallen onto his knees in front of her.

She stood preternaturally still, a single finger extended, her face serene, as if watching a beautiful sunset. Instead, she watched Stefan choke on his own blood, one knife-sharp fingernail penetrating the centre of his throat.

His gaze shifted away from the Rakshasi's face to Maya, his expression apologetic. He coughed, and blood dribbled down his chin as he tried to speak.

"See, Maya. You cannot save him. This is really all your fault, you know." Priya's eyes turned amber. "Because of you, I ended up in purgatory. And only because of you, was I able to get out. I swore to find you and make you pay any way I knew how. All those girls? They were part of my mission to purge the world of stupid little females like you. In the end they proved far more useful as followers to do my bidding, but you are the one they can thank for dying." Priya laughed at Maya's confused expression. "Have you not looked in the mirror lately, Maya Rao?"

Maya found it difficult to concentrate on Priya's words. She was revealing the reason for the murders but the sight of the dying boy, and of Priya's uncaring expression, did something to Maya.

She'd had had to kill those poor girls-turned-demons because of Priya. That was bad enough, but this was worse. Her rage plumbed deep down, to a place beyond even Maya's conscious knowledge, and pure fury erupted like a volcanic explosion.

Fire burst from her mouth, a wide stream of superheated flame that engulfed the surprised Priya who did nothing more than stare at Maya in shock.

Flames encircled the Rakshasi, incinerating her almost instantaneously. Maya barely paid attention as Priya disappeared in an explosion of fire.

She sank to her knees beside Stefan, ignoring the ash and flakes of soot that drifted slowly to the bare floor.

Maya shoved her hand over the wound in Stefan's neck, but she was too late.

He lay there, eyes open, staring at the bare rafters of the hut.

A noise at the door drew her attention and she shifted to see Claudia standing there framed by the night outside, a look of horror crumpling her usually unaffected face.

They'd succeeded in their mission.

Kill the demon.

Save the girl.

Losing the boy was not part of the plan.

CHAPTER 21

The next day, back home in the relative safety of her bedroom, Maya reflected on the mission, and its ultimate failure.

Sure Priya was dead. They'd succeeded in ending her reign of terror. They'd even managed to understood Priya's intention, the reason she'd killed all those girls.

Maya.

Looking in the mirror had done the trick. How they'd missed that throughout the mission was beyond Maya, but what reason had they had to connect the girls to her? As far as they'd known, the girls were of similar coloring to each other. Nothing more.

Maya's heart was heavy, the memory of Stefan's face still so fresh in her mind. She'd gone through the rest of that awful night, and the entire trip home, in a blur, walking around in a bubble that protected her from sensation.

Claudia had tried repeatedly to get her to talk, had spoken to her for long periods, alternating between extolling Stefan's virtues, and stressing the dangers that constantly existed in their line of work. Reminding Maya that all those murders hadn't been her fault. That it was all on Priya alone.

Although the words had made sense, there was a serious disconnect when Maya tried to weigh them against the loss of the boy, against the loss of the lives of all those girls.

They'd arrived home not two hours ago and Maya had decided it was time to call Kali. The visions, and her ability to see what was happening through Priya's eyes, they were two things that Maya shouldn't have been able to do. That particular talent had nothing to do with blood or fire.

Kali had some explaining to do.

Maya sat up on her mattress, and reached over to open her rucksack. Within a side pocket, beside Chayya's brass pot sat the Kapala. A shudder ran through Maya as she placed it in her palm and removed camphor and frankincense.

She scrabbled inside her night-stand drawer for a safety pin. Ready, she pricked her finger, then waited for the bead of blood to swell. She wiped it off inside the bottom of the skull-bowl, then lit the camphor and the sambrani in close succession.

All done, she placed the smoking skull on her nightstand, and waited.

The room filled with the pungent sweet woody scent of the resin, and Maya unconsciously took a deep breath. She'd always loved the smell of frankincense, and having an excuse to light some now was a rare pleasure.

Only problem was the smell now took her back to that awful hut outside of Budapest. Maya pulled free from the dark memories and watched as the smoke rose, curling around and around as it reached the ceiling and disappeared into nothing.

Strange, there were no complicated prayers to perform, no Sanskrit chants, no convoluted rituals, no transcendental trances that would call the gods to Maya.

She simply had to ask.

Now, as she waited for Kali to arrive, she wondered what it would be like to recall her previous lifetime as the revered Mother Radha.

Her parents had often expressed a deep love and reverence for the Mother, and it was always hard for Maya to reconcile the fact that they were essentially talking about *her*.

But it was a bit of a leap of faith for Maya to accept she was one and the same as Radha. Maybe the day would come when she would believe she deserved that comparison, but right now she couldn't see the past even if her life depended on it.

With another soft sigh she got to her feet and pulled on a pair of worn sweats that bore the marks of numerous training sessions; a sprinkling of holes, edges hardened where the polyester had melted, a smattering of rips made by daggers and swords.

Slipping on socks and sneakers, she grabbed a hair band as she headed out the door. She dragged her thick locks into the confines of the elastic band as she entered the garage, the only place she was allowed to use for training. She was well overdue for a training session and her bout with Priya and her demon horde didn't count. Not as far as she was concerned. If she really had to think about it, she'd say it had been too damn easy.

Sure, she'd gotten injured in the process, but the wound had already knitted together. Maya slipped a hand beneath her shirt and ran her fingertips over the ridged scar. As soon as they'd returned to the hotel, Maya had sent small bursts of heat to the wound, hoping to ensure it didn't get infected. But, when Claudia had insisted on taking a closer look, they'd both been shocked to discover that the gash in her side was no longer a raw, bleeding mess.

The edges had come together, the wound had sealed itself, and a thin scab had already begun to form. Maya sighed and left the wound alone, more so because touching it brought Stefan to mind. Refusing to speak to his parents when they'd come by to the hotel had been cowardly, but, though Claudia had suggested it would be good to have the Hand of Kali console them, the last thing Maya wanted to do was face the parents of the boy she'd let die.

And that wasn't the least of her worries. She still hadn't heard from Nik, and because of Priya's confidence, Maya had a knot in her stomach that leaned toward believing what the demoness had to say. But Maya refused to dwell on it. Just the possibility of having Nik gone forever would mess with her concentration.

Now, she touched the pendant at her neck, a part of her hesitant to call him. He'd told her to, but she didn't want to be a burden. Only, Priya's claims bugged her far too much for her to worry about it.

Right now, all that mattered was that he was okay.

Maya gripped the pendant within her palm and thought of Nik, sending him her thoughts and asking him if he was okay. That was all she knew to do, so she tucked the necklace inside her shirt and hoped she'd done it right.

Gritting her teeth, she took a place in the center of the room. She pulled her iPod out of her pocket, and a few taps later she had her playlist going. Then she stuck her earbuds in her ears before tucking the player deep within her pocket.

The music was soft rock, with a heavy base and a good dose of dramatic in places, the kind of sound Maya enjoyed when she wanted to block the world out. She grinned as she wondered what the goddess Kali would think of her taste in music. This was certainly no Hanuman Chalisa. And as the Hand of Kali, surely she would be expected to uplift her culture first?

With a shrug, Maya softened her knees and settled into a comfortable pose. She turned on her heel, and faced the back wall, drawing deep inside, reaching for her fire energy, pulling it swiftly to the surface. Aiming at the metal-lined wall, Maya blasted it with ball after simmering ball, supremely glad that her dad had covered the walls with a metal that absorbed the heat from the flames. Glad because her fury, and her grief, only fueled the fire, bringing the fireballs to temperatures so hot that a light sweat was beginning to coat Maya's cheeks.

Soon, she danced around the carpet, melding the martial arts moves her dad had spent so many years teaching her, with the flow of her limbs that best drew the fire from her solar plexus. In a low spin, she swung her arms wide before drawing them together in front of her chest. Then she pushed out hard, putting a bit more strength into the move, and the fireball flew hard, slamming into the metal wall with a thunderous grunt.

The metal shuddered, growing hot where two dents had been punched into it by the heated flaming balls.

"As your power grows you will find that human creations, no matter how technologically advanced, will not be able to stand in your way."

Maya spun around, her arms dropping to her sides a little too late as she recognized Kali's voice. She watched in horror as a stray ball of flame flew straight at Kali's head and a squawk of shock and fear echoed around the room.

She registered almost absently that the sound had come from her own terrified throat.

Kali didn't even flinch.

The fireball sailed past her face, close enough to burn a trail across her blue cheek. But even as the fire hit the far wall, Maya could see the goddess's skin remained undamaged.

Maya's jaw hung open as she stared in horror at what she'd done. Her stomach hurt, as if a rock had been thrown into it, heavy and hard and filled with black fear.

But Kali merely smiled serenely and flicked the pads of her fingers against her cheek, swiping at the trail of soot; all that remained of the passing fireball, and the only damage it had caused to the goddess.

The edges of Maya's vision darkened and she knew she was about to faint from the shock of almost harming a god.

Why Kali had appeared behind Maya so suddenly, was not even a question she would voice.

The goddess certainly hadn't taken long to arrive and Maya wondered if it was such a good thing that Kali was so eager to teach her this next power. She had enough to worry about without adding the frustrations of a new ability to her list of daily problems.

Kali reached out with one long finger and placed it beneath Maya's chin, putting only the slightest pressure on it to close Maya's mouth.

Maya blushed, feeling the heat surge from her face to the rest of her body. To hide her embarrassment, she took a slight step backward and greeted the goddess, placing her hands together in Namaste. The goddess reciprocated, smiling softly as she came to stand in front of Maya.

Kali's proximity made Maya's heart jitter but she forced herself to calm down and concentrate. Kali was here to perform a task, not babysit fan-girling females.

"Are you ready, Maya?" the goddess asked, her eyes trained intently on Maya's face, while an amused smile curved her lips. She tilted her head to one side and seemed to see right through to Maya's soul.

Probably not the best time in the world to tell fibs. She nodded slowly, not wanting to appear over confident.

"We can get started then," said Kali.

Her gold bangles jingled as she took a step closer and placed her finger in the middle of Maya's forehead.

And then everything fell into darkness.

CHAPTER 22

Maya blinked, but her sight didn't return in entirety. She sucked in a short breath and searched the darkness for a hint of a shape, for the smallest suggestion of form in the dense shadows that steeped the space around her body. She reached a hand out, fingers scraping the empty air in front of her, tentative and afraid of what she may touch, what horrors she may encounter. Her hands shivered slightly and, as hard as she commanded them to still their shuddering, her muscles refused to listen.

In fact, her fingers, hands and arms all seemed to be straining, performing an action she had not requested. They seemed to be tightened in a posture that was unusual, and strangely filled with latent power.

Somewhere around her the wind shifted the hair on her forehead, and rushed in the trees, leaves shivered and whispered from above, and light began to filter through to her eyes very slowly. She wanted to call out to Kali, to ask her where she'd brought her, but some strange instinct bade her swallow her question and wait.

Patience.

The muscles in her fingers curled, tight, and straining and as her vision cleared she found herself focused, staring straight ahead at the nock of a bow. Maya swallowed her shock as she slowly took stock of her stance, fingers curved around the painfully taut string of a bow, muscles bunched and tight as she pulled hard and held the pose, waiting for something.

Movement in the trees beyond the bow caught Maya's attention and a streak of amber shifted into view and then was gone. Something prowled within the forest, watching her as she watched it.

Maya could feel a sense of confidence rise within her chest, an emotion that put her a little off balance. Why would she feel confidence while aiming an arrow at some creature that moved within the thick forest of trees?

And then the leaves shifted and the animal came into view.

And Maya let the string go, feeling the release of power as the arrow flew into the air and the gigantic bow shuddered within her grasp. Her eyes were still trained on the majestic creature that had emerged from the dense forest.

It happened so slowly, as if she was underwater and every action took ten times longer to perform, every flicker of brain activity taking a dozen times longer to process. The Bengal tiger stared at her, as if unaffected by its impending doom.

As if it was saying 'I will not bow to you'.

She could have sworn a sense of pride emanated from the animal, a sense of intense belonging to nature in its purest, most primal state.

And then the arrow buried itself deep within the tiger's left eye.

CHAPTER 23

The tiger dropped heavily to the jungle floor, the sound barely an echo as Maya began to stride toward the creature. She didn't want to go, but as hard as she tried to force herself to stop moving, as much as she strained to tighten the muscles in her legs, to command her body to stop moving, it was useless.

She trampled the long grass as she walked, and soon stopped beside the massive cat, its length almost ten feet from head to tail, and stood so very still, watching as its chest heaved, as it struggled for breath.

The tiger shifted its head and turned its gaze to stare at Maya. A part of her screamed that this cannot be happening, especially since she knew she'd never willingly harm such a beautiful animal, but another almost alien part of her could feel the emotions surging through her; satisfaction, pride. That part of her was happy in a very controlled, calculated way, with a sort of arrogance that Maya knew she didn't possess.

She stiffened, recognizing that odd twist in her gut. Much the same as during her vision of Priya watching Deb in the shack, hungering for her blood. Was this what was happening? Was she having another vision?

Maya slowed her breathing and paid closer attention to her movements, intending to sink to her knees. She wanted to check if she could do anything to help the tiger. But again nothing happened. Her muscles no longer obeyed her. She remained standing tall and stiff, staring at the big cat, that strange compartmentalized part of her feeling no remorse at all.

She stood unmoving, watching the light fade from the tiger's eyes, only blinking when the cat heaved a final reedy sigh and closed its eyes for the last time.

Only then did Maya find herself turning away from the animal and walking back to the clearing, spine stiff, head held high. Only then did Maya see the people gathered there, waiting for her. People who'd been standing behind her as she'd shot the tiger, watching her commit such an atrocity.

The small group watched anxiously as she made her way through the knee-high grass. A massive creature, pale as chalk, stood behind the group, moving its ponderous trunk this way and that. Maya swallowed her shock at the sight of the white elephant, an animal she knew did not exist. But there it was, standing tall and majestic, draped with fabric woven with gold thread that glinted in the warm sunshine. Atop the elephant's back was a golden howdah.

From what Maya knew, this type of howdah was a seat fashioned for royalty or nobility, nothing like the ones tourists used when visiting Asian countries that offered elephant rides.

A gold-etched domed canopy shaded the howdah's single occupant, who tipped his head at Maya. The action seemed to be one of approval yet the man's dark face hid his expression too well.

Another man walked up to Maya, accompanied by a slim, dark-eyed woman. Both were dressed in black and red, long, knee-length overdresses, with gathered pants tied at the ankles.

The man sported a plain red turban on his dark head, while the woman's eyes were heavily lined with kohl, her long hair held back in a plait the fell almost to her knees.

A voice said, "Is he satisfied?"

Maya started, unsure of who had spoken and then the turbaned man said, "Sire, he is very pleased."

Sire? Who was this man that she'd joined in the weird vision?

The woman stepped forward and offered Maya a beautiful coat, and waited, head bowed. Maya found herself nodding and flicking a finger at the man who took the garment and held it out. She raised her arm, offering the bow to one of the men gathered at her side and simply held it out in their direction. There was a certain superiority in her bearing and she remained puzzled, disliking the emotions.

One servant grabbed the weapon, while the first man shook out the coat, the sun glinting on the golden handwoven garment as Maya slipped her hands into the silk-lined sleeves.

Okay.

A white elephant, a superior father, a bunch of servants, lots of gold and someone calling her Sire.

She currently occupied the body of a man, and an important one, probably nobility if not royalty. She wished she could find a mirror to get a good look at him, then immediately prayed that he wouldn't do anything icky while she remained confined within his body. The last thing she needed was to piggyback him while he visited the toilet or got jiggy with it with a female companion.

Maya shuddered. What had Kali intended throwing her into this position? Was it a memory perhaps? Something from her life as Radha? No, that made absolutely no sense at all.

Now, she forced herself to pay attention as her host walked between the gathered servants and stopped beside the elephant where another servant held onto the reins of a much smaller animal.

A beautiful camel, its hide pale as fresh cream, stood there, watching him with giant liquid black eyes. The camel also bore a seat on its back, and this one was considerably smaller and looked a lot lighter, more of a large saddle, thank goodness. It seemed like such a cruel thing to do, even if you were special or royalty or whatever.

The servant holding the reins clicked his tongue and the dusky camel folded its knees and dropped smoothly to the grass.

Maya's host strode toward it and placed a foot on the small gold-plated step suspended from the seat. He moved with grace, pulling himself up onto the silk-cushioned seat and as he sank into them, the warmth of the fabric heated by the midday sunshine soaked into her skin.

Another servant moved closer, holding onto a long pole which turned out to belong to a large umbrella. The white fabric gleamed, throwing cool shade over the seat, and Maya watched as he placed the staff of the umbrella into a holder at the back of the seat.

The sun burned Maya hands and she had to pull them into the cooler shade, and only then did she realize that all along she'd been sheltered by an umbrella, that someone had stood behind her at all times, holding the long-handled umbrella over her. Talk about a privileged hunt, umbrella held over you while you aim at and kill a beautiful animal.

She knew by now that she was restricted; unable to do anything unless her host performed the action. Maya gritted her teeth, impatient to know the reason for this whole experience. And hoped there really was one, in the first place.

The camel ride wasn't comfortable in the slightest, the height from the ground, the rolling gait of the animal, the shifting of the seat at every step, all making her feel slightly seasick. Her host didn't even take the time to look out at the scenery, that way she could at least have learned more about where in the world she'd landed. All he did was stare at the intricately carved screen in front of him, his shoulders hunched over awkwardly.

God, he was boring.

But, despite his lack of movement, Maya could sense his emotions, of which there were a tumultuous tangle; frustration, a burning anger, and a sense of self-importance that seemed to color his every thought.

He was beginning to seem more of an asshole the longer Maya remained stuck within his body and privy to his feelings.

What she really wanted to do was to swivel around and get a better look at the man sitting on top of the elephant. She was still in shock at the sight of the white elephant and couldn't help wondering if it was an albino, an anomaly or mutation, or if it was an entirely different species.

And the man on the elephant's back stirred Maya's curiosity even more. A darkness seemed to emanate from him, a sense of deep simmering blackness that had nothing to do with his coal-dark skin, a darkness that made Maya want to shiver right down to her bones.

Was he the father of her host?

It certainly seemed he had some kind of hold on the man whose body Maya was possessing. He'd wanted his approval, that much was clear. But Maya had also sensed a dissatisfaction and a touch of resentment in his need for that approval.

But why? It would make sense if he was the father since respect for one's elders had long been a strong Indian trait. And, that brought Maya back to the most important question: where in God's name was she?

Indian yes, modern no.

She was stuck somewhere in the past, probably in the Indian sub-continent. It didn't take a genius to figure *that* out.

Now, if only this damned host would look up she'd be able to get a better sense of her environment. Something deep within the pit of her stomach told her that when she finally did find out where she was, that she wasn't going to like it one bit.

Stupid instinct was probably right.

The ride seemed interminable, the heat penetrating Maya's lungs like an insidious python, lazy and suffocating. Her host's head popped up at last and he lifted a hand, the movement a weak wave, but it must have meant something to someone because within seconds a large tray seemed to rise beside the rolling camel, laden with food and a fat golden goblet covered with glittering gems.

Maya made a face as her host reached for the drink. Why the heck would anyone want to drink from something covered in jewels? It seemed weird and a little bit wrong.

Her host didn't mind very much. He drank deeply and Maya began to feel a sense of satiation.

And then she blinked.

Every emotion and every physical reaction she experienced was courtesy of this anonymous individual within whose body she remained trapped.

Maya gritted her teeth and then forced herself to relax. She had to wait this out. Kali would have had a good reason to leave her here without telling her a single thing.

The camel moved far too slowly, and only when Maya's head threatened to explode from heat and boredom, did her host lift his head to gaze out at the countryside.

The sky was strikingly blue and bright with the midday sunshine. They traveled along a dusty road, but its neat edges and flat surface implied it was well taken care of. The road cut a path through a thick jungle where trees and bush leaned towards them, almost reaching out to grab hold of them.

Every now and then, bright patches of sky peered down at them from within the high canopy, and the calls of dozens of animals filled the air. Had this been some kind of safari or holiday adventure Maya might have appreciated it more, but as it stood she remained in limbo.

Soon, they left the thick jungle and the procession moved slowly toward a brilliant green valley, where a glassy lake took possession of the land. At the side of the expanse of water sat a magnificent white palace, surrounded by a silvery moat fed by the lake.

It rose like something out of a fantasy story, domed spires, carved filigree screens, columned towers and high walls guarded by a regiment of archers and armed guards, weapons drawn.

Not so serene after all, then.

Peacocks called all around Maya, and she found her attention settling on the gardens within the palace wall where the proud feathered males strutted, fanning out their shimmering blue-green tails, preening to an enamored audience of dull brown hens.

The birds made up for the sobriety of the guards, but Maya paid only brief attention as she winced against the bright sunlight.

Up ahead, a wide stone bridge spanned a river of rushing water. The camel's feet hit the stone surface of the bridge with a series of dull thuds, followed closely by the elephant which lumbered along behind them in no apparent hurry. The impact of its gigantic feet sent ripples of thunder through the stone.

The procession slowed and Maya, or rather her host, looked down at the gathered servants lined up on either side of the door, in expectation of it opening. Then, Maya's host lifted his gaze in the direction of the giant golden gate that blocked the entrance to the palace grounds, and she sucked in a shocked breath. The door, rising thirty feet into the air and covered in a layer of gleaming gold, was a weapon in itself.

Gigantic metal spikes stuck out of the door from twenty feet high all the way to the bottom. The deadly tips glistened, each sharpened to such a fine point they were very nearly invisible.

The gates opened slowly, a deep grinding emanating from somewhere within the twenty-foot-thick walls. The doors shuddered as they opened and the grandeur of the gates made Maya feel small and insignificant. But the camel started its loping walk again and Maya immediately forgot about everything except how much she now wanted to throw up.

What would happen if she threw up? Would her body back in her dad's garage hurl her last meal all over the floor? Or would her host find himself upchucking his snack for no good reason?

Maya focused, although she did give in to a little smile. Option two would be by far the more amusing one.

Inside the gate, they headed sedately up a stone path that cut through brilliant green lawns edged with beds of beautiful and exotic flowers. The details were hard to pin down because her host had the annoying habit of not studying his surroundings long enough for Maya to see anything properly.

But she was at his mercy, and he'd probably seen the view a million times. No reason for him to gape around like a tourist if he lived here. But, Maya wanted to see the beauty of the gardens which reminded her the Taj Mahal, with its expansive pools and beautifully manicured lawns.

Even if her host owned all of this, she wouldn't be impressed because she already sensed he'd not be the kind of person she'd like or want to get to know.

Talk about being judgmental.

She gritted her teeth as the procession headed up the hillside, curving to stop abruptly before another set of golden doors. The entrance to the palace was guarded by a pair of red-coated red-turbaned men, whose mustaches were generous black caterpillars weighing down their top lips.

Their deadly-serious expressions made Maya want to giggle,

and to her surprise, a similar amusement surged within her host. So he had a sense of humor.

Score one: host.

The camel halted in front of a set of wide marble steps that led up to a columned verandah. She couldn't see how far the verandah went. A servant came running, holding a set of stairs aloft. But her host waved him off and jumped off the camel, landing expertly on the ground, much to the displeasure of the servant.

Maya's host strode inside the palace, traversing a front room that was larger than the entire bottom floor of her house. Divided by a path up the centre of the marble-floored room, numerous seating areas were scattered around the space, tapestry-covered seats and cushions repeating the golden theme, sitting side-by-side with elegant white fabric and the darker more luxurious black.

The furniture was either heavy carved dark teak or spindly-legged gold-painted things that looked too fragile to use. At the back of the room, two staircases rose on the left and the right, curving to enter the upper level at opposite ends of the room.

This place was beginning to make even Lord Shiva's palace look like a barn.

Maya's host sprinted up the stairs and headed right, only coming to a stop in front of the dark man who'd watched so coldly from the top of the elephant. Now she could see his face more clearly, glassy black eyes, hooded by thick brows, a blunt nose, wide nostrils that seemed to flare constantly with latent anger. His high cheekbones and thick mustache gave him a dangerous air.

Clearly not the friendliest of people.

The elephant had deposited the man directly onto the second floor of the palace. Behind him, at a set of stairs that led to the creature, a group of servants busied themselves removing the howdah, and another man fed the poor animal some unidentifiable branch of leaves.

Her host lifted his chin, a hint to his well-hidden defiance. As he reached his side, the man turned toward Maya. When he began to speak, she blinked, surprised.

She couldn't understand a word he said and yet she understood everything. The sound of the words made little sense to Maya, but she found herself knowing the meaning. As if she had some kind of magic translation device in her head. She'd been able to pick up on her host's emotions, so maybe her link to him allowed her to also understand his thoughts.

"You did well. But emotions will get you nowhere. What must I do to teach you the benefit of hardening your heart?"

Her host cleared his throat. "Sorry. I'll do better next time." Despite his apology, Maya sensed that he still rebelled against the older man's instruction. She wondered again if they were father and son, a relationship that totally lacked affection.

A name popped into her head, one related to this odious man. Bana.

It was a thought she'd picked up from her host's mind. Seemed she was getting better at understanding him.

Bana laughed and the sound echoed coldly around the room. Behind him the elephant stepped away from the balcony as a guard locked a carved screen in place.

"For too long you have allowed people to prey on your emotions, and the time for that to end is now."

His voice cut deep into Maya and she knew if he'd been speaking to her, she would have probably wanted to cry. The ice in his tone, the cruelty in his gaze; the man seemed to be evil. And she didn't miss how his words made her host feel.

"You came to me remember?" Bana's voice was so close to Maya's ear that she jumped. But, unsurprisingly, she found her body didn't obey. She just stood there in her host's body, seeing something other than what the man had hissed into her ear.

A vision of Bana, smiling and chatty, playing master at a table filled with men whose faces blurred, irrelevant to her host. Bana's voice echoed in her head, saying "You are more than what these people think. If you want to be more, call me. I want to help you. If you will let me."

Her host's discomfort was clear and she sensed he didn't entirely agree with Bana on how things had gone down. But he didn't contradict the dark man.

He just said, "I remember. I also remember you said you'd help me be more. How does killing a tiger help me become more?"

The man smiled, his expression sly as he walked over to a table set with a bronze pitcher and half a dozen goblets, all carved with dancing maidens, fruit and waterfalls. "Did you get a good look at the tiger?"

Maya's host seemed perplexed. "Yes. I killed him and you insisted I watch him take his last breath." Maya could sense he was repeating the words more for himself, as if he couldn't believe he'd agreed.

"And what did you see?"

"A tiger dying, that's what I saw," snapped her host, now impatient and growing angry.

"And that is all you saw? Just a tiger dying?" When her host didn't answer, Bana chuckled and asked, "So there was nothing familiar about the creature at all?"

"Familiar? Why would the tiger be-"

And then he was running.

CHAPTER 25

He was flying down the stairs and through to the back of the palace, along corridors that blurred into themselves until he reached a garden at the back of the palace that was twice the size of the one out front.

The expanse of green lawn stopped only when it reached a thick stand of trees; her host's destination. He dove within the trees, slapping palm fronds aside as he searched for something.

He didn't stop until he found what he was looking for.

For a moment Maya was frustrated as her host lifted his face and stared up at the snippet of sky high above them. But when he blinked away hot tears, she sensed something terrible was about to happen.

Her host looked down and Maya's gaze fell upon the tiger. It lay dead on the grass that carpeted the little jungle.

And now Maya knew why the creature had stared at him, why it hadn't fled the sight of a man with an arrow.

Noises behind them urged the man to turn and glare angrily at Bana, whose face was a few shades darker from his exertions. He'd walked all the way there. Imagine that.

He stood watching, ice in his eyes, a strip of gold glinting in his hand. Her host's attention focused on Bana's hand and Maya recognized the strap. A golden animal collar.

"Why?" The shout was filled with grief and Maya knew then that the animal had meant more to the man than just being a part of his garden. He cared for the tiger. And the loss struck deeply.

Bana flung the collar and Maya followed it as it flew in the air and landed beside the tiger's lifeless paw.

"Why? Because you need to know what treachery feels like. You killed a pet, but it's just like killing someone that you care about. Like friends or family. It's exactly what those closest to you have done to you all these years. They've lulled you into believing they cared for you, that they had your best interest at heart, but in truth all they wanted was to control you. In the end, they always betrayed you." Bana snorted, then began to pace the grass, his leather shoes passing so close to the corpse of the tiger that Maya almost flinched.

"Malik did nothing to me. He was only ever my friend." Maya's host spoke, his tone harsh as he turned his gaze from Bana to his pet. Visions filled Maya's mind.

A little boy running wildly through waist high grass, a tiger cub close on his heels, bouncing around behind him like a live-wire.

Laughter rippled beneath Maya's skin and she sensed a happiness in those memories that her host seemed to yearn for.

Bana laughed harshly, the sound pulling Maya straight from her host's memories as he turned to face the older man. Maya could feel his fingers curl as rebellion filled his heart, fury and grief melding to push him to a dangerous edge.

"He was merely an animal. He would have given you up in the end. There is always someone else more important." Bana paused as he drew closer and came to stand right in front of Maya's host, where he was unable to avoid the penetrating ice of the man's gaze. "Always someone else more important, isn't there?"

The tight fist he'd made tightened even more as something

seemed to break inside of the man whose mind Maya possessed. "You are right," he said exhaling hard.

He gave the dead tiger one last glance and swallowed down the bubble of grief that seemed to rise from within.

He'd convinced himself that Bana had been right, and yet his heart still rebelled against his mind. Good for him.

When he spun on his heel and strode past Bana and out of the little forest of green, Maya wanted to wail in anger. She couldn't believe that he'd fallen for the dark man's manipulations. Maya wanted to jump out of her confinement and blast the old creep to smithereens. He deserved to be a pile of ash after what he'd done to her host. She'd known people like him existed but hadn't been face to face with such a man before.

"He is right," her host whispered angrily. *There is always someone more important, always a better best friend, always a closer loved one. Mother has Father, friends have better friends. I am always a third wheel, the outsider, the newcomer. I have had enough of it. I am more powerful than all of them, and I will show them what it means to cross me.*

Maya stiffened, her mind filled with a wave of his emotions. But she was more angry than sympathetic.

What the hell are you thinking? she yelled. He wouldn't hear her, but she was too frustrated to care.

Maya had barely gotten the words out when her host flinched, giving her such a fright she gasped loudly. He misstepped and stopped in his tracks, tilting his head as if he strained to listen to something on the wind.

She could feel his tension again. Had he heard her? But that wasn't possible. She was just an observer here. Someone stuck here to watch the devolution of this man's mind. The success of Bana's manipulation.

The brilliant lawns and dazzling peacocks barely penetrated Maya's limited scope of vision as her host strode briskly back to the palace, his jaw clenched almost as hard as his fingers. She paid little attention, seething in the morass of her own anger as the hot sun beating down on her head faded away.

Only when a voice called out did Maya bring herself out of her fury long enough to pay attention. She found they'd left the garden and were now inside the cool lower hall. Her host stopped and turned to address the summoner.

As he did so, Maya caught sight of his reflection in gigantic gold-framed mirror that leaned against the wall beside them. He was taller than Maya, much younger than she'd expected, his features and his bearing regal.

This man was a king, that much was true.

Her heart stuttered as she recognized him.

Kas.

CHAPTER 26

It might have been the utter shock of seeing Kas's familiar face in the gilded mirror that sent Maya flying back into her own body in her father's garage. If not, Kali may have had something to do with her sudden return.

Either way, Maya had had no control of her ejection, or of her travels home at all. Thank goodness her journey back to her own body hadn't ended with her stuck in a stone wall somewhere half way across the world. Perhaps she ought to be thanking the enigmatic goddess for her accuracy.

Back within the home of familiar muscle and bone, Maya blinked a few times and swallowed hard against the urge to throw up. The jump from Kas's body back into her own had been too fast for her to handle. She found, from the sudden turbulence in her gut, it was taking a negative toll on her poor stomach.

Bending over at the waist she wrapped a hand around her torso and took a few deep breaths. *Please don't throw up*, she begged herself. She wasn't in the mood to clean up any messes. Not after this trip. She very much preferred jet-lag to the feeling of being twisted in ten different directions, coupled with the sense that she wasn't all together yet, as if she'd left a part of herself back in Kas's body. Wherever he was right now.

As her breathing slowed and the tumult in her stomach settled, Maya's mind reeled, still caught up in processing everything she'd just experienced. Surreal didn't even begin to describe it.

How is it possible that she could have been inside of Kas? Was it something that Kali had done to her?

Maya blinked again and straightened her body. She was in exactly the same spot as she'd been before she'd found herself in Kas's body. And so was Kali.

She found the goddess sitting on the floor, eyes closed in a perfect meditation pose. Her wrists lay relaxed on her knees and she seemed to exude peace. Something Maya craved now more than she'd ever done.

Her mind simmered with everything. Bana, Kas, the tiger.

Oh, that poor tiger.

Kali opened her eyes slowly, as if emerging from a dream, and gave Maya a soft and encouraging smile. The corners of Maya's mouth twitched in response, but the smile she gave in return was lacking numerous levels of happiness. She couldn't help being annoyed for having been left out of the loop. The least the goddess could have done was tell Maya what was going to happen. And why.

A little bit of advance warning would've helped Maya deal with the transition into the demon king's body. Not to mention that it would have helped her sanity too. Being stuck inside Kas's body was about as far from fun as Maya could have imagined.

Maya stepped closer to the goddess and dropped to the floor in front of her, but instead of mimicking Kali's pose she remained on her knees, her posture stiff. Now was not the time to get comfortable.

She cleared her throat and then asked, "Why did you send me

there?" She succeeded in keeping her annoyance out of her voice. No sense in offending the goddess.

"So you can see."

Cryptic.

Maya wasn't about to let go of her line of questioning. If Kali wanted to play evasion then Maya would show her determination. "Was it because of Kas? Er . . . Narakasura?" asked Maya, her forehead creasing with a frown.

Kali tilted her dark head to one side, her hair falling over her shoulder in rich waves, to pool in her lap, a glossy black waterfall. She studied Maya, her dark eyes watchful.

"Narakasura has played a significant role in the tasks you were asked to perform over the last few weeks. Is this why you feel familiar enough with him to call him Kas?"

Maya shrugged, a little unsettled by the goddess's scrutiny. "He told me to call him Kas. Apparently, that's the name he's been using in this . . . life."

Kas had managed to find a way to come back, reincarnated into this life despite history claiming he'd been killed forever by his own mother.

Kali nodded. "I understand. But you have a sense of sympathy for him. Why do you feel that way?" Kali looked like she genuinely wanted to know why.

And Maya knew exactly what the goddess was asking her. Why hadn't she killed Kas when she'd had the opportunity? She could have obliterated him when she'd gone to Swargaloka to rescue Varuni. And she hadn't.

She sighed. "He seemed . . . good. I don't know how to explain it. I knew he'd held Varuni prisoner, and I knew what he was capable of because I'd seen him kill Priya right in front of my eyes, but there was still a part of him left that seemed . . . that made me see him as human, I guess. Something about his eyes." Maya laughed. Her explanation must have come off as ridiculous.

A poor excuse for her failure. She shook her head. "I know it probably sounds stupid, but I can't explain it any other way."

Soft laughter rose from Kali's throat, but she wasn't laughing at Maya. The sound conveyed a warm kindness and an understanding that comforted Maya and made her feel less stupid.

"I know what you mean very well, my child. You used to have the very same ability the last time you walked this earth." As Kali mentioned Maya's previous incarnation she stiffened, rejecting the notion that the goddess would prefer Mother Radha to Maya herself. She had to pull herself away from her emotional pouting to focus as Kali said, "When I last knew you, you could sense a person's essence so swiftly it was almost magical. Almost the way most gods do."

"Most gods?" Maya frowned, completely side-tracked now by the mention of the gods. "I thought all gods would be able to do that?" asked Maya, feeling a ripple of unease again at the knowledge that the gods could see right through her to her deepest emotions.

"The gods whose powers are not waning have the strongest ability." In all the time that Kali had remained seated she hadn't moved, and yet she appeared as relaxed as when she'd first folded herself into the pose.

Maya on the other hand had begun to fidget, rocking slowly from side to side because her left butt cheek had chosen that moment to fall asleep. She cleared her throat and asked, "So loss of faith means loss of power too?"

A wave of sadness ran through her. She hadn't expected to empathize with the gods but she did. They were no longer as powerful or as influential as they once were. And now she'd begun to humanize them too, making them more real in her mind. So it wasn't surprising that she found herself sympathizing with them. It sucked that they would lose something so important just because people refused to believe in them anymore.

Kali nodded, seemingly oblivious to Maya's internal

muddling. "And not only do powers wane. Gods who have truly weakened also begin to fade."

"Fade?" A frown creased Maya's forehead. That did not sound good. "Like disappear? Forever?"

The goddess nodded, her blue-tinged skin gleaming in the garage florescent. Her eyes held an ethereal sadness, a mother unable to save her doomed children. "They melt away into the ether. Just like wind blowing the fog away."

Maya's shoulders fell, the weight of sadness and hopelessness too heavy to bear. "Oh. That is bad," she said with a twist of her lips. "Is there something we can do for them? To help save them?"

"Unfortunately, it takes hundreds of years of decline in faith before it begins to affect the god, and by then it is often too late to attempt a reversal. And for the minor gods, there is very little anyone can do. The worst of it is that those gods whose powers are fading, can sometimes, out of desperation, take advantage of the wrong powers to extend their lives."

"Deal with the devil," Maya mumbled, only realizing she'd spoken aloud when Kali laughed. "I'm sorry." Maya's cheeks reddened.

"No need to apologize, Maya. That is the basic truth of it. A few gods have rebelled and sought the dark powers to ensure they do not die."

"Are they so desperate to live that they would do such a thing?" Maya asked, curious. She knew a lot of people with different opinions on death and its finality, but few would make such deals just to live longer lives.

"Maya, you must understand that the gods have existed for millennia. To a human whose life span is on average seventy years, death is inevitable, something people sometimes welcome. But for a god, life lasts a long time, and there is an expectation that it will be long. So when one is used to extended longevity then when faced with the impending end, it is understandable that they would not take comfort from death.

"So what do fading gods have to do with Kas?" asked Maya trying to make the connection and failing.

"Because gods and demons work in a similar fashion. A long time ago the demons themselves attained their power by worshiping the gods. Their boons were also longevity, riches. Whatever they asked for. But when the gods that confer those boons begin to fade then they have little choice but to seek their survival elsewhere."

"So Kas is fading and is dealing with the dark powers so he can live longer?"

"It's a little more complicated than that but essentially yes." Kali held out her hand, the action indicating that Maya should take it. "Your sojourn inside Narakasura's head had its purpose and once you understand it well, you will be able to help him."

"Isn't he holed up safely somewhere down there?" Maya poked her finger into the carpeted floor.

And the goddess ignored her question. "Do you understand what it is you did just now?"

"With Kas?" asked Maya. When Kali nodded, she said, "I possessed him. Or jumped inside his head for a while."

"Good. And while you were inside his mind, what did you feel?"

Maya tipped her head and stared off into nothing as she reflected on her experience of being imprisoned within Kas's mind. In all that time, she'd had no idea it was him. Not until she'd caught sight of his reflection. But she'd been privy to his deepest feeling. "His emotions. I could feel them. Without being able to understand the actual words. It was more a sense of his mood."

"Anything else?"

"His memories. There were a few times when he remembered things from his past. Like when he was a little boy playing with his tiger." Maya stopped abruptly as a rush of ice skittered down her spine.

"What's the matter, child?"

Maya shrugged. "Nothing. It's just this man, Bana, who was with Kas. He made him kill his own pet tiger. I can't understand how someone could be so cruel and all just to teach Kas some stupid lesson."

Kali nodded, her face tightening with an emotion Maya was unable to define. "And what was the lesson he was attempting to impart on our young Kas?" asked Kali with a kind smile. She was trying to teach Maya something, and Maya hoped she wouldn't fail the goddess.

"He was showing him how much he couldn't trust the people around him."

"And what else?"

Maya frowned. Had she missed something in what Bana had explained to Kas? "Oh, and that emotional attachment is a weakness. It makes you vulnerable."

"Well done, Maya." Kali was nodding. "Then your visit was worth it."

"Is that why you didn't want to tell me where I was going?" Kali nodded. "I had the same experience with Priya back in Budapest." Maya offered the information. It all made so much sense now how she'd been able to see Priya in that hut. And she'd 'seen' it even before they'd left on the mission. Maya had assumed it was a premonition. But it had been a vision of the past.

"I know." Kali smiled. "The skill has been growing within you." The goddess certainly didn't mess around with words. There was so much Maya wanted to know.

With a nod Maya leaned forward taking a gamble on telling Kali the one thing that had bothered her since she'd returned. But when she opened her mouth she found herself hesitating. What did it mean anyway?

"What is it Maya?" Kali was beginning to frown.

Clearing her throat, Maya said, "There was something that

happened. I got really angry with Bana after what he did and when Kas seemed to be convinced, I kinda lost it."

Kali frowned. "Lost it?"

"I got mad. And I guess I yelled at him." Maya paused and looked away from Kali's penetrating gaze. The experience still unnerved her. Then she cleared her throat. "I think he heard me."

The room grew silent as Maya counted off the seconds before Kali responded. It wasn't that the goddess was angry or upset in anyway. She just looked unnerved.

"Did I do something wrong?" Maya asked, her voice low, afraid to send Kali into a sudden fury.

She needn't have worried. Kali shook her head and smiled. "Of course, you have not. I was merely taken aback for a moment. I hadn't expected this to happen so soon. It appears your intuitive power is much stronger than I had anticipated."

Intuitive power? Fear thrummed within Maya's gut. What else did she not know about her powers?

"What power?" asked Maya softly, her heart thudding wildly against her ribs.

"The power to control time."

CHAPTER 27

Hijacking bodies was one thing, changing time was a whole other ballgame.

Maya forced her lungs to function.

Inhale.

Exhale.

Repeat.

Why was she so stunned? She could wield fire, so what's so freaking insane about manipulating time?

A whole freaking lot, that's what.

Maya shook her head. This wasn't a joke. This was as real as it got. And she had a goddess waiting patiently for her while she worked through her little freakout.

"Okay," said Maya, forcing her head to move up and down. She had to re-assure Kali that she was really okay with all this crazy.

But the goddess was onto her and merely chuckled. "It is a lot to get your mind around, I know." She held out the palm of her hand and a folded newspaper appeared. "Here. Front page."

Maya took the paper and opened it up to reveal the bold headline.

Toddler Dies
Parents Under Investigation

SHE FROWNED and looked up at Kali wondering what an abused toddler had to do with time-bending.

"Let us go. You will need to see this before you understand." Kali held out her hand, and Maya took a step closer, still clutching the paper.

The moment she grasped Kali's hand the garage faded and a well-lit hallway appeared. It looked like an apartment building, and a nice one from the cream walls, white skirting borders and the random framed prints on the walls. It looked more like a hotel hallway, but it had a more lived in feel.

A weight pulled on her arms and she looked down. One hand clutched a paper bag filled with groceries, while the other reached into her pocket for a set of keys she knew didn't belong to her.

Okay, another body-jacking.

She slipped the key into the lock and jiggled it a little before it turned. As she pushed open the door, a child's excited yell broke the subdued silence of the apartment. When the baby came bounding toward her, Maya's eyes widened as she recognized the toddler from the paper. The dead child.

Maya found herself bending and placing the bag on the floor, as eager as the child for a cuddle. She opened her arms for the him just as he crashed into her, full of smiles and baby smells.

She held him close and breathed in his baby scent, and a potent rush of love for the child filled her. She stiffened, recalling the headline. This child had died and this mother, who only had pure devotion for him, was now accused of killing him. It didn't seem right at all.

She kissed his cheek a dozen times eliciting a tumult of high-pitched giggles before setting him free and rising to her feet. Maya watched him as he burbled babyspeak and toddled back inside toward the couch.

She stooped to grab the groceries and as she moved to close her door, the neighbor across the hall opened hers. Maya found herself both smiling in pleasant greeting, and stunned with shock at the neighbor's identity.

Maya's teacher, Ms Harris.

The demon.

CHAPTER 28

*A*ND JUST AS suddenly, Maya was back in her own body, back in her garage, too stunned to speak.

"Now, do you understand?"

Maya nodded, her throat hurting as she swallowed. "The demon killed the baby?"

Kali looked away. "The Rakshasi is one who feeds on innocence."

Maya let out a puff of breath. "That would explain why she's at our school."

Giving her head a slight shake, Kali said, "She is there because of you. She is keeping an eye on you for her Master."

Ice rippled through Maya's veins. "So this baby died because of me?"

"Not technically, but essentially yes."

Talk about not pulling any punches.

Maya stared at the goddess, shocked, feeling dead inside that she could be the reason that baby had been killed, the reason however far removed.

"Don't even think this is your fault."

"It is."

Kali sighed, the sound much like the way air rushes through the sails of a yacht. "If you believe it's your fault, then fix it."

"Can I?"

"That's what manipulating time can entail."

"Tell me how to do it," said Maya, realizing too late that her words sounded more like an instruction than a request. Belatedly, she tacked on, "Please," but the goddess seemed unfazed by Maya's lapse in respect.

"You must learn to manipulate the behavior of the person in whose body you exist."

"You mean Kas really did hear me?" asked Maya.

"You are stronger than I expected. You are ready to make an attempt."

"So how does it work? Do I tell her not to kill the child? Will that even work?"

"We cannot take that chance. You only get one opportunity to be in any one particular spot. I would much rather you start earlier and try to reroute the timeline instead of aiming to stop the murder alone." Kali paused. "And, Maya. Please remember. There must always be balance."

Maya nodded and waited as Kali outlined her tasks. The longer the goddess spoke the stranger it all sounded, but if it meant saving that little boy she knew she'd try anything.

AIR RUSHED around Maya as she swooped into Ms Harris's body. The teacher was making her way across her living room, picking up plastic drinking glasses and discarded paper towels on her way to the kitchen. She'd just picked up a pointy edged knife that lay beside a dried up piece of cheese when a woman appeared directly in her path.

Ms Harris shrieked, dropping everything on the floor and got possessed for her troubles.

~

MAYA SIGHED as she surged back into her own body and opened her eyes. This was getting easier each time.

"I couldn't save her."

"This time was not meant to be used to save her."

"What was it supposed to be?"

"I believe you call it 'recon'."

Maya grinned. "Now what?"

"What did you see?"

"A messy living room, Ms Harris cleaning and intending to go to the kitchen. A demon appearing and taking over her body."

"More detail, Maya."

Why was Kali beginning to sound like Maya's mom, tone of exaggerated patience included?

Maya sighed. "Living room, dirty plates, and cups and serviettes. Ms Harris picks stuff up. Then she picks up the cheese knife-" She paused. "Oh."

"Exactly," was all Kali said.

"Okay. Let's try this again."

"Remember, use your energy to force your suggestion to the surface. Get it right this time because the earlier you arrive each time the less you are able to control the actual event. Now, you can ensure she uses the knife. If you go in any earlier you won't see what you've already seen. If that makes sense."

Maya gave a nod. "Ready when you are."

~

MAYA LAY IN WAIT. If lying within an unsuspecting person's body could be described as lying in wait. Of course, Ms Harris had no idea what was in store for her today.

Ms Harris wriggled beneath her sheets and groaned, stuffing her face into her pillow before lifting it and shifting into a sitting position. Ms Harris stared at the fabric of her white pillowcase, streaked now with remnants of eyeshadow, lipstick, and foundation that she hadn't bothered to clean off last night. She ripped the pillowcase off the pillow and padded to the bathroom on bare feet, throwing it into the hamper before going to the basin and grabbing the toothpaste.

Maya would have jumped with shock at the sight of Ms Harris's reflection, but unfortunately she was stuck inside her teacher's body. Or rather her teachers very much underdressed body. Apparently all Ms Harris wore to bed was a silk negligee, its fabric so transparent it barely qualified as fabric. Maya averted her eyes and stared at Ms Harris makeup-smeared face. Geez. She was as bad as Maya in the makeup removal department. Raccoon eyes and lipstick streaked up her cheek. Yup, just like Maya.

Maya closed her eyes and sang loudly while her teacher performed her morning routine, only opening them when she was pretty certain she was clothed. Ms Harris headed into the kitchen, picking up trash and then she stooped to grab the knife.

Maya pulled the energy from deep within her, and focused it on Ms Harris's hand. Her teacher gasped as Maya took control of her fingers, tightening the digits around the hilt of the knife.

And then the demon appeared, with Maya well prepared. Maya had expected her, but Ms Harris stiffened, stunned.

She dropped the trash, but despite her fingers slackening their hold on the knife, they didn't let go. Because Maya held on with all her might.

Thrilled by her small success Maya tightened the muscles in her right leg and stepped back, willing with all her strength for her teacher to follow her direction.

Ms Harris didn't fight Maya, probably because she was moving away from the red-eyed creature, putting the sofa between them.

But even as Maya coaxed Ms Harris backward, the demon

followed step-for-step. And then she grinned, revealing hideous sharp teeth, and launched herself at Ms Harris.

But Maya was ready, putting the power of her fire behind her hand she pushed, forcing Ms Harris to throw her hand out in front of her.

Just in time.

The demon landed in front of Ms Harris, knife sharp fingers outspread, eager to end the teachers life. But instead of taking possession of the human body, the Rakshasi hesitated, staring at Ms Harris with the oddest expression, a strange amalgamation of surprise, frustration, fury and pain.

And then, in a conflagration of red and orange flames, she was gone. All that was left were little sparks of gold and flecks of black soot which floated to the white carpet on Ms Harris's living room floor.

Mission accomplished.

~

MAYA FLOATED BACK to her body, wondering how Ms Harris was going to handle her strange experience. Would she chalk it up to too much partying the previous night? Or would she assume she was going a little nuts.

Either way, the demon was dead and Maya had saved the boy's life.

Maya opened her eyes and Mother Kali had already left.

Paper crinkled in Maya's grip and she glanced down, opening the folded newspaper to see the headline.

Apartment Burgled By Crazed Woman
Residents advised to increase security.

Maya laughed. So that's what Ms Harris had told people.

But as her amusement died down she began to wonder how her actions had affected the timeline, especially where it had anything to do with Maya and her school.

She flicked her phone open and dialed Joss, who picked up on the second ring.

"What's up?"

"Ms Harris."

"What?" Joss asked, her tone clearly indicating that she'd concluded Maya was nuts. "What about Ms Harris?"

"She's free."

"Free from what, Maya?" Joss was speaking slowly and firmly, the way one did to naughty little kids.

"From the demon, Joss." Maya held her breath and waited for Joss's answer.

"What demon? What's Ms Harris got to do with any demon?" The lilt in her friend's voice as she asked the question told Maya that she would happily commit her right now.

Maya laughed. "Nothing. It's a long story. I'll explain when I see you."

"You are not going to get away with that so easily. Spill." The threat in Joss's tone was enough to make Maya burst out laughing.

"Where are you?"

"Spare room," she snapped.

Maya cut the call and turned on her heel.

The moment she'd confirmed that her attempt to save the boy had worked, a plan had begun to form in her mind.

CHAPTER 29

After Joss had left, Maya had time to sit and contemplate her actions. She turned the idea over in her mind, that time was so fluid, that a person could move through the past, could even manipulate people and their actions.

And despite the banter and teasing about how powerful she could be, Maya knew she couldn't be tempted to use this ability for personal gain.

She'd never done so, even after she'd received her fire power either, so why would she start now?

Maya, still exhausted from the flight, climbed under the covers and lay very still, her mind buzzing with possibilities. She'd expected to be way too energized to sleep, but within seconds she'd fallen into the numb slumber of the deeply fatigued, or the deeply troubled.

Maya just happened to be both.

She dreamed of a single face, red hair, eyebrows and cheeks.

She dreamed of a pair of curious eyes, of a boy who'd stared at her because he'd felt privileged to have even seen her. A boy she'd failed to save.

Stefan.

Maya sat up, suddenly wide awake, decisions and plans racing across her mind. She knew what she wanted to do, but a trill of fear ran beneath the anticipation.

Kali had said such power was not to be used lightly, and never to be used for personal gain. Was saving Stefan personal gain?

She'd be saving his life, yes, but wouldn't she also be satisfying her own need to feel better, assuaging her own guilt in her failure to keep him safe? Wasn't that just a different type of personal gain?

Maya shook the doubt from her head. Of course, it's not personal gain. She intended to save the boy's life. His parents would certainly appreciate the effort, even if they'd never know it had even happened. And what was the point of having such a power if she never used it to do good?

Maybe it's time she did something to define her own existence, something other than what she'd done in her previous life, something that would be just as worthy of Mother Radha.

She nodded.

She'll save him and deal with the consequences later.

As she settled back against the pillows, Kali's words rang through her head. "There must always be balance."

Maya frowned, wondering what exactly the goddess had meant by that, but she didn't let it trouble her too long.

She took a breath, calming herself.

Then she closed her eyes.

CHAPTER 30

When Maya opened her eyes, it was like rising from a deep, soundless ocean to be born into the eye of a hurricane. The stillness held a certain similarity but the mortal threat was vastly different.

She blinked and Priya's demon lunged for her. Stefan pulled the trigger and the demon went flying. Maya spun on her heel and ran to the boy who was still standing on the threshold, a glazed look in his eyes.

She grabbed the rifle and shoved him out of the hut. "Get back to the car if you want to live." She growled out the words and Stefan pulled back, shocked at the vehemence in her voice.

But she didn't care.

She just turned back to Priya, and the demon who was slowly getting back to his feet. She didn't give him a chance, just sent supercharged fire at him until he disappeared in a little puff of amber light. Second time around she knew better what it took to incinerate him.

Done, Maya turned to face Priya who'd launched into a run when her demon went down.

But instead of tackling the Rakshasi head on, Maya was

shoved roughly aside. Pain burst in her side and warmth began to trick down her hip as the impact ripped her stab wound open.

As she fell, Maya watched Claudia swipe a dagger at Priya. The demon's claws were long, but Claudia managed to skirt past her far enough that the demon couldn't touch her.

The hut was too small, the confines of its walls keeping them all cloistered together.

Too close

And, as Priya advanced, Claudia had nowhere to go.

When the Rakshasi plunged her dagger-like fingernail into Claudia's stomach, Maya let out a scream of horror.

She scrambled to her feet, her fingernails digging into the packed soil of the floor, and staggered over to her aunt. Her fury built in much the same way as it had the last time she'd been here, only much more potent.

Fueled by her anger, she destroyed Priya with a super-charged flare of fire and heat.

Then she found herself falling to Claudia's side instead of Stefan's.

Oh God, what had she done?

CHAPTER 31

Maya's heart crashed against her chest during the ride to visit Claudia. Sabala had pushed his nose against her hip until she let him get in the back seat with her. Now, he sat beside her in solemn silence, as if understanding what she needed.

The more she worried about what she would say and what Claudia's reaction would be, the more she twisted the little leather ties on the cuffs of her sleeves. She'd dressed on automatic, her subconscious in full force.

With her jeans, boots and silky blouse, she was already channeling Claudia. She'd been surprised when her parents hadn't driven to the local hospital. They'd entered the centre of busy downtown LA, and headed into a parking garage beneath a bog standard high-rise. Maya had paid little attention to the address, but her eyebrows had risen when they'd parked in a reserved space complete with her dad's name on it.

"Where are we going?"

"To see Claudia, honey. We promised to bring you," said her mom, looking over her shoulder as her dad pulled the handbrake and opened his door. Her mom's eyes held a hint of sadness and

Maya wondered if she was disappointed in her hurting Claudia. They'd assured her they didn't blame her but it was human nature to place blame, even if the person in question is their child.

She'd messed up and she did deserve their disappointment.

Now, she pushed away the niggling shame. "Uh?" said Maya. "This isn't the hospital."

Neither of her parents seemed to be listening as they alighted and shut their doors, so Maya followed suit, telling herself it was better to ask less questions right now. She'd rocked the boat plenty, and already felt like a piece of three-day-old pooch poop.

The parking space had proclaimed 'KALIMA' so maybe they were making a stop at the offices of the Kali organization before heading out to see Claudia. When she followed them into the elevator, Sabala close at her heel, her dad thumbed a blank button at the top of the bank of numbered ones. A floor with no number?

Stranger and stranger.

The ride within the multi-mirrored elevator was silent and Maya couldn't help but see the irony being stuck in a tiny space with a million reflections of herself to stare at. What better way to enjoy being disappointed in yourself than by seeing it multiplied over and over until you're cross-eyed, or nauseous.

Or both.

Maya chose to keep her eyes on the row of floor numbers above the doors, watching each one light up, then darken until suddenly none of them were lit. And yet the elevator came to a smooth halt at the unnumbered floor.

Okay, so nobody is meant to know what floor this place is on. Secretive much.

Maya frowned as the doors slid open and they entered a small cream-carpeted reception area. A surly security guard rose from behind a large desk and opened an inner door for them. He gave her parents a formal nod, and Maya a wide-eyed glance before lowering his eyes. The invisible dog remained invisible as the guard returned to his seat.

She snuck a look back at him as they entered the internal room but he paid them no further attention. Inside, another desk and this time an older man stood behind the smaller reception station, flipping through a stack of files, his face enigmatic.

He shifted his attention from papers to faces and gave a small smile, his features transforming from neutral to borderline cheery.

"Ah, Dev. She is waiting for you," he said, his clipped English matching his striped bowtie. His piercing gaze shifted to Maya.

A tiny nod; neutral was good.

Then he did a double-take as his gaze lowered to where Sabala stood beside her, supposedly invisible. He glanced back up at Maya, his eyes a fraction wider than before. Boy would he be good at poker. He held her gaze for a moment before flicking back to Sabala, as if he wanted to re-assure himself of what stood before his eyes.

Maya's dad offered the man a short greeting and a familiar smile before making a left and hurrying briskly down the hall. Her mom slipped a hand into the crook of her elbow and gently pulled Maya along.

"He's an adept," she whispered as Maya restrained the urge to look back at the old man.

"But he's-"

"Old?" asked Leela as they followed her dad. Sabala clacked along beside her, unperturbed by having had his glamor penetrated by a mere human.

Dev made a few turns, left, then right, then left again and seemed to be leading them to the other end of the building.

"White?" said Maya dryly.

"That's racist."

"Mom!"

Leela laughed. "Kali has had followers all over the world for hundreds of years. Edward McCullough is one of the founding members of the modern version of our organization."

"Modern version?" asked Maya.

They reached a pair of glass doors and Dev drew a card from his pocket, then swiped it through a little card reader on the wall.

"Organized, formalized, with infrastructure for making money to fund the rest of our work."

The door hissed open, as if the entrance sealed the area off so thoroughly that even the air didn't mix.

"Sounds so . . . boring," Maya said, nonetheless impressed. "At least you guys aren't unemployed, riding around in an old car with a bunch of weapons stashed in the trunk."

This section of the floor seemed no different from the rest, same decor, similar occupants except for the nurse behind a station on their left. She glanced up at them but barely paid any attention as they passed and headed down the corridor.

"Maybe not unemployed. But the car and the weapons pretty much sums it up," whispered her mom, her voice filled with laughter as she watched Maya's face.

Maya schooled her features as they reached a room at the end of the passage. The door stood ajar and they entered a deluxe hospital room, kitted out in a decor of oak and plush carpet, complete with fresh flowers and a big screen TV. The beeping of the machines dispelled the notion that this was a luxurious bedroom, bringing Maya to full awareness.

If the noises of hospital equipment hadn't succeeded in slamming Maya with a reality check, then the wheelchair tucked beside the door would have done the trick. Sabala sauntered over to it, then sat back on his haunches beside the wheelchair, his expression inscrutable.

Maya averted her eyes, refocused on Claudia who sat on the bed, the top half elevated so she was in a comfortable sitting position. She looked tired, pale, but in good spirits. She had a novel on her lap, something raunchy from the looks of it, and she didn't seem in the least embarrassed about the half-naked couple in an x-rated clinch splashed across the front cover.

Claudia smiled happily at the sight of her visitors, and a stab of pain ripped through Maya's heart. She'd soon be the one to single-handedly end that short moment of joy. She moved aside and let her parents gather beside the bed to complete their greetings. Even so she had no intention of waiting too long to get things off her chest.

Little point in approaching the subject with too much tact either, and as the conversation lulled Maya knew the time had come at last. This must be what it's like to walk the plank, or climb up on the gallows.

Dramatic much, Maya.

Claude glanced around Leela to get Maya's attention, so she moved closer and took a deep breath.

"So you have something to tell me, kid?" asked Claudia looking at Maya as if she was going to reveal a special surprise, as if it was going to be something good. Clearly, she was unaware of the bombshell Maya was about to drop.

Maya nodded, her throat feeling like she'd swallowed a handful of razor blades. "Hey," she said, her mouth twisting in a semblance of a smile.

"So? Tell me. Your mom made it sound very important." She gave Leela an unimpressed glance before returning her attention to Maya.

"It is, and you aren't going to like it. I'll understand if you hate me." In the ensuing seconds, breathing became difficult as a strange pressure began to compress her chest. She had to force herself to inhale slowly.

Claudia laughed, but the look she gave Maya was a little nervous. "Spill, Maya. You know how I dislike long moments of awkward silences." Sabala chuffed and Claudia grinned, searching the air in the hell-hound's direction. "Hey, pooch." When she looked at Maya again, her smile was gone.

Maya threaded her fingers, twisting the digits around and around each other. She held Claudia's gaze and said, "It's my fault this happened to you." She waved a hand at Claudia's limbs which lay unmoving beneath the silky coverlet.

Claudia gave a slight shake of her head, her forehead creasing in a triplicate of deep lines. She smiled. "Kid, I think you're a little confused."

Maya shook her head, her eyes growing moist. "No. It happened twice. The first time you were okay, but I went back to change things and you got hurt. There is always a price, but I didn't know it would be you." The words tumbled from Maya's mouth, a flood of terrible truths.

"Maya, this sounds nuts. What are you talking about?" Claude's voice held a note of impatience now, and Maya knew she'd better talk faster.

She cleared her throat. "Kali was teaching me how to go back in time and how to manipulate events. She helped me save a baby, and Ms Harris from a demon." Maya came to a sudden stop. The room was silent and even Claudia looked at her strangely, as if she was unsure whether Maya was lying, but also still intrigued by the possibility that it could be true.

"Who is Ms Harris?"

Maya suppressed a sigh. She should have known they would all have forgotten anything related to Ms Harris's demonic possession because Maya had changed the past which meant she'd also changed the present.

"My English teacher. She was possessed by a Rakshasi. She'd been watching me for a few weeks. Kali showed me a newspaper article where a baby had been killed. And when I traveled in time, I saw that the baby was Ms Harris's neighbor. The demon had fed on the baby and killed him. So I had to do something to save him. I went back and made Ms Harris kill the demon and the baby survived and now nobody remembers that she was even a demon. Not even Joss."

"So it worked. You saved the child. And Ms Harris?" asked Claudia, watching Maya's face closely, her expression inscrutable.

Not a good sign.

Maya nodded. "So I thought I would be able to fix what happened in Budapest the first time."

"What happened the first time?" asked Claudia softly. Her smile was strained.

"Stefan died."

"And I wasn't hurt?" And odd note reverberated in her tone.

Maya shook her head.

The silence burgeoned.

"So you thought you could go back and save him," Claudia said. It wasn't a question, but Maya nodded anyway. "And did you save him?"

That question must have been rhetorical because Maya knew that Claude was well aware that Stefan was perfectly fine. Except for the bump on the back of his head he'd received when Maya had shoved him out of the hut.

"I saved him. But Priya got *you* instead."

Another moment of silence passed, and Maya wondered what had happened to Claudia's dislike of them.

"And you think me being this way is your fault?" There was that note again.

"Of course, it is. You were fine. If I hadn't gone back *you* would still be fine."

"Maya? What are you planning?" The suspicion in her tone was enough to make Maya avert her gaze. Maybe if she didn't let Claudia see her eyes her aunt wouldn't be able to see the truth of it.

"I want to fix it." So, she knew she couldn't lie to Claudia.

"Fix it?" Claudia frowned, the vein in her throat beating rapidly. "How the hell do you plan on fixing it?"

"Kali said we could."

"And what happens if you fix it?" That note again. Maya

couldn't bring herself to say the words, but Claudia didn't seem to have a problem. "Stefan will die, isn't it?"

Maya nodded.

"Then there isn't even a question." Claudia spoke flatly. And her voice was calm. Not a hint of doubt. Maya's gaze snapped back to Claudia's face. "I will not exchange a boy's life for the use of my legs. And, even if you'd come to me and proposed going back to save him, I would have agreed, so don't go thinking this is entirely on you."

Maya frowned and shook her head. "But I went alone. I didn't ask you for your opinion. You didn't agree that I should go."

"Listen, kid. At least give me some credit. If you had told me about it, asked me what to do, I would have said that you should go. If it meant saving Stefan, I would have jumped at the chance. So even if we rewound everything, I'll still be right here." She waved her hands at her ruined legs.

"You're just trying to make me feel better."

"No. I wouldn't do that to you." Maya's eyebrows rose, a quizzical expression on her face. "I would never lie to you just to make you feel better. No matter what, the truth is always the better option."

At last, Maya sank onto the mattress beside Claudia's legs. The intense weight that had been pressing down on her had lifted, at least enough so she could breathe and relax a little.

"So what will you do now?" she asked, trying very hard not to look at Claudia's legs.

Was that what it's going to be like, always being careful where she looked and for how long?

Claudia snorted. "Just because I'll end up in a wheelchair doesn't mean I have to stop my work. A girl can be badass even if she's on wheels, you know."

Maya studied Claudia's face, a little suspicious, a little concerned. Was she just putting on a brave front, or did she really mean it? Claudia's grin was enough to convince her, at least eighty percent of the way.

But she still let out a sigh. "I'm still sorry, you know."

"I'm not, so get over yourself."

Maya snorted softly. She didn't miss the light sniff emitted by the cheeky pooch either.

She was a little light-headed with relief. She'd said what she'd come to say, a little off-kilter considering the consequences hadn't been as bad as she'd expected, like she'd put her back into lifting a heavy bag that ended up turning out to be empty. Off balance.

Claudia was going to be okay.

And that grounded Maya in her next decision.

She had to get to Patala. And given Nik's lack of response, there was one other person who could help her.

Chayya.

CHAPTER 32

The ride home was filled with one of those endless silences, the ones that are usually filled with accusations, self-recrimination and, in Maya's case, a healthy dose of self-pity. Not unexpectedly, Maya preferred to leave the dead air unrevived until they were stepping inside the equally silent house.

"Dinner?" asked her mom with a soft smile.

They paused in front of the darkened kitchen and Leela flicked the switch. Familiarity filled Maya, along with a hint of comfort, at the sight of their little kitchen, the table a reminder of good times and confidences given and taken. A reminder too, that her parents and Claudia, even if they were disappointed in her right now, would not give up on her.

Maya gave her mom a ghost of a smile and shook her head. "Not hungry," she murmured, taking a step to head upstairs. Then, the decision taking her entirely by surprise, she stopped and faced her mom. "I need to tell you guys where I'm going. Just in case."

"Where are you going, and in case of what?" asked Leela, her voice holding an interrogative air. She turned her gaze a faction, centering on Maya and that slight movement held a sense of a threat to it, the universal kind mothers used on their children when they want information and use body language to state that there is no alternative.

Speak or deal with the consequences, her eyes said.

Maya didn't need the threat.

Her windpipe whistled as she inhaled, and she gave a small cough, hoping she wasn't coming down with something. Time-travel may have all sorts of effects on a person, and seeing as she had nobody else to compare notes with, she figured it was best to be careful. Not to mention the last thing she wanted was to be plied the stock-standard turmeric-and-ginger infused boiled milk that was her mom's cough and cold treatment of choice.

Just gross.

"I'm going to Patala." She ignored the surprised glance and continued "The Rakshasi, Priya, said something that makes me worry that Nik is in danger. And he hasn't responded to my call either. After my experience in Kas's head, I'm more sure that I need to check up on them."

"Kas's head?" asked her dad as he passed them and dropped his keys on the kitchen table. He turned and faced her, folding his arms and sitting on the edge of the table. It was his talk-because-I'm-not-going-anywhere pose.

Sheesh.

Maya gave her parents a Cliff's Notes version of her surreal adventure when Kali sent her on her first foray into the timeline. Eyebrows were raised, faces paled and Maya counted at least half a dozen frowns when arrows, tigers, and mirrors were mentioned.

They were still a little raw after her revelation about having changed the past where Claudia was concerned, so she could hardly blame them. She did give them props for absorbing this latest pile of information with some semblance of calm.

"So. If you can travel through time, why can't you do that and find out where Nik is that way?" Dev's forehead scrunched as if he was trying to solve the puzzle of the question himself. "Okay. I'm going to guess that's not the easy way. You won't know where Nik will be unless you go back and join his time-line when he dropped you off in Prague."

Maya nodded. "It was easy when Kali just took me where I needed to go. And when I went back to my own past. But, if I join Nik in Prague, it may take hours to figure out what happened to him. And then I'd have to do the same with Kas if he's not with Nik in the underworld."

"Looks like it has the potential to become very confusing."

Maya nodded. "To be honest, I would have preferred jumping Nik in my bed-" Maya's eyes widened as her Mom's eyebrows rose a fraction and her dad's mouth began to twitch. "I so did not say that. What I meant was . . . never mind. Not important."

Maya turned, hiding her reddened cheeks and hurried out of the kitchen. "Make sure you take that invisible dog of yours with you."

The invisible dog snuffed as he clattered along the floor beside her and Maya gave her dad a thumbs up without turning around. She headed to her room and, leaving Sabala to watch from the doorway, began to dig around in her bedside drawer. She withdrew the small engraved brass container and gave it a satisfied smile.

She lifted the little hinged lid, and held her breath as a dark, smoky shadow wafted from the container. It curled in the air in front of Maya's face and then disintegrated into nothing.

Chayya's version of an emergency smoke signal.

With her call to Chayya completed, Maya hurried to change. She wanted to be ready to leave at a moment's notice.

As she turned to the closet, the shadows in the corner of the room darkened, thickening to a gloopy mass. The room seemed to grow smaller as the cloud of darkness closed in on Maya. She had a smile on her face even before the goddess Chayya material-ized in front of her.

"That was quick," said Maya, before greeting the goddess with a Namaste.

Chayya smiled and returned the greeting, but even as she straightened from the shallow bow, she asked, "You needed my help?"

Maya nodded and explained. As she spoke Sabala sauntered forward and curled himself around the goddess's legs.

Chayya nodded, as she ran her fingers along the top of the hell-hound's head, the expression on her face unreadable. And for the first time since Maya had met the benevolent goddess of shadows, she couldn't read her face. Chayya had always been easy-going, relaxed. But today her smile was thinner, the skin around her eyes tighter.

"Is everything okay?" asked Maya, worried now that she may have disturbed the goddess. "I hope I didn't call you when you were busy."

Chayya shook her head, the movement loosening a few threads of shadow from her dark hair. They floated around her, before disappearing into nothing. "No, Maya. You did not disturb me at all. Had I been occupied, I would have waited to complete my task before coming."

Maya smiled. The goddess was nothing if not truthful. She cleared her throat. "Will you be able to take me?"

Chayya inclined her head. "As soon as you are ready, we can leave."

Maya nodded, "I've just got to change. If you have something else to do I can wait." Maya offered, praying the goddess would say no.

But Chayya shook her head and Maya gave her a grateful smile, then hurried to grab a change of clothes, dashing into the bathroom to change. Chayya headed for the seat by the window.

She returned to see Chayya had sunk into the silky cushions

with Sabala's head on her lap. Maya raced about, packing a small rucksack with a sweater and her Madus. Her fire was enough of a weapon, both portable and invisible, but Maya liked to believe she had some form of backup she could use without having to fry her opponent before talking to him.

In under five minutes, she was ready. Flinging open her closet door to grab her jacket, her hand paused. Plastic crinkled as the red-and-gold Valente she'd worn to visit Lord Shiva on Mount Kailas, moved back and forth on the railing. She glanced over her shoulder to see that Chayya was watching her, again with that odd expression.

"You have something to ask me, Maya?" asked the goddess. As usual she could read Maya all too well.

Maya cleared her throat. "You took me to get this dress so I could wear something nice to meet Lord Shiva." Maya gave the dress a last glance before facing Chayya. The goddess had been meant to return the garment after Maya had used it, but she must have forgotten because there it had remained. "Why did I have to get fancied up when Lord Shiva is a symbol of austerity, when he does not stand for extravagance or luxury?"

Chayya smiled, her dark eyes lighting up. "I have been waiting for you to ask."

Maya's eyes narrowed as she studied the goddesses pleased expression. "I'm beginning to wonder if that was a test," she said dryly.

"It was," said Chayya cheerfully.

"Why?"

"Because we had to find out what type of person you were before your powers grew stronger."

Maya inhaled. "What would have happened if I wasn't the right type of person?" She suspected she already knew.

"Your powers would have been bound until you entered your next life cycle."

"I guess I passed?" asked Maya. There seemed to be no end of manipulation when dealing with the gods.

"How do you humans say it? With flying colors?"

Maya shrugged, unsure how to be impressed with Chayya's revelation. "What was so good?"

"You showed that you lack materialism. Yes, you thought the garments were beautiful, but you didn't revel in the luxury of it. It was more an appreciation of beauty as opposed to a need to live in excess. You could easily live with nothing."

Maya wasn't so sure about how happy she'd be to have nothing, but Chayya had managed to figure her out. She'd never been the kind of person who hankered for luxury. She was just as content with homemade clothes as she was with store labels or big brand items.

But, she could certainly see herself living with the barest essentials and still being happy. Give her toothpaste, soap and toilet paper and she didn't much care about silk or diamonds or real oak.

Maya shut her closet door with her foot, and said, "Okay. I'm ready." Now that it was time to leave, she couldn't wait even one more second.

Chayya got to her feet before giving Sabala one last pat. "You stay here and watch over Maya's family."

Maya frowned at Chayya's instruction. "Why can't he come with us?"

Chayya turned her gaze to Maya and opened her mouth. She looked like she wanted to tell Maya something, but in the end she closed her mouth again. She shook her head and smiled, a reassurance that seemed a little faded around the edges. "It's best if he remains here. Your family could do with the protection. And you don't need him to watch over you in Patala."

Maya nodded. The odd edge to Chayya's voice, the strain in her composure said she had damn good reasons for her suggestion. She wasn't about to challenge a goddess and she did agree that Sabala would be more useful here than with her in Patala.

Chayya drew closer and held out her hand. Maya placed her fingers in the goddess's palm.

The goddess sighed. "Maya, I need to warn you. Just before you called to me, I was given some concerning news." Chayya paused, and Maya wondered if this was the reason she'd been so stiff and strained. "We have discovered that Patala has been warded against all other gods. I was just asked to enter the palace to investigate, so your timing could not have been better."

That certainly explained it.

Maya nodded. "So we could be walking into danger?" She didn't need to add that Nik and Kas could also be in some sort of danger too.

Chayya smiled. "Yes. So let us be careful."

She tightened her hold on Maya's hand, and then the bedroom shimmered and faded away, to be replaced by the garden in front of Yama's palace.

Maya heaved a sigh of relief.

Then ducked as an arrow came flying at her head.

CHAPTER 33

Maya lay on the grass, her face low to the ground, thanking her luck that she'd covered the tips of her deadly sharp Madus with the fancy little cone-shaped caps her dad had given her.

If she hadn't, she'd now have a pair of holes in her side, a scar to match the one Priya's novice had given her.

Maya twisted around, wondering who the heck was crazy enough to be shooting arrows in the garden when people could be walking around, just like she and Chayya had just done.

And then Maya gasped. Chayya was sitting beside her, leaning against the base of a banyan tree, one hand to her stomach.

Her fingers clasped the feathered end, and she looked a little surprised. Maya spun scrambled along the ground, keeping as low as possible in case there were more idiotic archers in the vicinity.

Reaching the goddess she peered at the injury, surprised to see that the wound was not bleeding.

"Can you move?" she asked Chayya, glancing around them for a position that would provide more cover. "We need to get to safety."

Chayya smiled and nodded. She leaned forward slightly, then peered around at her back. The head of the arrow had passed right through Chayya's abdomen, and appeared to have no blood on the iron tip.

So gods don't bleed? wondered Maya.

She said nothing, just watched as Chayya reached behind her and snapped off the arrowhead. With a sigh, she straightened then pulled the arrow out of her stomach and tossed it aside.

Maya watched in fascination as the arrow landed within the grass a few feet from them.

"What's going on?" she whispered. Her eyes searched the grounds, hoping to see the archers.

"I don't know, but I should have come earlier to help."

Maya snorted. "They would just have shot you earlier."

Chayya chuckled softly and Maya stared at her for a moment. She'd just been shot in the stomach with a freaking arrow, but now she's chuckling. Maya blinked, trying to remind herself that she was looking at a goddess, not a normal human being.

"You are probably right, Maya." Chayya slid lower and touched the ground just in time. An arrow slammed into the tree-trunk, and would have gone through her eye if she'd remained where she'd been.

"Who the hell is shooting at us?" Maya asked through gritted teeth. "Surely they recognize you, even if I'm not a familiar face."

She stared between the leaves of a jasmine bush in front of her, more than a little sick to her stomach.

Yama's underground garden had been a beautiful place, the animals being the highlight, especially the peacocks. Now, one of the largest males lay just beyond the bush, his body still, his neck almost severed, probably by a flying arrow. Whoever these people were, they had no mercy.

Which didn't bode well for Maya.

But she'd come to find Nik and see if Kas was okay, and that was what she planned on doing. She adjusted her position again, watching the furthest end of the garden where the lawn ended and the palace began. She could see movement on the shallow verandah, and guessed the archers were among those shifting shadows.

A flash of color moved again, dark red, a little hint of black. Maya squinted and managed to make out two men, both bearing bows which were now empty of arrows.

She watched as they hunkered down, scanning the garden through the elaborately patterned screens. They were safe behind the screens, with Maya unable to hurl her fireballs and burn them to a crisp.

She had to get closer.

Maya glanced around at Chayya who was on her stomach watching through the trees with Maya. "Can you get to them?" whispered Maya.

Chayya nodded. "I can. I will distract them for you."

She disintegrated into snaking shadows that swirled and danced, then turned and streaked across the garden, a demonic black cloud that seemed alive.

Arrows slammed into the dark swarm of shadows but they simply passed through and stabbed into the lawn. Maya ran behind the cloud, keeping her distance and hoping that Chayya was able to hide her.

Arrows whizzed past her ears, a little too close for comfort, but Maya kept running. Chayya reached the stairs and swarmed up onto the balcony, enveloping the three archers. Startled, they spun around, batting at the shadows, all three disconcerted enough to be distracted.

They didn't see Maya creep up the stairs and sit with her back against the balustrade. She snuck a glance around the corner and sent a fireball at the archer closest to her. She kept the flame tempered, low enough not to kill, but hot enough to singe, just in case they were the good guys.

When the ball of fire hit him full on the back, he yelled and spun around, his amber eyes enraged. Maya contemplated for a moment the consequences if he really wasn't a bad guy, but she no longer had a choice when he ran straight at her, arms flailing, empty bow going wild.

He was a foot away when Maya burnt him to a crisp.

She didn't wait to watch the last bits of him disintegrate. She ran past his remains, straight at the second demon, aware now that whoever they were, they certainly were not on the good side.

The second demon went down in a ball of flames, flailing back as he fell. Chayya in her shadow form, was busy driving the last demon insane as she immersed him in her darkness. She'd grown heavy, opaque and exuded an almost evil feel. One that sent shivers up and down Maya's spine.

The goddess who'd been so calm and serene had a serious dark side.

Chayya materialized and slammed her semi-solid fist right into the demons chest. Whatever she did with her fingers inside his body, it ended his life within seconds. Before she even removed her hand from his torso, he was disintegrating into soot and amber sparks.

Maya heaved a sigh of relief. "What now?" she asked, urging her heartbeat to slow down,

"Now, we hide," said Chayya before disintegrating into shadows again. "And I know just the place."

She floated down a slate-tiled corridor, heading towards the rooms Maya and Joss had been given when they'd come to Patala the first time.

On the way, they passed dozens of plants and trees which now lay on the floor, their hand painted pots smashed to smithereens, soil strewn across the tiles.

Maya ran lightly, following Chayya as she headed through the open double doors, into the central lounge area that lead to six rooms. The once beautifully-patterned brass doors now hung on broken hinges, as if they'd been smashed open in a frenzied search.

Chayya chose a room at the furthest end, two doors away from the one Maya had once occupied. They hurried inside, their feet making no sound on the marble tiles as they locked the door behind them.

The room bore a striking resemblance to the one next door, brass pots and vases, beautiful paintings on the walls, luxurious silk cushions and bedcovers. It even contained the steaming bathing pool, half hidden by a forest of potted trees and a beautiful painted screen depicting Krishna dancing with his maidens.

The goddess crouched low and duckwalked closer to the three doors on the far wall that led to a balcony. Maya followed and hid beside the screen to peer out of the door closest to her. The balcony opened out onto a central courtyard on the other side of the palace.

A small rectangular garden occupied the space below, a lone peacock wandering around miserably, warily watching a group of half a dozen demons, all armed to the teeth and looking particularly ferocious.

Maya backed away slowly, retreating inside the room. Turning to Chayya she asked, "What are we going to do?"

Chayya glanced at the courtyard and appeared a little stunned. Maya assumed Patala didn't exactly get taken over very often.

"We must wait and assess the situation. We must find a way to ensure Lord Yama and Nikhil are safe." Chayya cleared her throat and her eyes seemed to lose focus a little. Neither she, nor Maya, were battle hardened.

Maya nodded. "So, we go from one room to the next, secure the building, then get to the main hall?"

Chayya nodded. "You will need to be very hard, Maya. These demons are strong. Show a moment of weakness and it could spell the end. You must go into this well aware of the dangers.

And you must promise not to be rash." Maya opened her mouth. The hard expression in Chayya's eyes made her snap her jaw shut. "You cannot risk your life."

"Not even for Lord Yama?" asked Maya, her stomach hardening. She tried not to think about Nik, tried not to think about how she would handle it if something happened to him. So she didn't mention his name, but from the tender understanding on Chayya's face she knew the goddess was aware of who was on her mind.

"Not even for Lord Yama," said Chayya. Her voice sang with sadness. "You are far too valuable to risk your life. You can certainly attempt to save him, but should the danger be too great, I will have no alternative but to take you back home."

Maya nodded. The goddess wasn't exactly giving her a choice. She probably knew Maya had no intention of obeying her, but she pretended otherwise.

Probably for the best.

CHAPTER 34

The last thing Maya wanted was to waste time hiding out. The balcony outside the room did provide them with a good view. They could see into the rooms on the other side of the courtyard, as well as a few yards into the rooms on the ground floor.

Chayya pointed across the way. "That is Lord Yama's private dining room."

"Can't you go all smoky and check it out?"

Chayya was studying the open doors to the dining room, but glanced at Maya as she responded. "It would be dangerous to assume that such a well-guarded room would not be warded. Or at least contain measures to warn the attackers of my entry."

Good point.

"But if an arrow can't kill you then how can these creeps stop you?" Maya didn't like the idea that Chayya would be vulnerable.

Chayya's attention had returned to the dining room. The rust-colored silk drapes fluttered in the wind, shifting deeper inside the room. Deep enough for Maya to catch a glimpse of a foot and a set of chair legs.

"I may not be able to die through normal means, but I am not immune to dark magic. Anyone with magic powerful and evil enough can bind a god. Perhaps it won't be for long, but it would be enough that our plans could be destroyed."

Maya grunted. "So we enter the room as a last resort. Especially since there are people in there, the last thing we need is to get the hostages killed."

Chayya's dark eyes shifted to Maya, a honeyed brown flecked with shadows that seemed to shift and undulate as Maya stared. The goddesses voice broke through her trance. "I see you are observant." Then she sighed and turned back to her gazing. "I can see at least four people, each seated around the main table, all very still."

"Very still?" asked Maya. "Are they tied up?"

"In a sense, yes. There are no ropes, though. I would say it is a spell of sorts. One that will immobilize them for as long as their abductors desire."

"Do we know who they are?" Chayya's forehead creased. "The hostages, I mean."

The goddess's head jerked left and right, one sharp movement that bore a sense of tempered fury. It gave Maya a rash of goosebumps. "I cannot say just from their feet. But it could be Lord Yama."

"Or, it could be someone else and they have him hidden in another room." Maya sighed. "Or, he could have managed to evade them and is now completely safe, getting help."

Chayya said nothing. She could probably tell that Maya was trying to make herself feel better. More than that, she was hoping that none of those legs at the table belonged to Nik.

Maya's chest tightened, making it a little hard to breathe. The mere thought of Nik being in danger, of Nik hurt and in need of help, paralyzed her to the core.

She took a shuddering breath. "We should get going."

The goddess shifted, her sari rustling. "One room at a time."

"We head for the main hall?"

Chayya nodded and then became shadow.

Maya followed the undulating shade as she headed out of the room, checking the living area and each of the rooms while Maya stood watch.

A voice filtered to Maya. Disembodied, it echoed in her mind. "Empty." Chayya.

Creepy, but the goddess had turned into an effective spy. She followed as Chayya entered the corridor outside.

For the second time in the last hour, an arrow came flying at Maya. This time it sliced open the sleeve of her leather jacket, and nicked her arm. Pain heated her skin as blood welled to the surface and began to trickle down her arm.

She sent a pair of flaming fireballs at the two demons bearing down on her, then clamped her fingers against her wound, paying little attention to the squawks of pain and horror as they were devoured. Instead, she drew her heat from her core and sent it straight to the mouth of the wound. She left it to do its work as she scampered down the passage after Chayya.

Chayya, working in her shadow form, was a force to be reckoned with. She cleared room after room, with Maya frying the odd demon guard. The pair managed to make it all the way to the double doors of the main hall without being skewered by arrows or swords.

Once they'd ascended the grand staircase and entered the wide corridor leading to the main hall, they found the hallway occupied only by the people in the painted frescos adorning the walls.

The ten-foot-high carved brass doors that led to Lord Yama's main hall stood ajar.

Maya and the goddess shared a glance. "That can't be a good sign."

"I do have to agree with you. The lack of guard at the main hall is curious. Either they have all gone." Chayya fell silent but her unsaid words rang like a bell in her ears. Or they were all dead within the hall.

Maya swallowed hard and pushed the door wider slowly. The giant brass hinges made no sound so if the hall was occupied, their entry would go unannounced. Small mercies.

Inside, the grand room, with its elegantly pained columns, and its walls containing ancient relics from around the world, appeared to be deserted. Maya and Chayya stood there for a moment, staring at the dais where one of the royal guards lay mortally wounded. Most of the demon guards would have disintegrated into nothing once they'd died, so this man must still be alive. They crept closer and his eyes shot open, startled and afraid. He relaxed only when his frantic gaze settled on Chayya's face. Everyone in the land of darkness and shadow would recognize their goddess.

He even seemed relieved to see Maya, though she wasn't sure why. She certainly hadn't met him before so he wouldn't recognize her by sight.

"Are you okay?" she asked softly, keeping her voice down just in case.

He gave a short nod then pointed at his side. When Maya tilted her head to get a better look, the pool of blood in which he lay sealed the deal. It smelled rancid, even for demon blood scent. He didn't have much time left. Maya turned her attention back to him, wanting to lie to him to make him feel better he waved her into silence before pointing at one of the fat pillars beside the main dais. Her heart tightened at the sight of the small table where Chandragupta had kept the giant book of the dead. Now the table was in pieces and the book lay closed on the floor its leather bindings scuffed in places.

Beyond his book, Yama's right hand man lay propped against a column, blood dripping from his mouth.

"Lord Chandragupta," said Chayya, her gasp shattering the room's silence. She flitted to him, half-solid half-shadow, landing beside him in full form. Maya drew closer and remained at his side as the goddess checked his wound and patted his cheek.

His eyelids fluttered and Chayya looked up. "I should take him somewhere safe. I shall return immediately. Stay here." She pointed a commanding finger at Maya before grabbing hold of the scribe's shoulders and disappearing.

Maya glanced around at the dying demon and found herself hurrying over to his side. Demon or not, nobody should die alone. She sank to her knees, not caring of she soiled her jeans with demon blood.

He seemed to be fading, blinking only when she touched his arm. When he looked at her his eyes widened, his dark skin going ashen.

It took Maya precious seconds to realize he was not looking at her. And then it was too late.

A pair of strong hands grabbed a hold of Maya's arms, while the sharp tip of a knife was pressed against her throat.

"Don't even think about using your fire. You'll be dead before you can blink."

Maya obeyed.

CHAPTER 35

$\mathcal{M}$aya tried to inhale without getting herself impaled. The only problem was the idiot with the knife didn't seem to care that simply moving her to a standing position would draw blood.

She gritted her teeth and wished he'd move to her side so she could breathe a little heated air into his stupid face. But he remained safely behind her, holding one of her arms curled up high behind her back. Her other hand remained within the fierce grip of a second demon who faced her palm straight to the ground.

Smart, these two.

They knew her. Knew her power and how it worked.

And that worried her. How did they know her so well? And were they expecting her? Neither of them had seemed surprised to see her. In fact, their attitude bordered on triumphant, and that Maya didn't like either.

They marched her down the corridor past the main hall, heading in a direction that Maya guessed would take them to the dining room off the private courtyard. It didn't take long to get there as Yama's palace wasn't very large. Certainly not as expansive as the one Kas had lived in during his previous stint on earth.

They reached a bronze door, hammered with a convoluted leaf and flower pattern. While still holding Maya's hand, the second demon grabbed the large doorknob and pushed the door open.

He was there, right in front of Maya. She could have grilled his ass. But something stopped her. They were bringing her to the hostages. What if killing the demon in front of whoever was in charge could endanger the lives of his hostages?

Maya was shoved deeper into the grand room, and brought closer to a large table. It gleamed like black stone and Maya guessed it was a piece of rock fashioned into a table. Probably obsidian. Not an extravagance for a god who lived this far beneath the surface of the earth.

Around the table sat four people. A stranger who looked at Maya as if she was nothing more than a filthy cockroach, Lord Yama and Nik.

And Kas.

Maya eyes widened as she took in the sight of them all sitting so still at the stone table. They didn't even look like they were breathing.

Only the odious man, a pink scar running from the corner of his lip to his temple, seemed able to move. Just Maya's luck the creep would be the one responsible for taking over Patala.

When he gave Maya a cold smile, his scar crinkled and Maya's stomach tightened.

"The Hand of Kali. Welcome." He didn't look welcoming.

Maya just stared at him, the dagger still pressing a little too close for comfort into her neck. Her chin remained slightly raised, making it obvious to everyone at the table that she was hurt. Nik's eyes narrowed while Yama's darkened, both not thrilled to see Maya in their midst. She wasn't sure if they were angry at the treatment she was receiving or, at her for being present.

Her attention moved to Kas, who watched her in a similar manner, a combination of concern and annoyance.

The demon in charge raised a hand and Maya was shoved forward. The knife remained where it was, only now the demon used a little less pressure, allowing Maya to straighten her neck.

"Are you alone?" asked the scarred demon.

Maya nodded, feeling the point of the knife cut into her skin again. She aimed a short nod in the direction of her captor. "Is this really necessary? I'm not going to use my fire." Not just yet.

He flashed a set of very white teeth at Maya, and she suppressed a shudder. "I don't believe I can trust you, Maya Rao. Your elusiveness has cost us a lot of time. But now that you are here, things will be much easier."

"What are you talking about?" Maya asked, trying hard to keep her voice even and unaffected. She suspected he already knew she was very much invested in the health of Nikhil and his father, but she certainly didn't want to appear the frightened female. "What exactly do you want?"

He shifted forward on his chair and glanced at Kas who sat completely still beside him. Kas glanced at him, his expression serene, as if he wasn't really being held hostage. Nik, on the other side of the demon, did appear affected. His eyes were wide, as he directed his gaze quickly at Kas and the demon then looked back at Maya.

She knew he was trying to tell her something, but she just couldn't figure out what it was. It must have been important for Nik to take such a risk but thankfully nobody noticed. The demon's attention lay with Maya and Kas.

Then he sat back and sighed. "This has been an eventful exercise."

"Who are you anyway?" asked Maya, failing to hide the bite in her voice. "What exactly are you hoping to achieve?"

"I'm Gopal. And, hoping is not the word I would use." He laughed. "We have achieved our goal. Yama has been removed from his role as god of the underworld. He no longer rules."

"So, what? Do you intend to take his place?"

"If not me, then someone else will." He said.

A soft grunt emanated from beside Nik and Maya glanced over to see an infuriated Yama, struggling so hard against the magic that held him that he looked about to burst a blood vessel.

Gopal sighed. "My Lord, there is no point in struggling. You will only be frustrated. The magic is stronger than you."

Maya snorted. "Magic stronger than a god. I doubt that very much."

"Of course you would, human. Magic can be stronger than a god, especially when it uses that gods own power against him," he snapped. Then he paled. Too late; he'd given away the workings of the magic binding his hostages.

He cleared his throat and got to his feet, flicking his fingers at the demon holding Maya. "Take her to the dungeons. Them too." He pointed at Nik and Kas, and a group of demons moved closer, appearing almost like magic from behind Maya. Gopal's wave of a hand must have done something to the magic because Kas and Nik were able to stand and walk, or stumble, as the demons shoved them toward the door.

Maya glanced at Nik, and didn't miss the furious look on his face. Again, he stared deliberately at Kas and Maya wondered what was wrong with him. Did Kas need her help? Was he hurt where she couldn't see the injury? What was Nik trying to tell her?

As the demon guards closed in to remove the two younger men, Yama began to struggle again. And Gopal nodded his head.

One of the demons took that as a go-ahead to hit Yama on the back of the head using a short, heavy club. It looked like a police baton, only shaped like an aubergine. Despite its odd look, it managed to render the god unconscious.

Maya didn't have much of a chance to study Yama's condition. She was hauled away after Nik and Kas, stumbling along as the demons shoved her forward. Despite her curiosity, she was beginning to tire. Where was Chayya and why hadn't she returned?

Maya paid close attention as the demons led her through the corridors and down two levels into the palace's jail. It was unusually small and unusually clean. Constructed of stone blocks, the cells populated less than one-tenth of the floor area of the palace, comprising of only a dozen small cells. Either people behaved themselves very well in Patala, or Yama dealt with his criminals in a much more permanent fashion; one that didn't require imprisonment.

Nik, Kas and Maya were shoved inside the first cell, and hearing the door slam shut behind her made Maya feel a little hopeless. The guys sank onto the wooden seats beside the door, Kas looking exhausted, Nik's expression still furious and still glaring at the demon king.

"Nik?" asked Maya as she put a hand to her neck to assess the damage. "Are you okay?"

He finally pulled his eyes back to Maya's face but it seemed Gopal hadn't fully removed the spell and Nik was still struggling to talk.

Maya looked at Kas. "What did that oaf do to you?"

Kas shook his head, a defeated expression on his face. "He just roughed us up a little. Nothing too serious."

"Why can't Nik talk?" Maya eyed him. It seemed odd that he was able to speak but not Nik, and from the bulging veins in Nik's temple, the demigod was too pleased about it either.

"The magic may take a while to fade." Kas leaned forward, paused a moment as if taking his time to regain his equilibrium. Then he pushed himself slowly to his feet. He studied Nik for a moment, then took the few steps to where Maya sat on a low cot.

Sinking onto the padded mattress beside her, Kas shifted

close. Maya's eyes narrowed as she studied the demon king's face. He seemed relaxed, and was getting a little too close for comfort.

But she didn't react. Not until she knew what he was up to. His behavior seemed suspicious, a little skittish. Maybe he thought she was part of this whole endeavor to overthrow Yama.

"What's going on, Kas?" Maya asked softly. Across the room Nik was shaking his head slowly, glaring at Kas. Maya's heart gave a tiny jump. Nik was able to move his head now.

That must be a good sign.

Kas sighed beside her, bringing her attention back to him. "They've taken over Patala, Yama is out of commission, and we are imprisoned."

Maya snorted. "Tell me something I don't know." She shook her head. "Why? What could they possibly hope to achieve?"

"Controlling Patala is a huge thing, Maya. Dethroning Yama is even bigger." Kas paused, as if he needed the air in his lungs in order to speak. He shifted again, his right hand remaining at his side, hidden from view. His fist was clenched and Maya empathized as he tried to hide his frustrations from her.

That clenched fist said a lot about his mental state. Perhaps this whole event was as upsetting to him as it looked to be to Nik.

When Maya glanced up at Nik she stiffened. His expression was now calm and even, no bulging veins, no frustration, no glaring.

What the heck is going on here?

"Nik?" Maya asked, rising slowly to go to him. "Are you okay?"

Kas held on to her arm and pulled her back to the mattress. "You'd better stay put. The last thing we need is for the guards to come barging in here and put us back into that stupid trance." Kas jerked his chin in Nik's direction. "He's finally freed, so don't get him bound again."

Maya's gazed shifted to Nik. "Are you okay?"

Nik nodded, although his expression was dark. He wasn't usually this terse when he spoke to her and Maya assumed it had a lot to do with the upheaval in the palace. Not every day does one's father get ousted.

He cleared his throat. "I'm fine. Now."

Maya nodded, not entirely sure what she should say, and a little uncomfortable with Kas witnessing their reunion. "So where to from here?" she asked, eager to find a way out.

Kas shrugged. "We behave. We've been lucky so far, haven't we Nik?" he asked Nik a little too pointedly. Maya studied his face but his expression remained neutral and unaffected.

Nik merely nodded.

"You guys do realize this is bad, right?"

"Of course, we do." Kas was a little too calm for Maya's liking.

"But, Lord Yama isn't able to do his job. I don't see how you can be so calm." Maya pointed a finger at the ceiling. "We have to do something."

Kas just looked at her as if was getting a little ahead of herself. As if this was too big to tackle. But Maya wasn't afraid of too big. They had to do something soon.

Or it was going to get a little crowded upstairs.

CHAPTER 36

The silence hung in the air, strained and bearing a hint of a threat. From Nik's tight expression, Maya sensed something else was going on, but she still wasn't keen on asking questions in front of Kas.

Kas was still sort of the bad guy. Technically.

She still had no idea what had happened to him when Nik brought him here from Ravana's dungeon.

Ravana?

Her hands were slowly going numb, the ropes bound so tight they were cutting off the circulation. Maya sent waves of fire to the surface of her skin, trying hard to burn the ropes off.

But nothing happened.

She kept at it until Kas said, "Don't waste your time. The ropes are warded. . . . Probably."

Maya glared at him, angry that he was probably right.

But sat forward and her sudden movement made Nik flinch. She frowned but continued. "Is this Ravana's doing?"

Nik laughed and Kas joined, the sounds clashing in both tone and level of amusement.

Odd.

Kas cleared his throat. "No. It's not Ravana's doing."

"Then who?" Maya asked, turning on him. "You sound very sure that it isn't Ravana. What do you know that you aren't telling me?"

Kas stared at her for a few seconds, although the moment seemed to stretch for eons. Then he shifted his gaze to Nik. From their expression, Maya guessed they exchanged silent words, unsaid meanings, and then Nik cleared his throat.

"We've told you everything, Maya. All we know is what Gopal has already told us." There was something strange about Nik's voice, about the way he looked at Maya. Something Maya just couldn't put a finger on. She inhaled, intending to interrogate him further, but a noise at the door drew her attention.

A demon guard stood outside, visible through the bars on the small window set in the door. Metal grated as he turned a key into the lock and then metal squealed as he pushed it open. Another demon stood behind him, bearing a tray of food, and Maya's eyes narrowed. Fragrant steaming rice, curried meat and vegetables, fried spicy snacks. Such a spread for prisoners?

The first guard entered and pointed an arrow at Nik's neck. Nik slid off his chair and walked to the opposite wall, taking the hint well enough. The second demon set the tray of plates and drinks onto the table and was slowly backing out when Maya let out a cry.

She bent over, hissing as if in pain, and swallowed her surprise when Kas shifted away from her. She would have expected him to check on her first, given she'd thought they were somewhat friendly, if not friends. But he stood away from her.

She lifted her chin, stiffening as the demon hovered before her, holding his spear in Nik's direction, looking from Maya, to Nik, to Kas, unable to decide what to do.

"Check her, you imbecile. Something must be wrong." Nik was yelling but the demon didn't budge.

He seemed to be waiting for something.

"Why are you waiting?" Kas shouted. The guard jumped. "See if she needs help."

Only then did the demon come closer to check on Maya. And though she wondered why he'd obeyed Kas, Maya had other things on her mind.

The demon bent over her, his hand closing over her shoulder as if he meant to straighten her. She did straighten. But instead of revealing the reason for her pain, she send a blast of fire straight into his face.

Using her mouth.

He'd thought her bound hands would save him.

Too bad.

The demon grabbed his face, slapping at his skin as he tried to put the fire out. Maya didn't let him succeed. Instead she sent another blast of fire at him, this time catching him in the upper chest. His hands, bent in front of him as he slapped at the fire on his face, were now also alight and he began to scream.

Maya gave an annoyed sigh, sent another fireball at him, and put him out of his misery. Killing demons was one thing, but she wasn't cut out to torture people.

While the guard disintegrated, Maya rushed at Nik. "Let's get out of here." Nik didn't move. "Nik!" she yelled at him but he avoided her eyes.

She was about to scream at him when he said, "Just calm down Maya. Things are not what they seem. Things and people."

"What are you talking about?" she hissed. "We need to get out of here. Use your magic and take us home."

Maya found she was almost pleading with him. But a small part of her sensed that her efforts were futile.

"He can't. The cells are warded too." Kas's voice broke through Maya's concentration.

"How the hell do you know that?" She looked at him over her shoulder.

He shrugged. "It's logical."

Maya turned back to Nik. "I don't have enough power, Maya. Not to break these wards."

Her stomach clenched with fear and Maya looked back at Kas. "Can't you help? Put your power together with Nik's and help us get out of here." Her voice held an edge that she'd tried and failed to hide. She was slowly losing patience with the both of them.

"Don't waste your breath on him. He's the last person who would help us," said Nik, his tone a little too harsh.

Maya turned to face him, worried when darkness shadowed his eyes and the almost palpable hatred in his expression, as he stared at Kas over her shoulder.

"Why won't he help us?" she asked.

Even as the words left her mouth, pain stabbed into the muscles of her back. She gasped, shifting to look behind her, unable to touch the area with her bound hands.

She caught a flash of metal, a sword or knife. Then someone appeared in front of her.

Arms wrapped around her and the room went black

Maya opened her eyes gradually. The room buzzed with voices and movement, but she paid little attention as the pain in her back held her in limbo. She could still feel the blade inside her flesh so her moments of unconsciousness had not been used to her advantage.

She groaned and tried to turn, the softness of the mattress beneath her only making her hurt more. "Don't move, honey." Her mom's voice was soft in her ear.

Fabric rustled and Chayya knelt before her. "Maya. We have attempted to remove the blade but it has an unusual tip which is making it a little difficult."

"Unusual?" asked Maya, taking a short painful breath. Despite the strong temptation, she refrained from sending any fire toward the wound for fear of sealing the flesh round the blade.

"We've done a makeshift x-ray." Her father's voice filtered over her shoulder. "The blade has a barbed tip. It's a stiletto type weapon, the tip turning in three places like a fishhook. The edges are sharp. So in essence three tiny knives sliced their way into your body, and now we won't be able to take them out unless you undergo surgery."

"Just fabulous," grumbled Maya.

Dev laughed, and so did Chayya, but Maya didn't see anything amusing about her situation. "There's too much at stake right now for me to be lounging around. Isn't there another way to get the knife out?"

"There is one thing you could try, but there is no guarantee it will succeed."

"At this point I'd do anything as long as it gets me on my feet asap," said Maya dryly.

Chayya sank to her knees again so Maya, with her head on her pillow, could look directly into her eyes. "Now, tell me. Are you able to focus your fire, in a fine-tuned manner?"

Maya frowned. "Like, aiming it at specific areas?"

Chayya nodded. "Very specific, very small areas?"

"I think so," said Maya, honing in on what Chayya was getting at. "You want me to use my fire to melt the knife?"

The goddess nodded. "Just enough to lump the metal together and make it easier to remove."

"Maya, it's a possibility," said her dad, coming round to kneel beside Chayya. "It may not work. So give it all you got, but don't be disappointed if it doesn't work."

Maya sighed. "Yes, Dad." The worry in his voice made her need to reassure him that she was strong enough to deal with the task.

Then she turned her gaze to Chayya. "What do I do?" she asked the goddess. Usually it was *Kali* giving her advice on how to heal herself.

"First, feel your way around the knife. Feel the weight and the density of it."

"Almost like doing an x-ray with my mind?"

Chayya nodded. "Yes. From what your father has explained in terms of the process, it is very much like that. Although you would get a mental feel for it rather than an image."

"Okay, let me try."

Maya let the room fade away and concentrated on her body, pulling power from her solar plexus. The energy tingled mildly, then fell flat. With a sigh Maya tried again.

This time she accessed all her chakras, forehead, neck, solar plexus, until she had them all open and emitting energy. She pulled at the vibrations, using them to power her journey further into her body until she reached her back.

"It's so strange," she whispered. "I can feel the knife, and almost see it at the same time."

"It is working." Chayya sounded satisfied.

Maya didn't respond. She continued to concentrate, to feel her way around the shape of the metal, defining where flesh ended and weapon began. At last she said, "Now what do I do?"

"Concentrate your fire on the metal and try to smooth out each of the three hooks. Try to straighten them so the knife will slide out easily." Chayya's voice was soothing, a much needed calm when Maya was almost shivering with nerves.

Maya swallowed and followed the instructions, focusing heat and warming the metal near the point. She could feel her flesh tingle and begin to heat up, sensing the hot knife against it. She had to work fast, or risk searing her flesh to the metal itself.

Maya aimed her heat and used the energy from her chakras to coax the curve of metal until it began to straighten. It took longer than she expected, more because she was afraid of hurting herself. It was the strangest feeling, being able to sense her own organs within her body.

But in the end, she'd managed to straighten all three prongs lying them flat in line with the blade of the knife. With a whisper of breath, she released the energy, and relaxed.

"You can take it out now," she said softly.

Behind her, Maya's mom took hold of the handle and began to pull gently. The blade shifted, sending sparks of agony through Maya's body, but she absorbed the pain, breathed through it as her mom shifted the knife and continued to pull on it.

At last the knife slipped out, and Dev moved to stand. "Not long now, Maya. We just need to clean the wound and stitch it up."

Maya coughed and cleared her throat. "Don't worry about it dad. I've got it covered." She grabbed for his wrist, ignored his surprised frown and held on as she drew her energy and focused on the wound.

Now that the knife was no longer there, Maya could heal the wound, close the blood vessels, seal the raw edges.

Almost done.

Perspiration dripped along the side of her face. And then, her mom's gasp of surprise made her smile.

At last, she let go of her dad's hand and took a deep breath. Thank goodness it no longer hurt so badly.

Maya cleared her throat again and moved to sit up.

"Maya, it's too soon for you to be moving around like this," said her dad, sounding annoyed.

Leela laughed. "From the looks of this it's definitely not too soon." Seems she was in a little bit of a shock.

Dev raised his eyebrows and moved around the bed to get a look at Maya's back. The silence told her everything.

"Okay, then," he said, surprised and impressed at the same time.

"Right. Stop moving around while I clean you up." Her mom's instruction stilled her movements and she only got to her feet when she received a soft pat to her shoulder.

"I should get changed," Maya said, her voice a little scratchy.

Leela shifted, standing in front of Maya with magical swiftness. "Don't you think you need to get some rest before you go charging off into the sunset?"

Maya opened her mouth to respond, but Chayya cut her off. "I can assure you that Maya does not need as much rest as most humans."

"Even when she's been injured and lost a lot of blood," asked

Leela, as she faced the goddess. Maya's eyebrows shot up as she watched mom argue with a goddess. The woman had brass ones.

Maya cleared her throat. "Mom, seriously. I'm fine. I've been learning to heal myself and I'm pretty good at it right now. Don't worry about me."

As soon as Maya spoke the words she knew they were the wrong ones. Her mom stiffened and drew herself straighter. "Fine. As long as you know what you're doing."

She rubbed her bloodied fingers down the front of her jumper and spun on her heel, leaving the room before Maya could say another word.

Maya let out a long sigh.

"I'll talk to her honey." Her dad's voice came from behind her. She turned to see him busy cleaning up the remnants of the first-aid kit. "Don't worry about her. She has to learn to deal with things."

"I know. But it must be hard for her. I'm her kid."

"Yes. You're her kid," said her dad. Then he leaned closer. "And you're also not her kid."

CHAPTER 38

I'm not her kid, thought Maya as she struggled to get out of her blood-drenched clothing.

There was no time for a shower, not in *her* mind anyway. Her mom would probably disagree, though. Maya threw her ruined jacket and shirt on the tiles and changed into fresh, virtually identical, clothing.

At least she didn't take long to decide what to wear.

She made a face as she tied her hair back with an elastic band, the strands were smeared with blood, sticky and matted in places. But she just dragged her fingers through her hair and considered the job well done.

A minute later, she was standing in her empty bedroom, wondering what it was she was supposed to be doing. All thoughts had fled from her mind, as if she couldn't even handle one thought.

And she knew why.

She was so off balance that she could hardly find it amusing.

"Geez," said Joss from the open doorway. "Did your folks just tell you you're adopted or something?" She had that look in her eye, the one she got when she was trying to be funny, but knew she was failing.

"Huh?" asked Maya, turning to her friend as she walked into the room. She could barely string two thoughts together and now Joss was trying to force her to actually use her brain?

"That look on your face. What's wrong?"

Maya pursed her lips, reluctant to say. She felt foolish enough. "Nothing, really." She shrugged. "Well, nothing that matters a whole hell of a lot right now."

"It matters if it's bugging you." Joss sank onto the bed, giving the bloodstains smeared across the coverlet a raised eyebrow. Then she focused her attention back onto Maya. Which usually didn't bode well.

"Even if it's bugging me, I can deal until this mayhem is over."

"Yeah, I heard." Her tone was dry and bore an undertone that rang with steel. "But, none of us know what's about to happen, right? The poop's hitting the fan big-time all around us." She waved her hands in the air around her head. "Nothing is predictable right now, so you probably should get things off your chest if you need to."

"Gosh, spread the doom and gloom, why don't you," Maya mumbled and sank onto the mattress beside Joss, neatly avoiding the dried remains of blood. She gave a heavy sigh and studied her hands. "It just hit me."

"What hit you?"

"I'm not their child."

"What the frick are you on about?" Joss scowled.

She shifted her gaze from her threaded fingers to Joss's big blue eyes. "I'm not really their child. They raised me yes, birthed me, yes. But, they knew from the start that I was someone else." Maya sighed and her shoulders drooped. "That still sounds so weird to me."

"I know what you mean." Joss nudged her. "But you can't think that way. Even though this is a second life for you, it's more your life to you than the last one will ever be. Unless you end up going back to experience it again first hand. Or is that second hand?"

Joss frowned as she looked up at the ceiling, thought about it for a second, then gave up.

With a wave of her hand, she continued, "Anyway, what I'm trying to say is, your mom gave birth to you, loved you, raised you, worried about you. I believe, for your parents, you are first their child, and second Mother Radha."

Maya stared at her friend. She laughed softly and gave a short shake of her head. "I cannot believe you just hit the nail right on the head the first time."

Joss had managed to put into words the very thing that had been bothering Maya. She had to admit that she'd been bugged about it for a while now.

"I'm smart that way." Joss snickered.

Maya smiled. "Thanks."

"Happy to help." Joss grinned then patted Maya on the shoulder. "Now, please get your butt downstairs. There have been developments."

"Developments? What developments?"

But, Joss refused to answer, just shooing her downstairs until they entered the living room where the flatscreen was on, the sound low.

Her parents and Chayya sat, eyes trained on the screen, expressions all sombre.

"What's wrong?" asked Maya, her gaze flitting from face to face, feeling her stomach drop.

Joss took her gently by the shoulders, turned her to face the television, and pressed down until Maya was forced to drop into the seat beneath her.

And then she understood why Joss had made her sit.

Poop. And fans.

A major news network covered what they claimed to be the story of the millennium. According to statistics, there are at least one hundred deaths per minute, worldwide. As of five hours ago, not a single death had been recorded worldwide. Scientists, reporters, medical personnel and government officials were in a frenzy.

Maya blinked.

"Never before seen phenomenon."

"Unprecedented drop in mortality rates."

"Hospitals record lowest patient numbers in history."

"Is this Armageddon?"

The silence in the room was deafening.

Maya inhaled slowly, trying to tame the wild beat of her heart before she expressed her shock, but her dad didn't give her the chance to speak.

"It's much worse than just this." He pointed at the screen.

"How can it even be any worse?" Maya whispered, sure she didn't want to know the answer.

"We've been getting reports from KALIMA. Worldwide. Mortally injured people are not dying."

Maya's eyes widened. But she didn't speak. How could she? He was talking about the undead. Zombies. She listened to his voice through the buzz in her ears.

"Gunshot wounds, car crashes, you name it. Surgical deaths where the patients didn't flatline."

"Dad?" asked Maya, her voice flat.

"Yes, Maya," he responded a little distracted by the beeping of his phone.

"Permission to use foul language."

"Not in front of the goddess," he said before taking the call, his expression barely changing.

Joss snorted and Maya glanced at said goddess whose eyes were focused on the screen. That was a sight Maya had to get her head around as well. So called mythical god face to face with modern technology. In the goddesses favor, she didn't seem in the least awed.

Chayya looked up at the same time, as if she sensed Maya's need to get things moving.

She shifted in her seat and said, "What is it, Maya?"

"Did you see anyone when you came for me?" Maya asked, replaying the events leading up to the knife plunging into her body. "I didn't see who stabbed me, and I was hoping you got a glimpse of him." Maya mentally crossed her fingers.

Chayya shook her head. "I got in and out very fast. I saw Nik and Kas. And another demon who appeared to be a guard. But, no, I did not see who stabbed you." Chayya's expression was sad, as if she'd failed somehow.

And Maya had to admit she was disappointed. She mentally uncrossed her fingers wondering why she bothered.

"It was either the demon or it was Kas." Maya didn't like her options.

"And let me guess. You're going to go with the demon. Aren't you?" asked Joss, folding her arms, not bothering to hide her annoyance. She'd never been a fan of Kas.

"At least give him the benefit of the doubt."

"Like hell, I will. He freaking stabbed you for God's sake, Maya." Joss's eyes widened and she glanced at the goddess sitting beside her. "I'm sorry."

Across from them, Maya's mom hid a grin.

"No need to apologize, child."

Joss blushed and gave Chayya a grateful smile. But nothing was able to bring a smile to Maya's face. Right now, the world was going to hell, and it's very possible that Kas had plunged that knife into her back. Something she did not want to consider because she'd trusted him.

And because she'd seen him in his previous life, seen the boy he'd been, seen the tortured young man, emotionally manipulated by the demon Bana.

But, there was one thing Maya did recall, a memory that made her blood go cold.

I will show them what it means to cross me.

CHAPTER 39

An hour later, Maya still sat in the living room. The TV was turned down but Maya kept an eye on the scrolling banner at the bottom of the screen.

New reports were coming on every few minutes and Maya wondered when the reporters would reach their saturation point.

Very soon, people will get over the mystical aspect of no death. And when they do they will start to panic.

Chayya had left a while ago to speak to the other gods, to get a better idea of what they knew. The goddess had insisted that the more information they had the better.

She'd been right, of course.

Maya's parents had been busy, on the phone with the other agents at KALIMA. Even Joss had been roped in to handle calls coming through the US call-centre. Dev's study was a hive of activity, and Maya was currently hiding out in the lounge, trying hard not to get up and pace.

Footsteps tapped along the hall outside the living room, drawing Maya's attention to the doorway, and when she turned around and her mom walked in with a glass of milk and a plate of baked goodies, Maya smiled.

Leela sat slowly beside Maya and handed her the glass, placing a plate of ginger cookies on Maya's lap.

"You should probably eat something before you go."

"I'm sorry about before." The words popped out of her mouth before she'd even decided to say it.

"It's okay honey. I'm just . . . I don't know. You'd think I'd be used to it by now, but clearly I'm not."

"Mom?"

Leela dragged her eyes away from the tv to meet Maya's eyes

"I'm sorry. I didn't mean to push you away."

Tears filmed Leela's eyes and she sniffed. "It's okay. I know you didn't mean that. It's just harder for me when I see you hurt or in pain."

Maya sighed. "You know, I used to wonder if you preferred Mother Radha to Maya."

Leela gasped softly at Maya's sudden admission. Her mouth formed a small 'o'

"I know I was wrong to believe that, but I did."

"Why would you even think that?"

"Because of the way you used to talk about her before I found out what I am."

Leela smiled. "We do tend to ramble when it comes to the Mother."

Maya laughed. "I guess I was a little jealous and more than a little confused."

"Of course, Maya. It's not going to be easy reconciling your old life with your new, especially when you cannot recall any of it. It will take time."

Maya tilted her chin at the tv. "Not if those creeps can help it. The world will be overrun with undead and overpopulated soon enough. Who knows what will happen if we can't fix this."

Her mom sighed, staring at the screen. A pensive air settled around her and Maya frowned

Then Leela cleared her throat. "It certainly has the potential to get worse. Unrest, rioting, unemployment, theft. If we're lucky, the authorities will be able to retain control long enough for us to find a way around this mess."

"If we are lucky," said Chayya from the doorway.

They both turned to face the goddess and as she entered, Maya set her milk and cookies on the table. Somehow food wasn't the least bit appealing.

"I'm afraid I do not come bearing any new information. What the gods have discovered is what we know already. They do have a few suspects in terms of who wants Yama's throne."

Maya and her mother shared a smile at Chayya's mention of the word 'suspects'

"It could be Ravana," offered Maya.

"Yes. He is on Lord Shiva's list. Bana is another option." Chayya paused, giving Maya an odd look.

"They suspect Kas as well?" she asked.

"Lord Shiva prefers to be thorough."

Maya nodded, her neck wooden. "And Kas as done little to redeem himself."

Chayya remained silent. "So only three names? Can we do anything to help track them all down? We know Kas is in Patala. Maybe if we find Ravana and Bana then we could rule them out?"

Chayya nodded. "Lord Shiva has sent out emissaries to all parts of the world. We will soon ascertain where the demon kings are."

"In the meantime, I'd rather not be sitting and waiting. What can we do in case its any one of them?"

Chayya inclined her head. "We expected you to ask just that question."

Maya wondered if she was that predictable but she kept her mouth shut. "Where do we start?"

"Lord Shiva believes that the most likely candidate is Naraka-sura. Are you familiar with the tale?"

"Only briefly," admitted Maya, ignoring her mom's admonishing glare. She should have known it well enough by now having heard it enough times.

Chayya smiled. "The short version is that Narakasura can only be killed by his mother Bhumi, the goddess of the earth."

"Can we find her?" asked Maya, then she stiffened at the strange expression on her mom's face. She looked uncomfortable and worried, but Maya decided it was best to give her space. She'd talk about whatever bugged her soon enough. "And why are we thinking of killing him?"

The goddess shook her head sadly. "I am afraid we have previous experience with Narakasura. He is relentless, and filled with a deep hatred. He will stop at nothing to get what he wants. And to answer your other question, Bhumi is in another reincarnation. We will need to find her and attempt to persuade her to help us end his life. It must be at her hand that he dies or he will come back."

Maya shivered. "Even if she believes us when we find her, what mother would agree to kill her own child?"

Maya glanced at her mom, taking in her pale skin. She looked positively sick.

"Mom? Are you okay?"

Leela nodded, her expression clearing as she pasted a smile on her face.

Looks like her mom wasn't ready to talk, so Maya asked, "How long will they take? I feel like all this waiting is only wasting our time. Nik and Lord Yama are still being held hostage. Kas could be our bad guy, and we are killing time waiting."

"What if you go back to Nik's past? Maybe when he arrived in Patala after leaving you and Claudia in Prague?" offered her mom.

Maya blinked. That was a good idea and a very weird one at that. "Um . . . I could do that but I'm not sure I really want to."

"Why not?" Leela frowned, then paused for a second as she thought about it. Then her eyes widened. "Oh. I see your point."

Maya nodded. Not even her mom would want to spend time in her dad's mind.

"Even if you wanted, to you would be unable to," said Chayya softly.

"Why?" asked Maya.

"Nikhil is the son of Lord Yama. He is a god, even if he is only genetically half. No god can be invaded by another being."

"Oh." Maya had never been more relieved in her life.

"What about if you try to go back in Narakasura's past?" Mom again, her voice holding an edge of worry. "That way you could find out once and for all if he is behind the whole thing." Her mom nodded, as if she thought her own idea was an excellent one.

And Maya couldn't agree more.

CHAPTER 40

Maya readied herself, taking a seat on the wide armed single sofa that didn't have a view of the TV. The last report had flashed a picture of a woman, burned in a car crash, being taken to hospital very much alive and in horrific pain. The newscaster claimed that scenes where people are in such agony were the hardest to bear, and that sometimes living wasn't the best option.

Maya couldn't believe she actually got away with saying that on live TV but it was soon becoming clear that the problem was affecting the way people thought about death. Right now, it was the last thing Maya wanted to see.

Chayya watched over her as she settled into the cushions and closed her eyes. The only time she'd done this before was with Kali's guidance, and with an event she'd physically attended.

A voice whispered, "Keep your thoughts focused on Naraka-sura. Find a point in time in which you were with him, then move back along the timeline."

Maya blinked and looked around. "What is it, honey?" asked Leela, her brow furrowed as Maya lifted her head and scanned the room.

Kali.

Maya could have sworn that was the voice in her head, but the goddess wasn't around.

Shaking her head, Maya relaxed again and closed her eyes. Her thoughts drifted back to seeing Kas at the table with Nik and Yama. She inhaled slowly, then let the breath out through her mouth.

Calm filtered through her as she settled on Kas, allowing her mind to flow into his consciousness.

And she gasped.

She didn't need to go back in time to figure out who had brought about the downfall of Patala. It was all there in Kas's head.

Look at her, he thought, his emotions filled with a latent anger. *She comes in here as if she is capable of saving Yama and his son. What a waste that she sides with them.*

Maya blinked, the shock of Kas's inner voice throwing her out of his thoughts for a moment. She had to start again, concentrate to re-enter his mind.

Bana was right. I should have worked harder to convince her to join me. Now that would have been a victory, having the Hand of Kali on my team.

Maya swallowed her shock. So it is Kas. He masterminded the whole thing. And he'd been the villain all along. Something she'd refused to accept.

Joss was going to have a field day with this information.

Priya was right, but she was still an infatuated female. Pity. Kas's thoughts focused on Priya's death, images of the abandoned shack flitting through his head. He must have sent people to check up on the Rakshasi and found the empty hovel. *She allowed her emotions to cloud her judgment. I gave her a second chance, but she used it for petty revenge against this one. Poor stupid, Priya. She was so far gone she didn't even realize what she'd been doing chasing and killing all those girls. That she'd made them into her own personal demon horde didn't make up for the selfishness of her actions. All she'd wanted was to get back at Maya, however indirectly.*

Wow, was that what Priya had been up to? Maya was horrified.

Now, she wished she was there to kill her again. All those girls Maya had killed were the ones that had gone missing. Maya shuddered and her stomach did a sickening somersault. In the end she'd killed them instead of saving them, and even the thought that they may have been too far gone, having been turned into demons and all, didn't make her feel any better.

Right now, all she wanted to do was to put her hands around Narakasura's neck and squeeze the freaking life out of him.

Unfortunately, a sojourn in the demon king's mind would prove useful, so Maya forced herself to listen to his thoughts again.

Through his eyes she could see herself looking a little shaken up, the demon holding tightly to her hands. She glanced at Nik and her skin went pale, her eyes filling with worry. Maya stiffened. Had her face always been so open for anyone to read? Her affection for Nik was so obvious to Kas but she had to wonder if it was because he knew her better than most people.

Narakasura knew her too well. Not a good thing.

How had she misjudged him so badly? She'd given him the benefit of the doubt over and over again. Was it because of her visit to his past, and the knowledge of what he'd gone through at Bana's hands? Had all of that contributed to Maya feeling sorry for him, making excuses for him?

She shook the thoughts off and paid attention as Gopal looked at Kas. Now it made sense what he'd been waiting for. A sign from the demon king, the okay to take them to the dungeons. Maya waited with the utmost patience as she followed Narakasura through the next few minutes, despising every second that she had to spend in his head.

Inside the cell he gave Nik a glare. *You better watch yourself, or she's a goner.*

Maya frowned. Those thoughts belonged to Kas, so why did Nik look so strained. He couldn't have heard the demon's words.

Then, the muscles in Kas's fingers tightened. He was holding something within his hand, but since he wasn't looking down, Maya couldn't tell what it was. All she had to go on was the sense of utter confidence Kas had that Nik would not make a move.

The demon king watched Maya walk toward the cot and followed her. She recalled paying little attention to his movements, and regretted it now. She'd ignored anything suspicious because she'd wanted to trust him.

Just look at her. So trusting. So blind. She doesn't see that eventually they will use her too. That all she is to them is a means to an end.

A rush of sadness and empathy ran through Kas, its strength and genuineness a real surprise. He really did believe that Maya was merely a pawn, manipulated by everyone around her.

Her stomach tightened at the thought. And then she shoved it away, locking it in a dark corner of her mind. Right now was not the time to be contemplating such thoughts. Right now she needed to glean as much as she could from the demon king's mind.

His gaze shifted. From Nik to his lap then back to Nik again.

No. Not his lap.

His right hand that lay on the cot beside his lap.

The knife held within his palm, hidden from Maya by the rise of his thigh.

Maya stiffened and the link was broken. She went rushing back into her own body and sat up with a gasp. Putting a hand to her chest, she forced herself to take a deep breath.

"What happened, Maya?" asked her mom, panic lacing her voice.

"It was Kas." Maya met her gaze, feeling a little faint and a whole lot stupid. "It was Kas who tried to kill me."

CHAPTER 41

"IF IT'S THE last thing I do, I'm going to kill him." Never before had such unadulterated, all-encompassing fury filled Maya's soul. Kas's betrayal had hit her full in the gut, and in the heart. How had her judgement been so wrong?

"Perhaps it is best you think along the line of arresting him?" suggested Chayya. When Maya looked up at the goddess with a frown, she continued. "The Hand of Kali was never meant to be an executioner."

Maya was silent for a while. Chayya had a good point. Maya was probably not the best person to be judge, jury and executioner, especially when her own judgment had been seriously skewed to begin with.

She'd trusted him.

Maybe the goddess suspected that Maya needed more convincing, because she cleared her throat. "Lord Shiva would appreciate the opportunity to speak directly with his devotee."

It hadn't been necessary for Chayya to mention Lord Shiva, but his name made Maya realize that all this nonsense could be laid at his feet. "He gave Narakasura that boon right? To never die except by his mother's hand?"

Chayya nodded while Maya's mom's face appeared shadowed, strained.

"One would expect that he'd have gotten the message by now that life and destiny have a way of getting around such boons."

"Yeah. Especially when Lord Shiva himself agrees with life and destiny."

The goddess laughed softly. "Which is why Lord Shiva would prefer to discuss this directly with Narakasura. But, of course, if you were unable to summon him to Mt Kailas, or if the situation so requires it, you have Lord Shiva's permission to end the dominion of Narakasura over Patala and by extension, the rest of the world."

"Kill him, you mean?" asked Maya. Too many words were confusing her tired brain. Chayya merely gave a nod in answer.

"As a last resort, of course. The ideal method of his dispatch would be at the hand of his mother."

Maya shuddered, giving her mom a sad smile. She'd never been more glad to have her mom right at her side during this awful time. Mother's killing their kids, something Maya wished she didn't have to contemplate.

Maya sighed and sank into the cushions behind her, feeling exhaustion take her over. No surprise there, she thought. All the time-travel does take it out of a girl.

She heard her mom ask her if she was okay, heard Chayya assure her it was just time-travel fatigue and that it's probably good for her to rest. A part of Maya wanted to protest, but her vision darkened and she fell asleep

CHAPTER 42

*M*aya opened her eyes to a world of darkness.

But this time it wasn't dense and black and filled with nothing. This darkness was a beautiful, expansive night. She'd never dreamed of the milky way, or of outer space before. Even the words *outer space* made her think Star Trek and Star Wars, not reality.

But here she was, floating weightless, the blazing sun to her right, in a sea of stars and planets and pale dust that swirled around innumerable tiny worlds.

Spectacular.

And spectacularly strange, too. Maya never dreamed of space.

She blinked, finding she was strangely conscious in this dream. If it was a dream. She was more aware than she'd ever been before in a dream.

Light shifted, crashing off something to her right. Maya urged her body to move, expecting it to be like swimming in a thick soup of black. But the lack of gravity had little effect on her movements. Lord Shiva sat in the air before her, his cross-legged pose so familiar, his indigo skin glowing with an angelic light. He floated on nothing, much like Maya, and yet he didn't move either.

He was the god she'd known all her life and yet he was different. Today the tiger's pelt he usually wore around his waist had been replaced with a piece of fabric that looked like it had been ripped straight from the milky way beyond the god's body.

Planets spun and stars twinkled within the silky swathe of material wrapped around Lord Shiva's hips. More aspects of the god seemed to stand out to Maya, as her awareness returned to her only in small drips. Lord Shiva's usually blue-tinged skin was now a deeper navy, sprinkled with stars, the rushing river that often flowed from his moon-bedecked hair was now an ethereal milky way that trailed off around his mountainous shoulder and disappeared into the cosmos.

Even the trident he held was no longer gold. Fashioned from the stars, it was a bright glowing thing that looked like diamonds and moonlight.

The sight of Lord Shiva, so large, so majestic, made Maya feel a little faint. She looked up at the face of the god in his true form. Her awareness heightened and she watched him without a breath. He was the creator, the preserver and the destroyer and yet so many people focus only on the last of his functions.

Seeing him in this form convinced Maya that those acts of destruction were merely the natural cycles of life, the things that symbolically ended a process. He killed darkness with light, but darkness was not dead, merely contained, controlled. He ended life, but it was not permanent. Life returns with reincarnation or rebirth in some form. He killed ignorance with knowledge, but ignorance had an infinite number of forms, so destruction continued for the good of everyone.

Lord Shiva, his aspect so large that Maya had to crane her neck to see his face, opened his eyes. She shivered inwardly, refusing to show how intimidating the experience was. Just when she began to feel the pull of the muscles in her neck, strained from staring up at the god's face, her body shifted and she rose in the air.

She floated higher until she was abreast of the god. Her gratitude was forgotten as soon as she met his gaze. Within each eye an entire universe shimmered and twisted, and within the space of a breath, she knew beyond anything she'd ever known before, that Lord Shiva *was* the universe, he *was* creation, and existence personified.

How strange that an outer-space dream would result in her understanding the complications of Lord Shiva.

Maya swallowed a gasp as Lord Shiva blinked. "Thank you for coming, Maya," he said, his voice deep yet soft.

The god's voice enveloped her, echoing slowly around her ears. She knew that outer space was a vacuum, that gravity was zero and that no sound traveled there. Yet she heard the musical notes of the god's voice in her head.

She hesitated, unsure how to respond. Saying 'My pleasure' certainly didn't seem appropriate, especially since she hadn't been asked. And if it was a dream, it meant she was talking to a figment of her imagination.

On the other hand, if this was real she would be disrespecting Lord Shiva to his face.

She decided to go with the assumption of reality. It was safer.

But, before she could open her mouth to speak, Lord Shiva tilted his head to study her and he said, "Do not be afraid, Maya. I decided to bring you here," he waved a hand at the view around them, "in order to show you the essence of our being."

Maya swallowed hard and nodded, once, twice, before going very still.

Lord Shiva seemed okay with that. He probably dealt with nervous humans on a daily basis. "The universe is who we are, intrinsically." He spoke and again his voice echoed in her head, more real now than a dream. "Even as individuals, we form part of this cosmos, every act we perform, every thought we have, has its effect. Like a pebble in the water, the waves flow out, impacting all it touches. A never ending consequence as each ripple causes more ripples, and they in turn have effects further along the way."

Maya had heard that saying before, but had never thought of it in terms of a universal effect. She'd taken it more figuratively.

"This is a much better depiction of how it works." Lord Shiva flicked a finger and beside him light exploded.

Like a fireworks show, bright white light burst from a single point, expanding until it formed an oval shape. Tiny suns flickered from pinpoints of light, swelling until they looked like fiery planets. They began to spin in a ring, that expanded and contracted until it settled into a full circle. Maya began to suspect what was appearing before her, when more light exploded within the circle and began to form into the shape of a dancing man.

The Nataraja.

The Dance of the Cosmos.

The image of Lord Shiva himself formed within the brilliant circle and as Maya looked closer she gasped in amazement. Each spinning sun was more than just a glowing orb. A universe of suns and planets and stars, that shone blindingly bright, spun along the perimeter of the circle, constantly circumnavigating the Creator.

Maya was in awe.

Within the Nataraja image, Lord Shiva's face and body glowed with the light of a million suns, emanating such power, such emotion that hot tears trickled down her cheeks. All of a sudden, she was overwhelmed.

"The universe is you," said Lord Shiva softly. "And you are the universe."

CHAPTER 43

$\mathcal{M}$aya shifted her gaze, reluctant to look away from the stunning Nataraja for fear that it would disappear. The thought of not being able to look upon it again made her feel inexplicably sad.

Lord Shiva smiled when Maya met his eyes, but he said, "A long time ago there was nothing. None of this existed." He waved a hand around him. "Then one day life just was. And I just was. I am the giver and the taker. Omniscient, omnipresent and omnipotent."

All-seeing, all-present, all powerful. Never before had those words held such power for Maya.

"No churning?" Out before she could stop the words.

Well done, Maya.

The god laughed and a dark star shivered nearby. "No churning. Some myths are truly just metaphors."

"Narakasura's story certainly wasn't." There went her big mouth again.

"Unfortunately not. And we must try to put things right."

Taking that as her cue, Maya asked, "What can I do?"

"You can help me fix my mistake."

"Mistake?"

Lord Shiva nodded sadly. "Narakasura is an errant child. I should have stayed his hand a long time ago, but when a boon is given, a god is meant to keep his word no matter what." He fell silent, as if lost in his memories and Maya waited until he looked back at her again. "He was a deserving disciple. Good at heart. Loving, kind, pure of soul."

"What happened to him?" asked Maya. She'd seen the sweet little boy he had been, and knowing how he'd turned out made it all the more sad.

"Sometimes, no matter how pure of heart one is, it is the way one accepts outside influence that matters. Narakasura's faith was so pure, so true, that I gave him the gift of a long life. The only caveat, which he himself placed, was that he should die by his mother's hand."

"And he thought it would be hard to find a mother who would willingly kill her own child." Maya recalled the very question she'd asked not too long ago.

Lord Shiva nodded, a sad smile on his lips. "He thought he had tricked me well, and perhaps he was smart about it. If he had not been swayed from his path, we would not be here today contemplating taking his life for the second time around."

"And Bana swayed him," said Maya, bitterly.

"Banasura had a big role in swaying Narakasura's faith, and his belief in the people around him. As you have witnessed for yourself."

Maya sighed. "I wish I could have changed it."

"Perhaps that could have helped." Lord Shiva nodded, but then he gave a small shake of his head. "But, sometimes destiny finds a way to put things back onto the true path."

"Then how do we fix it?"

"By ensuring Bhumi kills him, and this time by ensuring his soul is contained so he cannot be reborn."

"So he won't be allowed to be reincarnated?" Maya wondered if gods did this kind of thing often. Reincarnation was meant to be the inevitable next step, unless a soul was sent to Patala or to the Heavens.

"I do not believe he deserves the privilege. He has done great wrong, but sending him to Patala is dangerous. He has cultivated too many negative relationships that it would be like sending him home. It would not amount to punishment."

"So how would we contain his soul?" Maya wanted to ask about Bhumi, but she was a little unsure how to approach the topic.

Lord Shiva held out his fisted hand. He turned it around, palm up, and opened his fingers to reveal a little brass pot with a lid that screwed on. The container was covered in writing and Maya watched as the letters danced, shining, growing larger then fading. A dazzling spectacle of words that Maya didn't understand.

"When he dies, and his soul leaves his body, place it in this container. Once the lid is closed the metal will seal itself and it will no longer be able to be opened. The vessel is indestructible, warded by old magic, so nobody can penetrate the metal to get at the soul."

Maya took the pot from the giant palm, trying not to stare at the lifeline that split his hand down the center and glowed, a deep cavern filled with stars, and slipped it into her jacket pocket. She wondered what had made Kas so special to deserve such a great gift, and one that he eventually disrespected.

As if attuned to her thoughts, Lord Shiva sighed, the gusting breath shifting Maya a few feet backward. She glided to a slow stop as he said, "When people have faith in their gods, their trust and their prayers do not go unheard."

Maya winced. Startled by the accuracy of his words, she glanced up guiltily at the god's face but he didn't appear displeased or angry. Clearly privacy was not an option, so she'd better watch what she thought.

"Many people receive boons, even if it is not given in person. In times gone by, gods would visit their faithful and grant the gift in person, but times have changed and limited our access to the world. Perhaps I was wrong with Narakasura, perhaps I should have chosen better but at the time he was the right choice. Gods grant their boons, then leave the humans to live with that boon, to manage that gift in a way that will justify having received it. Too often they fail. And they fail because humans are fallible. They are not perfect, which is essentially what is so beautiful about them."

Not so beautiful when they abuse the gifts they're given. She winced when she caught the small lift to Lord Shiva's lips. He'd heard.

But the god seemed to care little for Maya's errant thoughts and she assumed he had much bigger things to consider than her inability to control her mind.

"The gods do not interfere with human life and action. They allow things to take their course. And sometimes, even when a person believes they should receive a god's help, they will not, only because destiny has other plans."

Maya squinted at Lord Shiva, trying to figure out if he was talking about abandoning her in Lanka. When he laughed she knew he was.

"I did abandon you, Maya but for a good reason. Redemption comes in many forms. Your interaction with Narakasura has shown me that he does not deserve to be annihilated."

"Annihilated?"

That sounded pretty harsh.

The god inclined his head, his eyebrows hooded, serious. "I can obliterate him from existence if I so wish. His soul will not live on, he will not be destined for another plane. He will just simply cease to be. That would be the ultimate punishment for someone like Narakasura, but I have decided against such a sentence. He has you to thank for that."

"Me?"

"You showed him kindness, friendship. And it stirred something within him. Brought him back to a time when friendship was a true thing. You spared his life in the first instance," Lord Shiva said, pausing while Maya nodded and apologized but he ignored her words and continued, "and because of that simple act, he was able to see that not everyone wanted something from him. That some people were just being kind for the sake of kindness."

"He remembered what it was like before Bana started in on him?" asked Maya, still feeling her fists clench at the memory of the older man's viciously cold face as he'd taunted the young Narakasura. That was tantamount to brainwashing as far as she was concerned.

"Yes, he did remember. And when you ended up in Lanka with him, you gave him a chance at redemption. Both Nikhil and Lord Yama offered him a second chance because you believed in him."

"But he betrayed that trust." Maya found it hard to tamp down the volume of her criticism.

"Yes, indeed he did," said Lord Shiva sadly. He stared off at the extraordinary view, and the moment seemed to stretch for ages. "But his heart did not remain hard. You chipped away at the walls he'd build around his emotions, Maya. And for that he will always be thankful. But do not expect him to show his appreciation. To him, caring is weakness and he will not reveal it to anyone. Just know that you did right by him. It is enough."

Maya nodded, a little shocked by the somewhat-apology and the revelation that she'd redeemed Narakasura somehow. She wasn't entirely sure how that made her feel considering she was still so furious with the demon king.

But she needed to focus, instead of getting distracted. "How do we get her to kill Narakasura?"

Lord Shiva leaned forward, the muscles in his arms and abdomen rippling. This time his hand extended and when he opened it, a weapon sat on his palm.

"This is the bow that Satyabhama used to slay Narakasura. It is necessary that the same weapon be used again. And there is something else you must remember, Maya," Lord Shiva's voice, though soft, echoed around Maya like a living wind, bringing her gaze from the bow to his face again. "Everything is connected. In some way, in some shape, everything is connected. Remember that. It will help you in the coming days."

Everything is connected.

Lord Shiva didn't seem to be in any particular hurry, but Maya cleared her throat, feeling like she should at least ask the crucial question. "How do we find Bhumi?"

"Bhumi does not need to be found."

If that was the case, Maya sure hoped she'd hurry and reveal herself.

"Why is she human?" she asked, confused as to why the earth goddess would wander the world instead of ruling from the heavens.

"Bhumi is the earth, the goddess of the soil and of this planet. She still rules from the heavens," Lord Shiva said in answer to her mental question. She was beginning to get used to it. "A god has many aspects. And the avatar is only one part of the whole."

"So the living avatar of Bhumi is just one aspect of her? And she still watches over her human form?"

"Yes. Bhumi knows what she needs to do. Just as she knew when she walked the earth as Satyabhama, so shall this living form."

"So how long do we have to wait before she finds us?"

"She has already found you." Maya frowned. That, she had not expected. "You have known her all your life."

Maya swallowed. "All my life?"

Lord Shiva nodded. "When you begged to be reborn, to be given the opportunity to serve once more, Mother Kali searched for the best home for you. What better place to leave you than within the arms of the goddess of the Earth."

CHAPTER 44

Maya blinked.

She found herself staring straight into her mom's eyes, a little disoriented and a little dizzy. Maya rubbed her forehead. then gave a short laugh. "Gosh, if that was a dream, then it was one heckuva dream."

"Honey, you just closed your eyes," said Leela, her expression one of patience. "I don't think you would've had much time to dream."

Maya's eyebrows shot up as she stared at her mom in shock. "No way, Mom. I had a long conversation with Lord Shiva. In outer space no less." Leela shook her head. "I know how that sounds but it was for real . . . I had no idea."

"No idea about what, honey?" Leela asked, her spine stiff.

Maya cleared her throat. "Everything I tell you is going to sound insane but just . . . give it a chance okay?" she said, her eyes narrowing on her mom's face. Only when Leela nodded did Maya continue. "It was amazing. I think it was Lord Shiva's true form."

Although Leela's expression began as skeptical, as Maya spoke, describing universes and stars, the great dancing god, the termination of Kas, Maya's influence and the fact that everything was connected, her mom's expression changed.

She nodded, impressed but her soft scowl revealed she was troubled. "What's wrong, Mom?" asked Maya, Leela's expression taking the edge off her excitement.

Leela shook her head. "Nothing, really. I just have this feeling that whatever is going to happen here on out isn't going to be something any of us like."

"Whoa Mom, you turning oracle on me?"

Leela laughed. "No, I do not have the sight."

Maya studied her mom's face. "Are you sure you aren't going to start telling me this is too dangerous?"

Leela shrugged, smoothing her expression out to a more acceptable serenity. "Of course not. This is your destiny. Who am I to tell you otherwise?"

"Er . . . you don't have a problem with me fighting one of the most powerful demon kings in the history of . . . history?" asked Maya, more than a little surprised she'd barely gotten a reaction from her mom.

Leela shook her head. "No. I think I have finally accepted that you will always be more than I expected. And . . . It's probably time we allowed you to do your duty. The Hand of Kali is more important than little old me."

"And what about Maya Rao?" asked Maya softly. Her throat hurt and she had to swallow the tears that threatened to well up.

Leela sighed and her lower lip wobbled. "Awww, honey. I didn't mean . . ." She gathered Maya close and kissed the top of her head. "You will always be my baby, you hear me. Always." She gave Maya a tight, almost threatening squeeze for effect, but instead of throwing her off, Maya reveled in the hug, feeling more relaxed than she'd been in a while.

Then she stiffened.

In the arms of Mother Bhumi.

Her mom's eyes widened, and Maya realized she'd said the words out loud.

Leela sighed and got to her feet. "So you know?"

Maya was glad she was still seated. Had she been standing she knew her knees would have given out. Her ears were ringing so loudly she could barely string two words together.

Her mom was the incarnation of Bhumi the goddess of the earth. Maya took a breath.

"Oh my god," Maya whispered, watching her mother's shocked expression. "Mom?" said Maya, wanting to know if it was true but unable to say the words.

Her dad's arm went around her mom's shoulders. Where had he come from?

Maya watched as he guided her mom to the nearest sofa. They sat together, both silent for a long moment. Her mom's face was bloodless, the corners of her eyes tight. Her dad looked a little green around the gills.

"Did Lord Shiva tell you?

Maya nodded, giving her dad a narrow-eyed glare. "Don't tell me you knew?"

Dev shrugged. "I knew. And it wasn't as if I could say anything. Not until we knew what we were dealing with."

"So all this time, with Kas out to get me, you knew the truth."

Leela shook her head. "No, it's not so cut and dried." Her mom swallowed, taking a few seconds before saying, "I'd had no idea until this morning."

The look on Maya's face was clear enough. She'd been tempted to roll her eyes, but had managed to hold back the urge.

"It is true," said Chayya from the doorway. "Most avatars do not know who they are until the time is right. And the time became right with today's events." Then Chayya turned and greeted Leela with a Namaste, her bow low and long, and Maya felt slightly sick. "Greetings, Mother Bhumi. I welcome you with all my heart, goddess of the earth, mother of all."

Chayya's voice was reverent and Maya understood, being in awe herself. For a lesser known goddess, Bhumi certainly had an effect on the rest of the pantheon. Even lord Shiva had only respect for her.

Leela cleared her throat and met Maya's eyes from across the coffee table. It all seemed so surreal and so strange. Her mom was an avatar of the earth goddess. But the revelation would never be enjoyed.

"Are you okay, Mom?" asked Maya, finally pushing to her feet and going to her mom's side. She put an arm around her mom's shoulder and glanced up at Chayya. How do you make someone feel better about killing her own child?

The goddess had no answers.

Leela nodded. "I'm okay." Then she laughed. "It's a lot to absorb, of course. But I'll be fine."

"But are you going to be okay to do this?" Maya dared to ask the question but a glance at her dad said that he knew she needed to ask it. There was no time to be gently with her mom.

Leela gave a weak smile. "I'll be okay, Maya. It's a little strange to think *the* Narakasura is my son, but just the knowledge has opened the feelings up inside of me. I know I should be okay with killing him, but suddenly it just feels so wrong." Her face crumpled as if she was about to cry but then she stiffened her spine and took a shuddering breath. "But I will do this. There is too much at stake." She glanced at the silent television set, the wide screen still reporting undead and worldwide crises.

Maya gave her Mom a tight squeeze. "I'm so sorry, Mom," she said as she leaned her head on Leela's shoulder.

They sat that way in silence and then, blinking back tears, Maya whispered the words, understanding now what Lord Shiva had meant.

"Everything is connected."

CHAPTER 45

"Okay people. Stop the soppy stuff and get back to work." Dev clapped his hands together.

Maya smiled. "So what's the situation? Other than my mother the goddess?"

Dev made a face. "Still no more deaths, still far too many undead . . . or not yet dead, or whatever they are calling it. God knows what it will be like if things don't go back to normal."

"Yeah, I'd rather they go back to normal and people accept it as a freak incident. This being the way life is from now on is going to suck."

Dev nodded. "All the phone lines are manned, Joss is keeping me updated, KALIMA HQ is running themselves crazy attending to the case. They are apprehending as many of the 'undead' as they possibly can. The less there are on the streets the better."

"Do we have the manpower for that?" Maya found it hard to concentrate on mundane information when she still absorbed the truth about her mom.

Her dad nodded. "The police are helping. And the hospitals are giving us the heads up as soon as new cases come in."

Maya sighed and got to her feet.

"I suppose it's time to go?" She looked at Chayya, and the goddess smiled and offered a nod.

Maya stood beside her mom as she spoke softly to her dad, ready to go to Patala. But killing Kas was the last thing she wanted to do. Especially when she was taking her mother with her so she can kill her son. It all sounded so weird to her ears, but even she was affected by the revelation.

She'd gone from calling him Narakasura to Kas, then back again when she'd found out he'd betrayed her. Now, he was Kas again because he was her mother's son, and her sorta-brother in a very convoluted way.

It was a total mind fudge but Maya had to suck it up and deal with it. So did her mom. A glance at the tv confirmed the news reports were becoming worse by the minute, and there didn't seem to be any let-up. Police and the army and navy across the worlds were being run ragged and there was no rest for anyone. How long could they hold them off before everything went to hell? That's what they'd want, what Kas would want.

Anarchy in the world meant it was ripe for the taking. He'd be like some sort of devil, rising up to conquer the masses. And then there'd be no help for anyone.

She had to do this. And so did her mother.

Maya patted her pocket and her fingers brushed Lord Shiva's little pot, safely hidden within it. Her mind and body had grown stronger, her wounds were well healed and she sent her gratitude and thanks to Kali.

Chayya shifted forward, and held out two weapons. Leela took the bow and arrow, Maya the trident. Chayya smiled and pointed at the bow that Maya's mom now bounced on her palm testing its weight.

"This bow belonged to Satyabhama, the avatar of Bhumi who killed Narakasura the last time he saw life in this world. It is fitting that you would select this very weapon, for it belongs to you. Let the weapon guide you, let Lord Shiva guide your aim."

No one mentioned anything about the guidance she'd need to kill her son.

Chayya turned to Maya and gave the trident a nod. "That is a Shakthi." Maya stared at the trident-shaped end of the weapon. The two side spikes were curved, meeting in a U shape. Despite its simplicity, it had always been known as a destructive weapon. The middle blade bore a red dot, the symbol of power, and Maya hoped the power of the Shakthi will help her through the next few hours.

"Now, you must leave." Chayya took a step forward and glanced at Dev. For a moment it looked like he'd insist they stay, but then he kissed Maya and her mom and stepped away. His face was dark, stubble grayed his chin, and there were circles under his eyes.

Maya gave him a reassuring smile, hoping it would make him feel a little better but his expression didn't change.

The sadness in his face was the last thing Maya saw before they disappeared.

CHAPTER 46

They arrived just outside the giant bronze doors to main hall within Yama's palace. Which made Maya frown.

"I thought we'd go straight to the cell for Nik and Kas?" she asked, holding tightly onto the bow.

Chayya smiled. "I had to make one stop. There is something here that you will need. This battle may be harder than you expect. The best way to tackle it is to be prepared." Chayya turned on her heel and headed down the corridor.

The path was familiar to Maya, one she'd taken with Nik when they'd waited to see Yama before their mission to save Varuni from Kas.

When Chayya pushed open the doors of the training room, Maya knew why she took them there.

"But we already have weapons," said Leela, staring around the grand open space.

"There is one thing that may benefit you. It is always best to be over-prepared than to be caught without defenses." That was certainly true.

The goddess entered the room, took the two steps down to

the training area sunk into the center of the room. She crossed the space, twice the size of a basketball court, then went to the other side of the room.

The sunken area was surrounded by a columned level and along the back, weapons from around the world filled the walls. One particular piece shone brightly, a golden sun that attracted Chayya.

She slipped it off its hook and brought it over, handing it carefully to Maya. "This discus belonged to Lord Krishna." Maya recalled it from folktales she'd read. Made of pure gold, it spun under some mysterious power. One hundred and eight serrated blades were embedded around the perimeter of the discus, making it one deadly weapon.

"Wow," said Maya, staring at the weapon. Despite her impatience to get moving, she was glad to receive the discus.

"Use it well," was all Chayya said, before reaching out with both her hands.

Maya glanced at her mom who gave her a short nod in answer to the silent question. They took the goddess's hand and disappeared from the room.

Chayya materialized with Maya and her mom in the middle of the bare stone cell. At first, the silence struck Maya as odd and she spun around looking for Nik.

She'd been thinking that maybe they'd made the wrong decision to bring the fight to such a tight space. But all thoughts of tight spaces flew from her brain when Kas, startled by their sudden appearance, flinched. His dark eyes widened as the group, probably surprised by the size of their contingent.

Unfortunately, Nik sat a foot away from the demon king. Kas barely paused, just lunged forward and grabbed a hold of Nik, his hand slipping around his neck lightning fast, a slim knife appearing within his grasp as if he'd picked if from thin air. He gave Nik the same treatment that his goons had given Maya. The cut on her neck had healed but the wound from the insult certainly hadn't.

Maya stiffened at the sight of Nik being threatened. She glanced at her mom, unsurprised at the fear reflected in her eyes. Great. Two terrified women were supposed to win this battle.

Maya choked back a laugh that bordered on hysterical, and said, "What the hell are you up to, Kas?"

He shrugged. "Nothing much. Just don't move, please? If you don't mind." He spoke as if they'd just met for a cordial dinner.

"What is wrong with you? Is this really necessary?" Maya asked, pointing at the knife that was now cutting into Nik's neck. She'd forgotten she was still holding the Shakthi, and only when Nik's shocked gaze fell on the weapon did she realize it.

"Well, considering what you're holding in your hand, I do think it's necessary." Kas had noticed too.

Maya snorted and let her hand drop to her side. "I hadn't planned on using it on you."

Kas narrowed his eyes. "Then, why are you here?"

"Don't be stupid, Kas. I'm here to save the two of you. Why else would I be here?"

"Oh?" he seemed genuinely surprised. "I thought you returned to kill me."

Maya sighed dramatically, shaking her head as she said, "Really, Kas. Why do you keep thinking I want to kill you? I don't have any reason take your life."

"You don't?" asked Kas, surprised. Maya could tell he'd thought she'd returned to kill him because he'd stabbed her. She had him well and truly off balance and she preferred that he stayed that way until she got the upper hand.

"You can drop the knife, Kas," Maya said dryly taking a step forward.

But Kas wasn't entirely letting his guard down. The knife pressed deep and blood trickled down Nik's neck. He remained still, but his expression revealed fury rather than fear. Kas didn't know how close he was to death.

But when Nik blinked, and looked a little cross-eyed, Maya's gut tightened. What had they done to him?

She cleared her throat. "What do you want, Kas?" Time to negotiate.

Kas grinned. "Get us out of here and then we can talk." He seemed very sure of himself, and though Maya hated that he knew she'd listen, she accepted that she'd do it anyway.

"Fine," she snapped. "Where do you want to go? Lady Chayya can take you."

Kas shifted his gaze to Maya's mom and watched her for a mom. "Do I know you?" he asked.

Leela stiffened, her hand tightening around the bow.

Kas laughed. "I won't bite."

"Leave her alone, and tell me where you want to go. We are wasting time while you stand there trying to bleed Nik out as you make you decision." Maya's voice was cold and the temperature matched the glare she gave Kas.

"Take me to your home. I do believe that would be neutral ground."

"No way. I'm not going to take you inside my house."

"Why not Maya? Don't you invite your friends to your home?"

Maya grunted. "Fine. Whatever. As long as you don't hurt Nik. Hurt him and you're no friend of mine."

"Strong words, little Hand." Kas laughed.

"What's so funny? How can defending someone's life be such an amusement?" Maya asked angrily. She was getting tired of him.

"Is that what you were doing? Defending him? A little hard to do from way over there isn't it, Maya?" Kas was taunting her and she'd about had enough.

"If you want to leave Patala you will need to come closer. Chayya can take us up two at a time."

"The wards," croaked Nik. He seemed to have forgotten the knife at his throat.

"Oh yes," said Kas. "I'd have to lower the wards so Nik can leave the cell. I almost forgot about that."

"Yeah, right." Maya rolled her eyes. "Release the wards, Kas."

"Once he releases the wards we can all go together. Nikhil and I both have the ability to transport humans across the planes, and the demon king can manage the jump under his own steam. Just don't let go of him." Chayya's voice echoed in her head and Maya had to force herself not to flinch.

Maya met Nik's eyes. "We go together?" He gave a short nod.

Turning to Kas, Maya said, "Whenever you're ready." She didn't hide the bite to her tone and didn't care if she hurt his feelings either. From his expression, the entire scene was just an amusement to him, which made Maya more angry.

He didn't speak, but the air around Maya grew dense, heavy, the pressure rushing in her ears. The magic surged out of the cell, and she could feel the odd absence of it, despite having been unaware of it to begin with.

"Let's go," she said, keeping an eye on Kas.

She didn't blink.

Not until they arrived in the hallway of her home back in LA.

Maya was staring right at Kas when he turned the knife and plunged it straight into the side of Nik's throat.

CHAPTER 47

*M*aya screamed and lunged, not caring that Kas had just winked out of existence. All her thoughts were for Nik as he fell to the ground. She caught him just as he landed, right before his head bounced off the wood floor.

She couldn't see through the tears that blurred her vision as she pressed her palm against Nik's neck. She scraped the back of her hand across her face, but didn't bother to wipe it as she leaned over Nik.

People were running around her, her dad for first-aid stuff, Chayya pacing and talking to herself Maya's mom on the phone with someone.

She wanted them all to go away. Nik's eyes were clear as he stared at her.

"Don't worry about me," he said, his words slurred from the blood pooling in his throat.

"Stop talking," she sobbed. She didn't want him to stop. What if she never heard his voice again? But her needs weren't important. "I have to concentrate, and you're disturbing me." She watched a smile flicker on his lips before he obeyed.

Maya focused.

It had been so much easier when she'd tried to heal herself a few hours ago. But now, with her mind filled with fear and on the edge of hysteria, her hands shaking and her heart going a mile a minute, she couldn't even summon her fire.

"Concentrate Maya, breathe and calm yourself. You are of no use to him, or anyone if you can't even control your own fire." Her mom's voice rang out, echoing through her head. She'd blocked everyone out so well her mom had had to raise her voice before Maya paid attention.

Maya inhaled harshly, the tears clogging her throat as she tried to pull herself together. Calm. She needed calm, even though Nik was dying at her feet, even though her mother was about to kill her own son, even though the undead walked the earth because Yama was nowhere to be found.

Shut up Maya. Get a damn grip.

The inner voice seemed to understand that she needed to be told what to do, and Maya finally allowed calm to filter through her veins and through her mind. It was taking precious seconds, but it had to be done or else she'd be a gibbering mess and won't be of any use to anyone, least of all Nik.

Calm at last, Maya pulled her fire, and after a few false starts she managed to draw the energy and bring it to the fore. As she call the power, she asked Nik, "Can you use your own fire to help me?"

He shook his head. "Demigods have powers but not when their magic is bound."

"Kas?" she asked. He nodded his eyes glittery with pent-up fury. Maya recognized that expression. He'd given her the same look when she'd been in the cell with him. He'd tried to warn her about Kas, but she hadn't understood. She sighed.

"Okay, then. I'll go it alone."

Chayya came closer at last. "I will assist, but you are more than capable of focused healing. You don't really need anyones help. And we shouldn't wait. The more time that goes by, the further Narakasura gets."

Maya nodded. She'd needed that reminder. And a glance over Chayya's shoulder at her mom's face told her that she too didn't appreciate the interruption to their plan.

Get in, kill him, get out. Simple enough.

Total fail in the end

Maya pulled the energy to her palms, leaving the fire behind. She leaned forward placing her blood drenched palm onto Nik's neck and concentrate.

She stiffened. "Nothing's happening."

"It's the wards. You must persist." Chayya's voice was soft and encouraging. "You can break the wards but he must be healed fast because his energy is fading."

What if he dies, thought Maya, suddenly too terrified to move.

"He won't die as long as you get moving," said Chayya in her head.

She glanced at Nik's face, her stomach tightening. He hadn't had the strength to remain awake. Was it better for him to be asleep? She shook her head. No time to wake him. She sent the energy into his flesh, seeking with her mind, the edges of the incision, the broken flesh.

Kas had run his knife right through Nik's neck and the deadly sharp point had penetrated the other side before Kas had tugged it out. The vicious expression on his face had hurt Maya deeply, more because she'd seen the hatred in his eyes. Hatred that had been so unnecessary because everyone had wanted to give him a chance.

Even Nik and Yama.

Maya cupped the wound on the other side of Nik's neck and concentrated working her way along the gash from one side to the other. As she went, she sent healing energy deep within the flesh, urging the cells to knit together, the broken blood vessels to close and the wound to heal. Perspiration dotted her forehead, but she kept going, knowing that every inch she healed meant Nik would recover well.

At last she reached the exit wound, sealed the gash then closed the skin over it. She had never been more impressed with the power of fire than when she sat back, soaked in blood, and studied her work. Both wounds on Nik's neck had healed. Scarred, but healed.

But, he still slept.

Maya glanced up at the goddess. "Why isn't he waking up?"

"He is not fully a god. His human body needs to take time to heal."

"Can you make sure? I did what I could, but I can't tell if I succeeded."

Chayya nodded and knelt beside Nik, her eyes studying the wound with a glazed expression. When she flinched, Maya knew something was wrong. Chayya's reaction also drew Leela closer.

"What's wrong?" her mom asked. Maya couldn't bring herself to speak as fear spiked through her heart.

"Something is wrong. The wards are down now. I am able to detect something that isn't entirely magic." The goddesses voice sounded stained and odd. As if she found it hard to speak.

Maya got to her feet. "What's wrong?" She wanted to say that she didn't need protection, she paused. Was the goddess protecting her, or was she just finding it hard to deal with what she'd seen?

Chayya looked back at Nik's sleeping form.

"He has been poisoned."

CHAPTER 48

"Kas?" asked Maya knowing already that it was him. "The knife?"

Chayya glanced around, almost frantic to find the weapons.

"Where is it?" Maya asked, her voice a little to high-pitched for comfort. Maya scanned the room.

"There, on the sideboard," said her mom. They were still standing in the front hall and someone had taken the knife and put it on the table out of the way.

Chayya didn't move. "I can see it from here. It's powerful. Poison and magic mixed with evil."

Maya found she couldn't breathe. Her heart was racing but she wasn't planning on letting Kas win. He'd duped her into trusting him and it just might cost her Nik's life.

"What can we do? Is there a cure?"

"Let me find out," said Chayya, before she disintegrated into smoke.

Maya straightened her spine as she watched Nik's sleeping face. He didn't look like a damned demigod. In fact, he didn't look very imposing at all, lying there unconscious on their hall floor. Damn you Nik.

Maya sucked in a breath and it ended up being more of a hiccuping sob.

"Honey, you can go wash up, we'll make him comfortable."

Maya met her mom's gaze, her eyes hard. "I don't have time to clean up. We need to go as soon as Chayya gets back."

"You should at least eat something," said her dad, looking up from the floor.

"The last thing I need is food."

"That's where you're wrong. No food, you fall on your face instead of winning the battle. You think that fire of yours will last if you don't take care of your body?" Her dad's eyes rounded as he glared at her, and she knew that look. Do as I say or else.

But he didn't need to threaten her. She actually agreed with him. Using her fire did make her hungry and she'd been fighting the pangs for a while now.

"Fine. I'll eat." She turned on her heel and headed for the kitchen.

"Not looking like that you won't," snapped her mom as she overtook Maya on the way to the kitchen. She stopped in front of Maya and pointed down the hall. "Wash up first. Nobody sits to eat while looking like a damned bloodthirsty viking."

Maya laughed. "Mom, everyone knows that the Vikings weren't the killers they've been made out to be. It's all there on the History Channel."

"And how do you think that matters to me," Leela asked, finger still aimed in the direction of the downstairs bathroom.

Maya sighed and left without further argument.

As she scrubbed her hands and washed her face she tried to calm herself. She was furious. What was she doing washing and eating when Nik was dying? The sane part of her said that she had to take care of herself, but the part of herself that was angry and grieving and vengeful, that part demanded she head out the door. Now.

By the time she returned to the kitchen the break was over.

Chayya stood beside the sink, her fingers linked in front of her. Her shoulders drooped and Maya's stomach churned. This didn't look good.

Dev came up to stand beside her and nobody spoke until Chayya broke the silence. "The poison is permanent. The only way to remove it is to kill the sorcerer who created it."

"The sorcerer? Is Kas still using that Balraj creep?" asked Maya. She certainly hoped not. The sorcerer had tortured Maya last time they were in a room together so she wasn't looking forward to meeting him again. Unless it meant the opportunity to burn him to a crisp. Only problem was the dude was a pretty powerful magician.

"No. Perhaps Balraj may have assisted, but the real owner of that magic is Narakasura. Only the creator can wield such a power against a god. And though Nikhil is not a pure-blood, he still bears the blood of a god. The magic will need to be just as powerful."

"That's a good thing, right? We kill Kas, and Nik is safe."

"It's only a good thing if we succeed," said Leela, her tone bordering on emotionless.

Maya schooled her features to hide her shock at her mom's words. And here she thought her mom would be a little reluctant to kill her child. Although killing her child did sound way worse that it really was.

Or was it?

Maya shook her head and glared at her mom. "Don't be such a negative Nancy, Mom. We'll get him."

Leela waved a hand in the direction of the front door. "He's gone. He could be anywhere. How the hell would we find him if he doesn't want to be found?"

A thought struck her, a little like a lightning bold. Maya smiled, feeling a little triumphant. "We make him come to us." It was a brilliant idea, and the expression on her parents and Chayya's faces confirmed it.

"Only problem is we don't have anything that will make him come back," Dev words echoed like a death knell, and Maya wondered if the weakness in her knees was from hunger or loss of hope.

She began to pace a thin line along the kitchen floor. Either that or fall flat on her face. She could hear the soughing of breath as they all sank onto automatic, breathing, thinking, hoping.

A few seconds later, her mom broke the strained silence. "I know how to bring him here."

Maya stopped and looked at her Mom. "Do tell. I'm all out of ideas," she said drily.

Leela gave a small sad smile. "What better way to bring him here than to give him what he wants."

Maya folded her arms and waited. "So what does he want?"

"A mother."

CHAPTER 49

"No way. No way in hell am I going to let you be bait." Maya almost yelled the words.

She'd even attracted attention. Joss hurried inside the kitchen her hair in a ponytail, her mascara smudged. She looked exhausted and worried now as she looked from face to face.

"What's going on?" she asked wrapping her hands around her waist. It seemed like she was already preparing for the bad news.

"Mom thinks it's a good idea to tell Kas that she's his mother. She thinks it will make him come back so we can catch him."

Joss's jaw dropped and her pale skin went whiter. She sucked in a breath. "I'm not sure *I* think that's a very good idea, either." Her voice was softer that her usual vibrant self, and Maya wondered if the whole undead thing was getting to her.

"I know you guys are worried about me," said Leela smiling at both girls sadly. "But, really, we don't have any other options. I'm only one person in this awful worldwide horror. If I can help end this, then I will do anything." She didn't say it but Maya heard it nonetheless. Her mom was saying she was ready to die to save the world.

Maya opened her mouth then closed it, not trusting herself. There was every chance she would burst into tears. Or scream at her mom for being so brave.

But, how could Maya shut her down?

CHAPTER 50

The room remained silent for a little too long and at last Maya sighed and shook her head. "Mom, are you insane?"

Maya knew it was a last ditch effort to change her mind, to make the idea seem silly, illogical. The expression on her Mom's face was enough to tell Maya that she was failing at her attempt.

"Maya, insane is the last thing I am being."

She was speakings slowly, which was a really bad sign. Usually, slow deliberate speech translated into seething anger. Strangely enough she didn't blow.

She merely continued, "I am doing the logical thing. And I can also understand your resistance to the plan."

"The plan?" asked Maya. "It isn't a plan, so don't call it a plan."

Her voice held an edge of hysteria that she knew she had to temper. They may not allow her to fight Kas if they thought she was losing her mind.

But her mom just shook her head. "We don't have any other options and arguing with me is only going to waste time. I'm pretty certain that even though Nik looks like he's just sleeping, he's probably getting worse as a result of the poison."

She looked over at Chayya and the goddess acknowledged her assumption with a sober nod.

Great.

"So what are you planning on doing? How in heck are we supposed to tell Kas that you are here. Anyone know how to tap into his mind?"

Three pairs of eyes stared at Maya as her words faded away into the room.

"Oh," she said. She was the only person that could access his mind. "Um . . . how about we just place an ad on TV. He'll see it. I'm sure he's holed up somewhere watching the news to see what a huge effect his actions have been on the world."

Her dad shook his head. "Maya, the last thing we need is to be publicizing this. We're keeping it as under-wraps as possible. It doesn't make sense to let the world know that this whole thing was strategic. People aren't ready to know the truth. Not yet."

"*You* know the truth and you're not locked up in a mental institution."

"True. But you have to admit we are a little different from normal." Dev smiled.

"Yeah. About that. Can I have a do-over please?" Maya asked.

Everyone laughed and even Chayya smiled. "Okay, so I guess I'm the plan then." She started walking, pointing a finger in the direction of the lounge as she said, "I'll be over there, time-traveling."

She stalked off to the living room and gave the television an angry glare before sinking into the sofa. Her lip quivered.

All that posturing and anger was taking its toll on her nerves. She wasn't sure how much longer she could manage.

Finally she conceded that perhaps ending Kas was the best way to solve the worlds problem.

And she had to do it fast, because who knew how long Nik had left.

She sat there for a moment, appreciating the fact that they'd all left her alone, thinking about where in time was the best to go to change things so Kas would get the message.

But all she got was a whole lot of nothing.

The last thing she needed was to tip him off before they left the cell in case he didn't let them escape. Best to leave that part the way it really happened.

Kas when he left Maya's house?

That was probably the best point in time to hijack his time-line.

Maya put her feet up and settled back against the cushions. She closed her eyes and relaxed, preparing to join Kas's mind.

She drifted back to the moment they'd arrived in the front room. She stayed with him as he stabbed Nik, trying not to remember her visceral reaction to Nik's injuries.

She held on tightly to Kas's mind as he melted into nothing, disappearing from the house. When he materialized, nobody was more surprised than Maya to find where he'd gone.

Around her tree's soughed, and the wind breathed between the leaves.

The clearing in which Kas had killed his pet tiger.

Maya's heart ached for the young boy. She pitied him, but she didn't want to feel any kind of sympathy. Not for him. Not when he'd hurt Nik.

She staunched her emotions, trying to keep them free from Kas's tumultuous ones. She'd done this so many times, and now she sensed even the most minor nuances of his feelings. And she didn't like it one bit.

I'm glad they know exactly who they are dealing with, he thought

And who are they dealing with, Maya thought back, deeply annoyed at his satisfaction.

Maya was startled when he replied, *They are dealing with me, Narakasura, demon king, the eternal one.*

"As if that's so incredible. What did Nik do to deserve being stabbed in the neck?"

Kas grunted, as if frustrated and it occurred to Maya that maybe he was actually hearing her thoughts. "He's a demigod. Spawn of Yama. Why does he get to be special and all I get is banishment and death?" His voice rang out around the clearing, uncertain and confused.

"Probably because he doesn't want world domination?" suggested Maya.

"He has privilege. He thinks he deserves what he has."

"I doubt that."

"Of course, he does. Walking around feeling all superior, looking down on me. He deserves what he got." His voice rose.

"You seriously need your head checked."

Kas stopped in his tracks, coming to a sudden halt, as if it occurred to him only then that he wasn't talking to himself.

She could feel him tense, feel his suspicions begin to rise. He looked around him, scanning the area, the expansive field of grass, the thick jungle encircling him.

"Who's there?" he yelled.

Maya wanted to laugh. Was he so stupid that he thought a voice in his head was talking to him from within a stand of trees twenty yards away?

"Who is that?" he shouted again.

"Calm down before you bust a blood vessel."

"Don't tell me to calm down. Who are you?"

Maya sighed. *"Look, it's not important who I am."* Maya shook her head unable to believe what she was about to say but doing it anyway. *"Your mother wants to see you."*

"My mother?" confusion flooded his mind. Confusion, and grief, and a lot of shame. Then he wiped then away. "My mother is dead."

Maya frowned. His avatar mother would be dead, but Bhumi was very much alive. If not the world would have found out by now.

"I think you're mistaken. I know where she is, but if you really don't care to see her, then I'm wasting my time and I'd better be going."

Kas stiffened and the muscles in Maya's face shifted as he raised his eyebrows. "Do I know you? Why do you sound so familiar?"

*"You are wasting time."*Maya sighed. *"Your mother is waiting to see you. Do you want to meet her or not? I can't hang around forever waiting for you to make a decision."*

Maya went silent, deciding to let him stew for a bit.

He did.

So many emotions all mixing together. Maya could barely define any of them and found it exhausting. He sure carried around a lot of emotion.

And a lot of anger.

At last he said, "Are you there?"

"Where else would I be?"

Kas paused, probably unsure of what to make of her response. He cleared his throat. "Fine. I'll see her. Where is she?"

He turned on his heel, as if he was listening around him for the voice.

"She is waiting for you at Maya Rao's house."

The words scraped their way up, and out of Maya's throat.

"What?" he asked, his voice rough. His mind flickered to an image of Maya's mom and he gasped softly. "I knew it. There was just something about her."

Maya said nothing.

She had to accept that he was pretty astute, but she wasn't going to give him any further praise.

"Who is she?" His voice shivered, desperate now.

Maya gritted her teeth. *"You'll find out when you get there. And don't waste any more time, please."*

She was done talking to him. She'd come to give him a message, not be his friend. Maya ignored him for the next few minutes as the echoes of his yells danced among the leaves and the branches of the jungle.

When he demanded a response she ignored him, and when he begged for confirmation of his mother's identity, she ignored him then too.

At last, with the sound of his voice still ringing in her ears, he stopped and Maya listened to his thoughts as he weighed the reasons for going against the non-existent ones for ignoring the invitation.

She almost pitied him for the sick feeling that pooled in his stomach.

Almost.

CHAPTER 51

K as solidified in Maya's front hall and it annoyed her immensely. The really nit-picky part of her brain was asking why he hadn't appeared outside, and knocked like a decent human. But there was the obvious answer to that question.

Maya pulled away from his mind, happy that he'd followed through on her request. She returned to her own body in the living room, and sat up with a jerk the moment she opened her eyes.

For a second, she teetered, a little off balance. And odd pressure seemed to push against her and she wondered if someone, perhaps her parents or Chayya, had strengthened the wards around the house. It would have been the smart thing to do and they were all more than capable.

From where she sat in the darkened room, she could see him standing still in the hall, his profile shadowed, his stance defensive. He was a loose cannon.

Maya pushed to her feet, fighting fatigue, and forced herself to walk to him.

"You came," she said, her voice traveling down the hall.

"Your powers of observation are unparalleled." Kas's eyes were cold but he was watching her with an odd expression. "It was you." He nodded after he spoke convinced he was right.

Maya sighed as footsteps echoed from the kitchen. "*Your powers of observation are seriously lacking.*"

Kas snorted. "Touché."

Maya shook her head. Who even says Touché anymore, she wondered.

"Where is she?" he asked

"I'm right here," said Maya's mom from behind him. They'd come up with minimal fuss, Chayya and Maya's parents, and the god and the husband flanked Leela, as if they offered her some form of protection.

Everyone there knew they couldn't.

"Who are you," he asked, his voice flat as if he was trying very hard to keep the emotion out of it. His body told another story; taut muscles stiff spine. Tense jaw. Even his fingers were balled into fists.

"I'm Leela Rao."

"Rao?" Kas looked at Maya then back at her mom and then her let out a short bark of laughter. "She's your mother?" he asked.

Maya nodded. "Your's too," said Maya gritting her own teeth at the admission.

He shook his head, "This is ridiculous. It's all a trick."

With a soft laugh Maya said, "Deep down you know its true. You saw it when Mom came to the cell in Patala. You knew then and you know now."

Kas turned his head to stare at Maya. "How the hell were you in my head?"

Maya shrugged. "I have skills," she said.

She caught sight of the smile that curved her mom's lips, but kept her attention focused on Kas.

He was the unpredictable entity here.

"What do you want?" Kas asked, biting the words out as he stared at Leela.

"I want you to stop this craziness. You're so much better than this." Maya noticed her mom wasn't addressing him by any name and she knew why. How do you get personal with a killer, even if he happens to be your son?

Kas sneered. "And what do you know about me?"

Leela took a step forward. "I know everything about you. I know that you were kind and innocent once. That a long time ago you loved those who loved you. And I know that you can be saved from this path that you're treading."

Bad move mom.

Kas stiffened, if that was even possible considering how tightly strung he was. He took a step toward her.

"You don't know anything about me. Whatever knowledge you have given to you by my true mother isn't enough for you to understand me." His voice and face were filled with bitterness. "You are just a sad version of her."

Leela smiled softly, her skin glowing. "Perhaps I am, but I am the only part of her here right now."

He stared at her for a long moment and Maya could feel the tension around her. Here they were again, in the front hall, confronting the demon king.

Kas shook his head. "No. You are nothing. All of you. Whatever you think you're trying to do here you will fail."

"What do you think we're trying to do, Kas?" asked Maya, taking a step forward. Behind her she held the discus, ready to aim it the second she got the opportunity.

"You want to convince me to be nice and normal. That I have family." He laughed and gave another odd jerk of his head, his expression bordering on deranged. "That's not going to happen because I know the truth."

"Why?" asked Maya, gaining his attention. "Because Bana told you that?"

He frowned and stared at her. "You were in my head then too? How-" he stopped speaking as he stared at Maya. At last, he moved his head sharply, as if the question was not important. "He showed me the way it really was. He opened my eyes to the way people used me."

"People didn't use you, Kas. Bana made you see things differently and it was the wrong way." Leela spoke softly as she took another step closer to him. Her bow hung at her side, and Maya knew she'd never be able to use it. Not at that distance. Still she continued to speak to him. "We never wanted to manipulate or use you. Nobody wanted to betray you. You were manipulated by Bana because he was a lonely, angry old man. And he succeeded in turning you into something you are not."

Maya watched her mom's face, entranced. Leela's skin shone and Maya knew it was no longer her mom who spoke. The goddess Bhumi was at last talking directly to her son.

Kas stood there, shock tightening his features as he stared at his mother's face.

He said nothing to her.

He just stabbed Leela in the stomach and disappeared.

CHAPTER 52

Maya's ears range, and everything around her moved slowly.

She'd watched, unmoving, as Kas plunge his knife into her mom's abdomen.

But, as if her faculties had been closed off from her, she hadn't processed the reality that her mom had been badly injured.

Not until her gaze drifted to the blood, thick and glistening as it soaked into the fabric of her mom's peach blouse.

Maya sank to her mom's side, caring little that she hit the wood too hard, barely feeling the jarring impact of bone to wood.

Her hands shook as she reached out to check the wound. For the second time in a few hours, she was frantically stemming the flow of blood from a wound inflicted on someone she loved, a wound inflicted by Kas.

Kas had disintegrated in a flash of pale light, which seemed illogical considering what he'd just done. A bright, blood-red would have been more appropriate.

Maya couldn't get her head around how Kas could have done such a thing to his own mother. What kind of heart does a person have to possess that would allow him to stab his own mother in cold blood? Maya's head began to hurt.

Kas was gone, but he'd left Maya and her mom behind. That didn't help considering they'd been meant to kill him.

Leela sighed and shifted to look at Maya. She lifted her head off the floor, supporting her body with an elbow and grabbed hold of Maya's arm. "We don't have time for this Maya. We have to go and find him," she said. "There is no time to lose."

Desperation filled her voice, edged with confusion. It couldn't be easy being in her position. He'd escaped, her son. He was gone, and she had to find him. Only it wasn't for another reunion. She had to find him to kill him.

But Maya shook her head. Despite their mission, despite what they had to do to save the world, she had to consider her mom's health. "Mom, the last thing we need to think about right now is Kas."

Leela's grip tightened, her skin pale with blood-loss and worry. "You don't understand, honey. He's too unpredictable. It's all just a jumble of emotions his head. The way he's feeling now, he can't be trusted." She shuddered as she took another breath. "And besides, we have a job to do and time is running out."

With her mom's determination staring her in the face, Maya couldn't deny that she was right. There were too many things at stake.

Leela pushed Maya's hand away and moved into a sitting position, only her faced revealing the agony she was in.

"At least let me heal of the wound," said Maya, putting a little steel into her voice. "You can't afford to bleed out before we manage to succeed."

Her mom glared at her, but she finally gave in when Maya's dad touched her shoulder. She glanced up at him and they shared one of those silent, meaningful looks.

Then she sighed and looked back at Maya, giving her a pained nod. "Fine. Just be quick about it."

Maya huffed, then proceeded to send ripples of her fire into the wound. The blood was sticky now, and coated Maya's palms. She ignored it and worked on filling the wound with energy.

"It isn't that deep." A small miracle considering he'd deliberately stuck a knife into her.

At last Maya sat back and said, "Okay. That's about all I can do for now."

When Maya got to her feet, Chayya stood beside her. "May I speak to you in private?"

Surprised, Maya nodded and followed the goddess into the kitchen, leaving Dev to help Leela to her unsteady feet, and guide her to the living room.

Maya barely came to a stop when Chayya said, "That blade was also poisoned."

The room stilled around Maya, even her breathing stopped. Those five words echoed over and over in her mind. And suddenly Maya's muscles numbed and she sank against the edge of the table, glad it was supporting her weight or she would have sunk straight to the tiled floor.

"It does not change anything, Maya. Narakasura must still be stopped. His death will release both Nikhil and your mother from the hold of the poison."

Heat filled Maya's veins and she shoved off the table and stalked out of the kitchen. "Then we stop him."

Maya paused in the living room doorway, watching her mom lying on the couch that Maya herself had occupied not too long ago. It somehow seemed fitting. She cleared her throat, the sound bringing both of her parent's attention to her.

"I think I know where Kas has gone. I'm going to go after him and finish this job."

"You are not going without me." Her mom's voice was firm, and Maya suspected she'd be wasting her time arguing with her. She said nothing as Leela got to her feet and straightened. "Where is my bow?" she asked.

"I'll fetch the weapons," said Dev, hurrying out of the room.

Chayya stood quietly on the threshold while Maya grabbed her rucksack from the front hall, checked it for the discus and returned to the living room. Her dad walked in, holding out the Shakthi. She'd thrown it aside when they'd arrived back from Patala with Kas and Nik.

Now, just the weight of the spear filled her with comfort and reassurance.

Maya met her mom's eyes and received a nod in return. She smiled at her dad and he seemed to hesitate, as if he wanted to come over and hug her or something, but he didn't move.

The three women converged in the centre of the living room, and the goddess took them all to the clearing in the jungle.

CHAPTER 53

He stood alone, his back to them, in the middle of the grassy field, as if he waited for them to arrive. He'd have known Maya would have guessed his destination and she wondered if he'd left deliberately to buy himself time, to take them to familiar territory.

When they materialized Narakasura turned to face then and Maya almost nodded. She'd been right.

In his right hand he held what looked like a freaking bolt of lightning. Maya remembered something in the lore about a weapons fashioned from lightning, something that had belonged to Lord Vishnu. She could be wrong though, she'd never paid much attention to the specifics.

It didn't matter now, because he swung the staff of vibrating power and aimed it at Maya. Light surged from the tip and shot out at her. She ducked just in time, smelling ozone as the lightning singed her hair before slamming into the grass behind her.

It was a close call, but both Maya and her mom kept running for him. Maya's stomached tightened, fear and nerves melding into a solid rock within her gut. But she had to overlook her doubts. Her mother's life, and Nik's, depended on it.

More determined now, Maya ran, reaching deep for her power and sent a volley of fireballs at Kas. Her aim was perfect, and they all hit their target.

And fizzled out on impact.

Kas laughed as Maya came to a stop. "Sorry about that, Maya. Your blood has proven quite useful." For a moment Maya was taken back to a stone table, to chains, to a sorcerer who gleefully slit her veins open, intent on bleeding her dry. Now she knew what he'd wanted her blood for.

So, fire was out. But Maya had other weapons, and so did her mom.

Leela sent an arrow flying at Kas, following it quickly with a second and a third. The first went wide, the second hit him in the arm, the third plunged deep into his thigh. Leela let out a harsh gasp, shocked at what she'd done, but Maya didn't let her dwell on it.

"Good job, Mom."

Before Leela could respond Maya released the discus, sending it spinning like a tiny UFO in Kas's direction. More than anyone else she was shocked when it hit him full in the chest. She winced as she imagine the damaged the serrated blades would have caused, but she couldn't allow sympathy to get in her way.

Maya and Leela ran closer, taking advantage of Kas's temporary incapacitation, Because it was only temporary. He was already getting to his feet when they reached him.

An arrow appeared in the middle of Kas's breastbone and Maya glanced at her mom. She hadn't wasted time.

A searing pain ripped through Maya's chest. She'd taken her eye off Kas assuming with an arrow to heart he was out of contention. How stupid could she have been?

Now, she glanced down at the open wound that traced a path across her chest. That was going to look amazing in a strapless dress, she thought as she turned her attention to Kas.

He'd fallen onto his back and Leela was already beside him.

Maya reached for the pot and its lid, glad she'd opened it in preparation, because right then she didn't have sufficient control over her fingers to assure any level of acceptable dexterity.

She watched her mom shift slightly and slide Kas's head onto her lap. He looked up at her, the strangest expression his face.

When he tried to speak, Leela said, "Shh. You don't need to talk."

But he shook his head, a small jerk rather than a smooth movement. "I do. I need . . . to say . . . I'm sorry."

Part of Maya wondered what did it matter that he was sorry. He'd caused unforgivable damage in his insane quest.

Her mom smiled down at him, her face glowing again as Bhumi came forth. Maya watched as the goddess traced her son's cheek and kissed his forehead. Whispered words of forgiveness and love floated on the air, and then a hollow silence that echoed its finality around the jungle.

Pain lanced through Maya, and the edges of her vision darkened. She stumbled closer and watched in awe as Kas's body began to glow. The pale light lifted away from his corpse and swirled around in the air above him.

Maya raised her hand, holding the pot close to the spinning glow. It only spun faster, a slim spout forming at the bottom end. The glow began to funnel its way into the pot, and then with a sudden rush of air it was all gone.

Her hand shook as she screwed the lid onto the pot and shoved it into her pocket. She didn't want to look at it right now.

She crawled over to her mom's side, struggling to keep her eyes open. "Mom?"

"I'm okay, honey." Leela spoke the words with a steady tone that implied she believed it.

Maya knew her mom didn't. Her lids were swollen, as if tears lurked beneath them, ready to fall, and Maya couldn't blame her at all.

When Leela opened her arms, Maya shuffled into her

embrace, ignoring the fiery agony in her chest and blinking hard against the darkness closing in on her. The wound could wait.

Her mom was more important.

And as she held onto her, Maya slipped into unconsciousness.

CHAPTER 54

When Maya opened her eyes again, she found she was lying in bed, covered with a light sheet. The day felt different, as if some time had passed since she'd witnessed Kas's death.

She lifted her head off the pillow.

Sun shone through the window, hazy rays warming the sheets, soaking into the skin of her hand, as if nature wanted to make her feel better.

Maya shifted. Throwing off the sheet, she swung her feet to the floor and padded out of the silent room. She wore a pair of old track pants, and a teeshirt, so thin it was almost transparent. The comfiest clothes she owned.

Two doors down the hall, she stopped just inside her parent's room. This bedroom too, faced the morning sun, and its brightness and warmth comforted her as she watched her mom who lay so still that Maya began to feel faint again.

"Mom?"

"She's okay, Maya." A voice came from behind her. "She's just sleeping."

Maya spun around and she found herself staring at Nik.

"You're okay?" she whispered, heat filling her cheeks.

He nodded, linking his fingers with hers.

"So the spell was broken?"

"Yes. With Narakasura dead, the power of the spell died with him." When Maya looked over her shoulder at her mom lying so peacefully on the bed, Nik said, "Unfortunately, although your mom is the avatar, she is still fully human. She will take a while yet to recover."

"How?" asked Maya, a tremor in her voice. "How are we going to help her?"

"Don't worry. Mother Bhumi will heal her, but it will take time."

"I take it Chayya is back to her duties?" Maya had to admit she missed the goddess.

Nik nodded. "Shadows need to be wrestled back under control and all that."

He winked and drew closer to stand beside her. They both watched her mom's sleeping form. And neither of them moved, even when Maya's dad walked past them into the room, bearing a tray of food.

Dev laid the tray on the nightstand and straightened to watch his wife for a few beats, then he turned and came to Maya. He kissed Maya on the forehead. "You did good, honey."

"You sure kicked ass, Maya." Joss walked in, bringing a glass of lemonade. She placed it on the table and strode over to Maya to give her a quick hug.

"Is everything okay? Undead back to being dead?" Maya asked, giving the bowl of dhal and lamb stew on her mom's nightstand a hungry look. The spicy dhal soup with pieces of soft meat floating in it, had always been a favorite of Maya's, and now the meal proved to be a distraction.

Dev laughed. "Yes, undead are now well and truly dead. And the living are back to dying like they're supposed to. When Kas died, the wards on the prisons in Patala were removed, and Yama was freed."

"Chandragupta?" Maya asked.

Nik nodded beside her, shifting so their linked fingers would remain out of sight. "Our favorite scribe is feeling much better. So much that he insisted on returning to his duties today."

"Really? How did he manage that," asked Maya, giggling at the thought of the heavyset scribe making his case.

"I believe he mentioned something about backlog."

They all laughed, and Maya gave her mom a quick glance, mostly to reassure herself that she was still there.

Then she cleared her throat. "So, I think I need to get off my feet before I fall on my face."

Joss shifted to help, but Maya waved her away. "I'm fine." But Joss ignored her. She tucked her hand into the crook of Maya's elbow and walked her out of her room.

Nik let her fingers go as Joss pulled her away. Strangely enough, she didn't feel bereft.

Joss guided Maya back to her bedroom, and when they reached the bed, the girls sat down slowly while Nik hovered on the threshold. Joss giggled, her eyes going from Maya's face to Nik's.

"Don't worry, lovebirds. I won't intrude on your time." She faced Maya, and nudged her softly. "I'm so proud of you and your Mom. I wanted you to know that. You're kinda my hero."

Maya raised her eyebrows. "Really?" she asked, smiling softly.

Joss nodded, her expression serious. "Yep. Well. Just until Robert goes Iron on us again."

"Robert?" asked Maya. Her faculties must be still a little clouded as the reference went over her head."

"Downey?" Joss rolled her eyes. "Junior?"

"Ah," said Maya, holding in the laughter. She grinned at her crazy friend. Only Joss would want to make a girl laugh when she had a bunch of holes perforating her body.

Then Joss got to her feet. "I have stuff to do."

"Where you headed?" asked Maya. Joss's expression was a little too serious.

"Mom and Dad just got back from Barbados. Family reunion." Joss made a disgusted face and headed for the door. "I'll be back in a day or so." With a wave she was gone and Nik moved closer.

He came to stand in front of her and held out his hand. Maya stared at it for a moment before glancing up at his smiling face. She lifted her hand and placed it in his palm. Then the room disintegrated and the sound of waves filled her ears.

They were back at her beach.

Maya smiled, scrunching her toes into the warm sand.

Nik sank to the ground, pulling Maya slowly with him. She didn't resist as her folded her into his arms. They faced the sea, watching the orange-tinged sun as it set the horizon ablaze.

Today there was no breeze, just warm still air. And Maya was grateful. She needed warmth and had no energy to summon her fire from within her.

She laughed softly, almost forgetting Nik was with her.

"What's so funny?" he asked, his breath teasing her cheek.

She tilted her head to look at his adorable face. "It's probably been the longest that I've gone without even thinking of my fire."

Nik nodded, a little too solemnly. "Eventually, it gets old."

"Thanks." Maya snorted.

He shrugged. "Everything eventually gets old as you get comfortable with it."

"And will *we* get *old* as we get comfortable with us?" She had to ask.

But Nik just smiled and curled his arm around her waist. "I think we will, but comfortable is a good thing. Comfortable is trust and honor and hope. I want us to have all that."

Maya leaned into him, suddenly filled with joy. He must have sensed her emotions because he bent his head and kissed her.

Heat filled Maya's veins, making her a little light-headed. Nik deepened the kiss, his lips soft and hot, and Maya found herself struggling for breath.

But she didn't care.

His arms were wrapped around her, his heart beating close to hers. This was what she needed.

Then she felt her fire rise to coat her skin, the heat simmering against Nik's own godly fire.

It was the most beautiful thing she'd felt in her life; their fire melding, joining with each other as their passion burned, singing a different chord of the same song.

Just perfect.

At last Nik released her and sank back onto the sand, pulling her with him to lay her head on his shoulder.

"I'm here, Maya."

She shifted her head to look at his face, wondering what he meant.

He glanced down at her, his eyes dark. "I'm not going back to Patala for a while. My father has given me some time to recuperate."

"Kind of him." Maya wasn't sure how that worked.

Nik smiled as he lay back again. "He knows that we all need time to regain our balance after this. He's visiting with my mother for the next few days. How do you feel about making a small trip to Florida?" His voice rumbled against her cheek.

She smiled. "I'd love that." With that one question, he'd made everything worth it.

They lay there for a while, staring in silence up at the blue sky, watching puffy clouds float by, listening to the waves crashing against the shoreline.

Maya put her free hand to her pocket to retrieve the pot which held Kas's soul.

It was gone.

In the end, she just patted her pocket and smiled.

With Kas finally where he belonged, the world going back to

normal, her mom on the road to recovery, and Nik by her side, even if it was for a short while, Maya was happy.

She was surrounded by people who loved her.

It couldn't get any better that that.

~ TO BE CONTINUED ~
Thank you for reading. The Hand of Kali Series continues with Fury & Virtue.

ACKNOWLEDGMENTS

To my amazing family for their constant support and
encouragement. I wouldn't be able to do this without you.
To my writing group BI50D for daily encouragement and
butt-kicks.
To the Inklings for walking this journey with me. We are
not alone.
To my fellow writers at RWNZ for always being willing to share
information and learn together. Write on.
And to my readers. For living in the worlds I create, for
becoming Maya's friend and loving her adventures just as much
as I do. Keep reading . . .

ABOUT THE AUTHOR

I have been a writer from the time I was old enough to recognize that reading was a doorway into my imagination. Poetry was my first foray into the art of the written word. Books were my best friends, my escape, my haven. I am essentially a recluse but this part of my personality is impossible to practice given I have two teenage daughters, who are actually my friends, my tea-makers, my confidantes… I am blessed with a husband who has left me for golf. It's a fair trade as I have left him for writing. We are both passionate supporters of each other's loves – it works wonderfully…

My heart is currently broken in two. One half resides in South Africa where my old roots still remain, and my heart still longs for the endless beaches and the smell of moist soil after a summer downpour. My love for Ma Afrika will never fade. The other half of me has been transplanted to the Land of the Long White Cloud. The land of the Taniwha, beautiful Maraes, and volcanoes. The land of green, pure beauty that truly inspires. And because I am so torn between these two lands – I shall forever remain cross-eyed.

Stalk Tee here:
www.tgayer.com
tee@tgayer.com

facebook.com/TGAyerAuthor

twitter.com/TGAyerAuthor

bookbub.com/profile/t-g-ayer